on monday the boxer howled

CASEY & SCOUT MYSTERIES · BOOK 1

ANN RUSSELL

APOCRYPHILE
PRESS

Apocryphile Press
PO Box 255
Hannacroix, NY 12087
www.apocryphilepress.com

Copyright © 2026 by Lisa Fullam & John R. Mabry
Printed in the United States of America
ISBN 978-1-965646-23-6 | paper
ISBN 978-1-965646-24-3 | ePub

Please join our mailing list at www.apocryphilepress.com/free. We'll keep you up-to- date on all our new releases, and we'll also send you a FREE BOOK. Visit us today!

contents

prologue

A shriek pierced the air, causing the terrier in front of me to jump just as I was getting a grip on one of his anal sacs. I tried to ignore whatever was going on in the waiting room, and finally succeeded in expressing the viscous fluid from one of the sacs that was causing so much discomfort, but the ruckus did not stop. Whoever had been shrieking was still at it, and a large dog was barking frantically in return.

"Ugh...mornings," I muttered. I turned to the terrier's owner and, at a normal volume, said, "Can you hold Captain Bly for a minute?" She rushed to the exam table and I pivoted toward the door, stripping off my blue nitrile gloves. As soon as I snatched open the door, the din erupted all over again.

I paused before launching myself into the room—just in case there was something *truly* dangerous going on—and took in the scene. A man in well-worn sand-covered overalls and a red plaid flannel shirt was barely holding onto a leash. At the other end of it, a German Shepherd mix was straining to get loose, hurling itself toward a cat on the other side of the waiting room. The cat was fitted with a harness and lead, but was not in a carrier. All of its claws were extended and dug deep into its owner's shoulders and belly as the terrorized feline sought protection and safety in what was, after all, a very unfamiliar and suddenly scary environment. Its owner's eyes were wide with shock, and she was now no longer shrieking but full-on screaming.

I opened my mouth to speak, but before I could say anything, our head tech Ellie inserted herself between the two embattled animals and held a warding hand up toward the dog. "Mr. Fields—" She had to yell to be heard over the racket. "Why don't you bring Rufus into Exam Room Four?"

Exam Room Four wasn't really an exam room at all, but more of a mud room that had a fold-up exam table for emergencies just such as this. We rarely used it, but it did come in handy on occasion. The problem was that the dog would have to pass right in front of the cat to get there.

I closed the door behind me and snatched at Rufus' collar. Even though I am a small woman, I succeeded in restraining him. "No, Rufus. No!" I commanded. The dog took no notice of me, but as Ellie continued to keep her body between the two animals, I was able to wrestle the Shepherd mix safely past the cat and her still-screaming owner. I waited until Rufus' owner caught up with me, and said, "Close the door, please."

He did. I could hear the woman outside crying now, but at least the screeching had stopped. "I'll be right back," I said and returned to Exam Room Two to finish my work on the terrier— anal sacs wait for no man...or woman.

Five minutes later I had finished expelling the other sac, and had given Captain Bly an affectionate pat on my way out of the room. Passing Ellie, I asked, "How is the woman with the cat?"

"Uh, that's Mrs. Bradshaw. Her cat's claws drew blood—I

counted about twelve puncture marks. Dr. Capra has her in back, giving first aid and trying to calm her down."

"And her cat?"

"Utterly traumatized. Just here for her vaccines, so hopefully we'll have her done and out before Rufus is finished."

I shook my head. I knew Mrs. Bradshaw was in good hands. Shelley Capra was the best vet I knew; she was also my best and oldest friend.

I paused by the door of Exam Room Four and snatched at the client's file. Rufus was here complaining of noisy intestines and diarrhea. I glanced at the owner's name to refresh my memory. Then I took a deep breath to calm myself. Once becalmed, I whispered, "Once more into the breach..." and swung open the door.

To my great surprise, Rufus appeared to be sleeping peacefully at his master's feet. I closed the door behind me and swung the folded exam table into place. "Hello, Mr. Fields. That was...quite a set-to out in the waiting room."

"That lady was insane, bringing a cat in here that wasn't in a box!"

"A lot of clients don't use cat-carriers," I noted. "I encourage you to take Rufus here to an obedience class. With a little training, I think you'll find that he's better behaved in public situations like this. And that would mean that you could take him more places. You can take a trained dog *anywhere*."

"Wait, are you blaming *my* dog for this?" Mr. Fields' face suddenly grew dark and tense. "It's only natural for a dog to take after a cat. And I don't want to train it out of him—Rufus is a ratting dog. He keeps my yard free of pests. I need him to chase after the critters."

"I'm glad he's a good ratting dog," I said patiently, "but again, with a little bit of training, he could be so much more. You could train him when it is and isn't appropriate to go into full 'hunting' mode. I'd be glad to recommend some training classes or even a private trainer. With a little work, Rufus could be a dog you could really be proud of in difficult situations like this."

His mouth worked like he was about to spit tobacco. He studied me, sizing me up in a way that made my flesh crawl. Finally he asked, "Are you saying that my dog was doing something wrong?"

I concentrated on keeping my tone positive—or at least neutral. "I'm saying that both you and Rufus might be happier if he was trained well enough that you won't be surprised at his behavior in situations like this."

"Oh, for heaven's sake, this is ridiculous." He stood and Rufus picked his head up for the first time. "If you're going to blame my dog for this, then I need another veterinarian—one that understands dogs."

He swung open the door and stormed from the room. Rufus' claws skittered on the linoleum as he got to his feet and scrambled after his master. The waiting room was empty—a rare but fortunate state of affairs at the moment. Just before Mr. Fields reached the front door, I called after him, "I'll be happy to forward your records!"

I imagine he snarled at that, but he didn't turn around. He did slam the door, however. The glass vibrated like a singing saw, but didn't break. I exhaled, feeling the tension in my shoulders release just a bit. I returned to Exam Room Four and snatched up the file. I'd have to write up notes on the whole incident, and it was the last thing I felt like doing. I threw the file on the counter behind the reception desk. Ellie was on the phone, but she gave me a look that conveyed sympathy and solidarity. I gave her a sad smile and picked up the file again. *Might as well get it over with,* I thought.

Just then Shelley rounded the corner. She motioned toward

the break room and I followed her in. She shut the door behind us. "Sit," she commanded. "And breathe."

I did both things, because in this and pretty much every situation, I trusted that Shelley knew best. Six months ago, I had been living in the middle of the country, in Naperville, Illinois. I had a happy-ish marriage, and a solid veterinary practice. Then I was accused of an ethics violation that almost robbed me of my livelihood. I hadn't done what I'd been accused of, but by the time the truth had been sorted out, I had lost most of my clients. Then my marriage fell apart when Dennis sunk all of our retirement savings into a fly-by-night cryptocurrency—without telling me. I realized I couldn't live with a man I couldn't trust, and Scout and I spent a month living off Arby's in an Airbnb and blowing through what little savings I had left. I felt like I had failed at the whole "adulting" thing. I was a professional failure and a romantic failure. I had never felt so low.

And then Shelley had called. We had been study partners at the School of Veterinary Medicine at UC Davis twenty years ago, and later roommates. When I had stopped believing in myself, Shelley had believed in me. And when she invited me to join the staff of her practice in Gold Valley in northeastern California, it felt like someone had thrown me a life preserver. I said "yes" without even thinking about it, and I had not regretted it for a second.

Shelley moved around behind me and began to massage my shoulders. "I don't—" I started to object, but it just felt so damn good that I shut up and savored it. I don't often have common sense, but every now and then a bit pokes through.

"You can't let guys like that rattle you," she said. I wondered how much she had heard. The walls *were* thin.

"It's not good business practice to alienate clients," I said.

"There are some clients we don't need," she countered.

I sighed. I felt like crying. I felt like apologizing. I wanted to say, *I'm sorry I'm single-handedly destroying your practice*, but I hate myself when I'm whiney. "How is Mrs. Bradshaw?"

As she answered, her fingers didn't stop kneading my shoulder muscles, which I was grateful for. "She'll live. I gave her some of those antiseptic wipes single-packs and invited her to wipe down the wounds—"

"Because you can't treat a human," I said with a grim smile.

"Exactly. I made her promise to go see her GP, which she did. Then I gave Pinky her vaccines and sent them on their merry way. I think Mrs. Bradshaw was more frightened than damaged."

"Cat claws can be a bitch," I said.

"I didn't say it didn't hurt! Just that she's going to be okay."

She finally stopped and sat across from me. Her long, golden hair had a natural curl to it that I had always either envied or admired, depending on my level of self-judgment. There was a box of Girl Scout cookies at the far end of the table. She leaned over and punched it toward me. There were exactly two cookies inside. I fished them out and handed one to her.

She took it and smiled. "I have a new Pinot Grigio in the fridge, just begging to be evaluated by two wine snobs with nothing better to do tonight."

"I'm so in," I said, popping the cookie into my mouth.

one

"What are you howling at, you silly bitch?" It wasn't a put-down. As a woman, I've been called a bitch many times, but as a veterinarian the loaded term had just come to mean what it originally had—a dog of the female gender. On the other hand, Scout *was* silly—she was a Boxer, after all. I studied her as her pointed ears stood up at attention, her front paws on the windowsill, and every brindle hair on her back quivering with excitement. Once more she raised her snout and let loose with a formidable "Awooooooooooo!"

This was not unusual. A visit from the mailman could elicit the same response. In fact, since it was mid-afternoon, I thought it might have been the mailman. But Scout's eagerness didn't pass.

I thought about getting up to look out the window, but the problem was, I was busy. I was sitting cross-legged with my back against the couch. In one hand was a flesh-colored scrap of plastic gel about the size of a mousepad. In the other hand was a needle pulling a length of PDS thread. I had been taking an online continuing ed class on new suturing methods and I was practicing. It was not going well. I had stuck myself twice with the needle, and had ended up tying the knot backwards—also twice. Every bit of me did not want to stop until I nailed it, but Scout was driving me nuts. I decided to howl back. "Awoooooooooo!" I responded, mimicking her exact diction to the best of my ability.

Strangely, she took no notice. Normally Scout loved our howling game.

"Fine," I said, and threw down the plastic gel. It landed on the hardwood floor with a disgusting "glop" sound. I groaned, ran my fingers through my hair and got up, sidling up to the window next to Scout.

She was still attentive—the tiny stub of her tail fluttering as fast as a hummingbird's wings. "What is it, girl?"

But the front yard of the small cottage we shared was empty. The flag on the mailbox was still up. *Not the mailman, then,* I thought. I turned to face her. "Don't tell me you see dead people."

Scout whined her protest. Then she pushed herself from the window and went to the door. Putting her snout to its bottom, she snuffled noisily.

"Oh, all right. I'll humor you," I said. It was unusual behavior for Scout, who was pretty matter of fact for a Boxer. I opened the door, put one hand in front of Scout's nose—a "stay put" gesture—and caught my breath.

"Tripod?" I breathed. He was Shelley's dog. Tripod looked up at me with his enormous, dark Labrador eyes.

"What's wrong, boy? What are you doing loose?"

In answer, he turned and began to lope toward Shelley's house as fast as his three legs could carry him.

A stab of panic tore at my gut. "Okay. Shoes," I said. Scout stood at the threshold, looking after Tripod, whining her concern. I found my sneakers and stuffed my feet into them, not bothering to untie them. I paused at the door. "I assume you're coming?" I said. Scout leaped through the door and began to give Tripod chase.

It wasn't far to Shelley's house, but as my anxiety rose it seemed to take forever. Like most vets, Shelley collected lost causes—stray cats, blind parakeets, diabetic gerbils, and dogs nobody else wanted, like Tripod. In my gut, I knew I was one of those lost causes, or would have been had it not been for her. Thank God for people like Shelley.

By the time her house came into view, I had lost sight of the dogs. The side gate was open, so I figured they had gone in by the dog door. I headed for the front entrance. I knocked first, but the only response was the dogs barking inside. I pushed open the door, and was greeted by a flurry of tails and kisses, as if neither of them had seen me for months. Normally, I reveled in such affection—a girl's got to get it where she can—but there was no time for that now.

The house was immaculate as always. Shelley was a bit of a neat freak, and that was true at the clinic as well, even by medical standards. This sometimes created some conflict with the clinic staff, and I wasn't unsympathetic toward their complaints—Shelly could be a hard boss at times, and her standards were high. But I forgave her that—I owed her, after all.

Greetings over, Tripod ran to the kitchen. I followed, my breath growing shorter with each passing footfall. Rounding the corner into the kitchen I clutched at the wall with one hand and covered my mouth with the other. "Dear God," I breathed.

I felt dizzy as I surveyed the scene. Shelley was face-down on the floor, her long blond hair splayed out in many directions like the spokes of a tire. There was a deep gash on the back of her head and a pool of blood the size of my fist beneath her cheek.

I leaped to her side and put two fingers on her neck. There was no pulse. Tripod was turning in quick circles, whining. Scout started howling again.

I pulled my cell phone from my back pocket and hit 911. "This is Dr. Casey Gibbons. I need an ambulance at 1085 Cherry Blossom, in Gold Valley. Hurry." I hung up before they could ask me any further questions. I simply didn't have time for them. I turned her over and began to press on her chest, utilizing a rhythm I'd employed two years ago when massaging the heart of a newborn calf. It had worked then. It was not working now.

I had given up by the time the EMTs arrived. When they entered the room, I was sitting next to her body, my fingers trembling, my back against the lower cupboards, my knees drawn up to my chin. Both dogs rose to greet the paramedics, but the paramedics didn't seem to see them.

"Are you all right?" one of them asked me. She snapped her gum, but her tone sounded genuine. I managed to snap out of my shock and looked her in the eye. "I'm fine. She's...gone."

"Are you a doctor?" she asked.

"Veterinarian," I said.

"Oh. Well, I guess you'd know. We still need to check."

"Sure," I said. They didn't need my permission.

The EMTs confirmed that she was dead, and made a note of the time. One of the other paramedics pushed a gurney into the kitchen.

"I don't think that's a good idea," I said. "In fact, I don't think any of us should touch anything, if we can help it."

"Why not?" asked the first paramedic. She snapped her gum again.

"Because this wasn't an accident," I said.

two

"Damn, Casey. I'm so sorry." Sarge poured me a cup of coffee, then set the pot down on the counter at Millie's Diner.

I stirred the coffee, but it was still too hot to drink. I glanced over my shoulder, out the double glass doors, to check on Scout. She was lying down outside, her head on her paws. I liked sitting at the counter, not just because I could talk to Sarge, but because Scout and I could keep an eye on each other.

"I just feel numb," I said. "The world doesn't seem real. *It* doesn't seem real, you know. I keep expecting to turn around and see her."

"It sucks," Sarge said. "She didn't deserve that."

"No," I said. I glanced up at Sarge and tried to smile. He was impossibly tall, with biceps that threatened to bust the seams of his T-shirt. His skin was so black it looked almost blue in the right light, and his hair sported the same military buzz cut he'd worn throughout his career in the Marines. I've seen pictures, and the guy hasn't aged a day in twenty years.

Somewhere, lost in the attic of some barrack at Pendleton, there must be an oil painting aging less gracefully.

And now that Shelley was dead, he was the closest thing I had to a best friend. I'm not sure he would see it that way—to him I was probably just an annoying but reliable customer—but at this point I didn't have a lot of people to choose from.

"Do you want to talk about it?" he asked.

"I don't really do the *talking about it* thing," I said.

"You sure you've got two X chromosomes?" he asked, raising one eyebrow.

A bell rung and he went to the window to pick up the hot order. He took it to Teri Apple in one of the booths. Returning, he picked up a dishtowel and began to dry some glasses. I could feel his eyes on me. It made me squirm a bit.

"I made them call the sheriff," I said.

"You don't think it was an accident?" he asked.

"I mean, it *could* be," I said. "The wound on the back of her head is consistent with falling and hitting her head on the counter, but—"

"But?"

"But she didn't have epilepsy, she isn't hypoglycemic, she isn't prone to fainting spells for any other reason, and she's as sure-footed as a mountain goat."

"You know, you just said 'is'," he said.

"Oh. Yeah. I guess I did." I sighed. "It's hard to make the shift."

"What did the sheriff say?"

"Inconclusive, apparently. But until or unless there's some evidence of foul play, they're probably going to rule it accidental. The autopsy report is due tomorrow."

"That might show something up."

"It might."

"Any blood on the counter?" Sarge asked.

"Not that I could see."

"That speaks in your favor," he noted.

"Please. You make it sound like I *want* her to have been attacked." I shuddered.

"It's not like that at all," he said, his voice suddenly sounding soft, incongruously so.

"Sorry," I pinched the bridge of my nose. "I'm not at my best."

"Your best is medium-testy on a good day," Sarge said. "I think you're doing just fine."

"Thanks...I think." I forced a smile. "How is Prince?" Prince was Sarge's Cavalier King Charles Spaniel. While Sarge was sweating at the counter, Prince lounged in a cushy run behind the diner. Sarge was in the terrible habit of sneaking him leftover bits throughout his shift, which by now had made for one very tubby Spaniel.

"Eh, a little off today. Hasn't had a firm stool in two days."

"Stop feeding him *foie gras*," I scolded.

"*Foie gras*, in this place?"

"Fine. Bacon grease."

"He does love his bacon grease."

"That's what I'm talking about. You've got to knock that off."

"I can't stop him eating grass, and then he gets these long strands of grass coming out of his poophole—"

"I think 'anus' is the word you're looking for," I said.

"You say 'anus,' I say 'poophole.' Seems like we're communicating just fine."

"Eating grass isn't going to hurt him. Think of it as herbal medicine."

"All I'm thinking about is pulling long strands of grass out of him before he comes inside."

"The things we do for love, eh?" I asked.

"Got that right. Just a minute." Sarge greeted a couple I hadn't seen before and showed them to a booth. He got them menus, then poured them some coffee. He came back and leaned on the counter again. "So can you find out what the autopsy says?" he asked.

I shrugged. "Anyone can. All autopsy reports are a matter of public record, at least in California."

"Huh. Well, I guess you'd know."

I'm sure my brow furrowed. "That's the second time in twenty-four hours someone has said that to me. Being a vet doesn't make me an expert in all matters medical and legal."

"If you say so," he said, and went to take the order from the new couple. He passed the ticket to the fry cook and came back to his station near me. "So what are you going to do to take care of yourself?" he asked.

I blinked. ...*Take care of yourself.* The words echoed in my head. I could tell they were English, but I had no idea what they meant. But before I could betray my incomprehension, Sarge pressed ahead. "You gonna take some time off?"

"Hell no," I said. "Are you kidding? Someone's got to cover Shelley's shifts." I looked at my watch, which sported Snoopy doing the happy dance. His paws pointed to the twelve and the eight. "In fact, I'd better get going."

"Well, what are you going to do if the coroner's report comes back...you know...funny?" he asked.

I didn't even hesitate. There were lots of questions I didn't know the answers to: How do you feel? What is the price of caviar? How does the stock market work? But I knew the answer to that question without even needing to consider it. "I'm going to find out who killed my friend."

three

My back ached. It had been a grueling shift thus far, and it wasn't yet noon. I was trying to see my own clients and work in as many of Shelley's as I could. But when you try to make everyone happy, no one is happy. That certainly included me.

In a way, I welcomed the hectic pace. It kept me focused on, well, anything but Shelley. Images of her lying on her kitchen floor flashed through my brain at random intervals. As much as possible, I pushed them out of consciousness and concentrated on the animal in front of me.

With a sigh, I took the patient file from its holder on the door of Exam Room Two and gave it a quick glance. There was almost nothing in it, which told me it was probably a kitten or puppy. I put on my best professional smile and opened the door.

"Good morning, Mrs... Brackenmeyer."

"Ms. Brackenmeyer, please."

"Of course. My apologies."

"It's all right." Ms. Brackenmeyer was holding an adorable

puppy against her chest. The woman was about thirty, with two-tone gray and dark brown hair that could not have been natural. A part of me wanted to inquire about the Bride of Frankenstein look, but it resisted the distraction.

"And who do we have here?" I set down the file and stepped closer, putting my hands in the pockets of my lab coat.

"This is Muffins," she said.

I wanted to say, *Hello Muffins, your cruel owner has given you a horrible name that everyone will regret when you turn into a fully grown dog*, but instead I kept it short. "Hello, Muffins." Muffins was impossibly cute, which was his evolutionary ace-in-the-hole. He looked to me like a Maltese and Yorkshire mix, but I couldn't be certain in a puppy so young.

"He's new to the family, so I thought I'd bring him in for a checkup."

"Very wise," I said. "I'm so glad you did." I patted the top of the stainless-steel exam table. "Put Muffins right here and let's check him out."

She placed the puppy on the table. His head moved up and down like a bobblehead figure. I held my finger in front of his eyes and moved it back and forth. His eyes followed the finger. Good. I pulled my stethoscope from my pocket and fitted the earpieces into my ears. I touched the drum to the puppy's chest and listened. I frowned. I moved the drum to another spot and listened some more. I did not like what I was hearing.

I pulled the earpieces free and put the stethoscope back in my pocket. "I'm sorry to tell you this, Ms. Brackenmeyer, but your puppy has a heart murmur. It's...pretty severe."

Her eyes widened and her hand went to her chest. "But... the breeder said he was in perfect condition."

"The breeder lied to you...or the breeder is an idiot and didn't know which end of the stethoscope to listen to."

"But—"

I shook my head. "We'll need to do some tests to be sure, but I've seen this kind of thing before—it's all too common in puppies, I'm afraid, especially puppies from disreputable breeders. I suspect Muffins here has Patent Ductus Arteriosus —we call it PDA for short."

"What is that?" she breathed.

"When a puppy is still inside his mother, there's a little opening between two blood vessels leading from the heart. Normally, that closes soon after the puppy is born. When it doesn't, you get the kind of heart murmur we're hearing now."

"Oh, my. What...is there anything you can do?"

"Yes. Less invasively, we could insert a transarterial coil to seal up the passage; more invasively, we could do surgery and tie off the ductus."

"And what will that cost?"

I sighed. "The transarterial coil would cost several thousand dollars; for the full surgery, you're looking at $10,000 to start. And you'll need a specialist—Davis is the closest."

"I just paid $3,000 for him!" There was outrage in her voice. "He's a full-blooded Morkie!"

I opened my mouth to say, *There's no such thing as a full-blooded Morkie. "Morkie" is not a breed. A Morkie is a mutt. You paid $3,000 for a mutt...* But I kept my tongue in check this time, thank God. "I'm sorry about that. I'm only giving you the facts. This puppy has PDA, and you have a very short window of time to correct it."

"I'll take him back to the breeder and demand my money back!" she yelled.

"You can. California has a 'lemon puppy' law that entitles you to a refund or exchange for the pup. I doubt anything good would happen to Muffins if you return him, though. You can also get treatment costs for up to 150% of what you paid for him, but that's not likely to cover the cost of fixing his problem." I sighed. "If you don't mind, can I ask who the breeder was?"

"Eureka Acres Dog Farm, just across the river."

This was Northern California, so across the dried creek bed. I nodded. The name sounded familiar, but I couldn't remember just why. "This kind of thing happens all the time. Disreputable breeders don't check for cardiac or other conditions in their breeding stock, and they produce litter after litter of damaged dogs." I gave Muffins a pat. "If it will help you, I'll be glad to write up our diagnosis—but I can only definitively document the heart murmur. To prove PDA, we'll have to do some testing—"

"And how much will that cost?"

I shrugged. "$800."

"Just write up the heart murmur, then."

"Yes, ma'am," I said. "Wait here, please."

"Maggie was right about you guys."

I was almost out of the room, but I stopped and turned back. "Maggie?" I asked.

"Yes. When you killed Champ."

I cocked my head at her. It took me a minute to realize what she was referring to. Champ had been one of Shelley's patients. She'd done what had seemed like a routine surgery, but the dog had died on the table. It had shaken Shelley up pretty bad, and I remember trying my best to comfort her. The fact is that no treatment is 100% safe, there is always risk, and there are always freak accidents.

"Dr. Capra did not kill Champ—"

"Maggie is fit to be tied. She's talking about suing."

I wanted to say, *Well, Shelley's dead now, so there's no one to sue,* but I held my tongue. *She's just angry,* I thought. I breathed deep and reminded myself that she was not angry at me. She was angry at the situation and she was simply lashing out. I counted to ten to take the edge off of my irritation. I brought forward my best bedside manner, but before I could say anything there was a knock at the door. Our head tech Ellie popped in, ponytail bobbing over her cartoon-patterned scrubs. "Doctor Gibbons, the sheriff is here to see you. It's about Dr. Capra, I think."

"Oh." I knew an interview was coming, but I was expecting a summons, not a visit. "All right. Tell him I'll be right with him. Do we have an open exam room?"

"Yes, one. Number Four. I'll make sure it's clean."

"Thank you." She closed the door again. I worried about the backup for our patients, but some things couldn't be helped, nor could they wait. I turned back to Ms. Bracken-meyer. "You can pick up the diagnosis and a referral to a recommended specialist from the receptionist. I'm very sorry about your puppy." And with that I left the room, grateful that I had not done more damage.

Once in the hall, I headed for Exam Room Four. I opened the door and a man about my own age in the tan uniform of a deputy sheriff stood and took off his hat. He had an acne-scarred but still handsome face, but he had become a bit doughy in the middle. He wore the requisite cowboy boots, and his collar was stained from sweat. California's Gold Country could get crazy hot in summer, and even late spring had its sweltering moments.

"Doctor Gibbons?" he asked, offering his hand.

"Yes," I said. I pointed to one of the two plastic chairs shoved against one wall. He sat, playing with his hat absently.

"It's a pleasure to meet you. I'm Deputy Sheriff Gus Tucker."

"Good to meet you, Deputy."

"I'd like to ask you a few questions about...well, about Miss Capra."

"Doctor Capra," I corrected him.

"Oh. Of course. Yeah. Sorry."

Why is this deputy nervous? I wondered. He didn't look particularly young or green.

"Uh...can you tell me what happened...when you found the body?" He pulled a Moleskine notepad from his front pocket and clicked a ball-point pen.

I related the events of the day before in as much detail as I could. He wrote furiously, only pausing now and then to ask a clarifying question. I must admit, I was relieved that he seemed to be taking me seriously.

"And why do you think this wasn't an accident?" he asked.

I shrugged. "Because I know my friend. It's a feeling, I suppose. But it's a strong feeling. I don't know how I know it, I just know it."

"I do know what that feels like. A lot of police work is built on hunches," he nodded. "But...we can't move forward with anything unless we have some evidence."

"What did the necro—uh, the autopsy show?" I didn't know if it had been done yet, but there was a chance.

"It's not scheduled 'til this afternoon," he said.

"Damn," I said.

"Did you see anything out of place? Anything unusual at her house?"

"No," I said. "But I wasn't looking for it, either."

"I understand. Do you know of anyone who might have a reason to want Dr. Capra...to want to hurt her?" He held his pen poised for my answer.

"No, but—"

"Are you sure? It doesn't need to be anyone who actually made a threat—just anyone who might have had a beef..." He looked at me hopefully.

Suspects suddenly crowded my mind, each clamoring for

attention. "Well," I said, "last week we arrived at work to find every window plastered with flyers from an animal-rights group."

"What group?" He was writing again.

"They call themselves the Freedom Pack."

"Do you have any of these flyers?"

"Shelley filed a complaint at the Sheriff's Office last Wednesday, and dropped off a few of the flyers then. We threw the rest away. Don't you guys talk to each other?"

I cursed myself under my breath. My temper often got the best of me and it threatened to do so now. I reminded myself that the deputy was just doing his job. "Sorry," I said. "I'm..."

"No, it's okay. It's tough when a friend dies. Believe me, I know." He gave me a far too compassionate smile. "Thank you for telling me about the report. I'll pull it as soon as I'm back to HQ."

"And then there's Margaret Edgerton."

"Maggie?" The deputy asked.

"You know her?" I asked.

He shrugged. "I kind of know everyone. Everyone does. You're still new, but you'll get there. What's up with Maggie?"

"Her dog Champ died during surgery—Shelley was the attending vet on that case."

"Ah...I'm sorry to hear about that. Champ was a good dog."

"Champ almost took my pinky off when I tried to give him a distemper shot."

"He's an excitable boy...was, I guess. Well, it's sad about Champ. Maggie holding a grudge?"

"I don't know this directly, but I've heard she was considering a lawsuit."

"There's a lot of distance between suing and killing," he said.

"I agree," I said. "I'm not accusing her."

"No," he said. "You're just answering questions, and I'm grateful."

I narrowed my eyes. This guy was being *too nice*. It was a little creepy. What was up?

"Anyone else?"

"Not off the top of my head, but if I think of anything—"

"Call me," he said, taking a card out of his breast pocket. "Anytime." He flashed me a smile that was exactly 1.5 times too toothy.

"Sure," I said. "I need to get back to my patients."

"Of course." He stood and I shook his hand again. "Pleasure to meet you, doc."

"And you," I said. He left and closed the door behind him. I stood in the empty room for a moment chewing my lip. After a few minutes, I walked into the back and made my way to the front desk.

I caught Ellie's eye and waved her over. "We're starting to back up," she said.

"Sure. I'm going right into two."

"Danny Case and Dorito."

"Listen, Ellie, do you know of anyone who might have wanted to hurt Shelley?"

She blinked, then her eyes moved back and forth. "Yeah, I can think of a few."

"Can you make me a list?"

four

The rest of the day was so busy it passed with a blur. I was dreaming of going home, feeding Scout, sinking into a hot tub with a glass of sauvignon blanc, and going to bed, hopefully in that order. As I gathered my things, it occurred to me that now that Shelley was gone, I had nothing tethering me to this town, or this practice, or for that matter anything or anyone except for Scout—and she was portable. Was I happier than I had been in Naperville? I didn't have a husband, but I was free to make my own decisions and I didn't have to answer to anyone. I hadn't made a lot of new friends, but there were definitely people I liked. I thought of Sarge and smiled. But I knew one thing—I wasn't going anywhere until I figured out what had happened to my best friend in the world. I owed that to Shelley. On that note of resolve, I headed for the door but was called back by a raised voice.

"Oh, Dr. Gibbons?!"

I closed my eyes for exactly two seconds, took a deep breath, then turned around, speaking in an even, unaffected tone. "Yes?"

I recognized the voice. It was Bea, our office manager. She was often holed up in a closet-sized office in back, but now she was waving at me from the reception desk.

"I need the books," she said.

"What books?" I asked. I had an impulse to look at my watch. I was losing precious minutes of bath time.

"*The* books. The accounting books. For the practice."

I scowled and shook my head. "What about them?"

"Well..." She looked uncertain, as if I should have clued in by now. "Dr. Capra took them home, and so they're...not here... and you know...I need them."

"Oh." I walked back toward the reception desk. "Can't you go get them?"

"That's si—" It seemed like she was about to say "that's silly" but caught herself. "I don't have a key to her house."

"Oh," I said again, not at my most articulate.

"Could you pick them up and bring them in tomorrow?" She gave me a hopeful smile.

"Sure. Of course," I said. "I'll have them for you tomorrow."

"Thank you so much, Doctor."

"No problem," I said. I held my breath and headed for the door again. No one stopped me this time, and I exhaled a great wave of relief. "Okay, small setback, then," I said to myself as I strapped into Old Blue, my pumpkin-colored Honda Civic. I would make a surgical strike for the books on the way home, and it would only lose me five minutes of bath time.

But of course it was not so simple. As busy as it had been today, as much as I had been mindful of Shelley's absence, the truth was that she was everywhere. Nearly every patient had mentioned her—either because they were Shelley's patient, or because they had heard the news from someone in the tiny town. I felt like she was looking over my shoulder—and not in a good way. The image of her splayed out on the floor intruded upon my thoughts; the memory of the gash in the back of her head stabbed at my inner eye. A rush of emotion made my throat swell and I swallowed it back down. I didn't do emotions well, and I certainly didn't want to deal with *those* emotions. Besides, I was too tired and there was too much to do.

I pulled up in front of Shelley's house and removed the key from the ignition. The place looked unnaturally dark in the twilight. It was also too quiet—Tripod was not leaping spasmodically at me, bouncing on his one hind leg. Everything was wrong.

I knew that Tripod was being cared for. Our head tech Ellie had taken him in, at least temporarily, and I was grateful for that. But Tripod did not belong with Ellie, lovely as Ellie was. Tripod had belonged here, but now...

I set the thought aside. It was not helping me complete this very simple task. As I drew my keys from my pocket and inserted the right one in the lock, I cursed the police department for not labeling it a crime scene. There should be yellow tape over the door. There should be a squad car outside. I shouldn't even be able to go in and retrieve the books. And yet here I was, entering the house where Shelley had died, where, I was increasingly sure in my gut, she had been killed.

I found the light switch with my fingers and flipped it. Light blazed in the familiar hall, and I followed it upstairs, directly toward the spare bedroom Shelley used for an office. I was tempted to walk around the place, to...to... I don't know. Perhaps sense her presence, perhaps to make sure there weren't any other bodies lurking about.

But one thing I did not care to see again was the kitchen. I knew her body would not be there. I knew there was no blood spatter or any other gruesomeness, but I still did not want to see that room. A kitchen was always the heart of a house, and now that Shelley was gone, that heart had stopped.

I turned the knob and switched on the light. Shelley's office was immaculate, like everything else in her life. There was a computer on her desk, its screen dark. A floor-to-ceiling bookcase was filled with medical texts and historical romance novels. The juxtaposition did not seem unnatural—it was very Shelley. At eye-level on one of the shelves was an antique manual typewriter—ornamental, it seemed. On the floor on the other side of the desk was a dog bed for Tripod. Its emptiness seemed to taunt me.

I turned to my task. It didn't take long to find the books. They were oversized ledgers, filled with yellow pages on which were recorded page after mind-numbing page of double-entry accounting. I snatched the books up and was about to leave when something else caught my eye.

String. On a bulletin board hanging over her desk, Shelley had fashioned different colored strings to pushpins, creating a random pattern on the cork. Also on the board were articles and photos. The headline for one of the articles was "Puppy Mill Angers Neighbors."

"Damn puppy mills," I breathed, and I paused to scan the article. Then I followed a string from the article to a black-and-white photo of a burly man in overalls. He looked like a farmer, with a grizzled face that did not look kindly or welcoming. If anything, it looked vaguely menacing.

I followed more of the strings, each of them connected to the puppy mill story in some way. I was beginning to get a picture of the local pet supply underground, and it wasn't pretty.

Setting the accounting books down again, I began to look at the other items on Shelley's desk. There was a manila folder titled "Eureka Acres." The name rang a bell. Then I remembered—that was the name of the puppy mill that Beverly Brackenmeyer had paid $3,000 for her mutt Muffins.

I opened the folder and sorted through the contents. I rifled through a stack of handwritten notes on lined yellow paper. There was also a 9 x 12 envelope adorned with diagonal, parallel blue stripes full of xeroxed photos revealing damning conditions. My eyes were wide by the time I finished skimming through the file. Shelley had documented case after case of defective dogs coming out of Eureka. *Eureka indeed*, I thought.

It was obvious that Shelly was gathering evidence, but for what? The strings on her bulletin board traced a pattern of disreputable dog breeders in the area, and the Eureka folder was filled with particulars. I searched for other folders and found them. Each contained reports of various kinds—sick animals, dead animals, unsanitary conditions. Some of the notes were printed out, some were handwritten, often scrawled on whatever was handy—the backs of envelopes, Post-it notes that had lost their stickiness. But none of the folders were as thick as the Eureka folder, not by a long shot.

I glanced at the computer. If Shelley had been working on something, it would be there.

I hit the power button and waited. As expected, it booted up to a security screen. It was a little too obvious, but I tried it anyway. "T-R-I-P-O-D," I typed. The screen flared to life.

Shelley was just as organized in her virtual life, which was helpful. It didn't take long to navigate to the documents folder and find a directory titled "Puppy Mills." Inside were several files, an mp3 of a podcast about dog breeders in Gold Country, and one Word file simply titled, "Exposé." I opened it.

It was an article, apparently one that Shelley herself was writing, as the "track changes" tool was on and I could see where she had been editing. Quickly, I opened her email client and attached the file to my own email address. I then attached the other files in the directory and sent it off. Then I shut the computer down.

I snapped a picture of the bulletin board and, placing the puppy mill files on top of the accounting books, scooped them all up. Pressing them against my chest, I headed out.

five

The next morning I opened the hatchback of my Civic and twitched my head toward it. "You coming?" I asked.

Scout left off whatever smell she had been investigating and jumped in the back. But she didn't stay there; before I had even reached the driver's seat, Scout had taken the shotgun position, upright and eager to travel.

I put the manila file folder on the floor in front of her and turned the key in the ignition. The little engine roared to life, and we headed out.

I rolled down the passenger-side window just enough for Scout to get her nose in the wind, and she sampled all the olfactory joys along the way. But while she was sniffing, my brain was racing.

I had felt excited to discover Shelley's research on Eureka Acres Dog Farm, but I wasn't surprised. Something had to cause someone to kill her, and I was just glad to have a lead, and something to stay busy with. Otherwise, I felt mostly numb. I wondered about that, and even wondered if I ought to feel guilty...but the fact was, I didn't. I didn't feel much of anything.

I turned my thoughts to the research Shelley had been working on. She had obviously been building a case against Eureka Acres, but to what end I didn't know. Still, I hoped it would be enough to get the Sheriff's department interested in investigating.

Shelley and I shared a general opinion that puppy mills were evil. They simply bred, produced, and sold puppies in as great a number as they could without any regard for responsible breeding practices, rarely provided adequate healthcare —either for the pregnant bitches or the puppies themselves— and rarely vetted the homes for their puppies. Most puppy mill owners were only concerned with profit and did not see their dogs as sentient beings deserving of respect, care, and love. They saw them as products—little better than meat. They catered to whatever the fad breed of the moment happened to be, with no regard for the ultimate fate of those dogs. Thus it is that animal shelters across the country are filled with chihuahuas and pit bulls that nobody wants.

I was so lost in thought that I did not remember a single detail of the journey as I pulled into the parking lot of the Nevada County Sheriff's Office.

Crossing the lot, I pushed open one of the wide glass doors and held it for Scout. She dutifully trotted in and waited for me, the stub of her tail moving back and forth slowly. She fell into step beside me as I crossed the atrium of the spacious county building toward the Sheriff's Office.

The deputy at the desk gave me a matter-of-fact smile, although her eyebrows rose a bit upon seeing Scout beside me. As usual, Scout was a perfect lady, heeling when I walked and sitting when I stopped. "How can I help you?" she asked.

I hugged the file folder to my chest and gave my best

professional smile. "I'm Dr. Casey Gibbon. I'd like to speak to the sheriff, please."

"*The* sheriff?" she asked, as if that was a big ask. "Or a deputy?"

"The sheriff, please. Or a detective."

"The detective I can do. What's this regarding?" She picked up a phone receiver and held it a couple of inches from her ear, her right hand poised over the buttons.

"That's something I'd like to save for the detective."

The deputy rolled her eyes and hit one of the glowing buttons on the phone's base. "Hey, De Marco, I've got someone here who wants to file...something."

She frowned as she listened. "Don't put that on me, you jerk. Take it up with Blake. It's not personal! Jesus. Okay, I'll send her back. Oh, she's got a dog." Her eyes moved back and forth as she listened. Then she hung up.

"Down this hallway"—she pointed to her left—"then take a right. De Marco's office is the second one on the left."

"Thanks," I said. "Is there always so much...drama?"

Her brow furrowed. "What are you talking about?"

"Nothing. Not a damn thing," I said. "Thanks for your help."

We set off down the hall and at the turn, I almost collided with someone familiar.

"Dr. Gibbons!" he exclaimed.

It took me a moment to place him, but then I knew. "Deputy Tucker. So good to see you again."

He pulled his hat off his head, revealing a head of sweaty, unruly black hair. "Please call me Gus. I hope you will, anyway."

"Gus. Sure." I shook his hand. I gestured toward my Boxer. "And this is Scout, the wonder-bitch."

"Scout?" Instantly, Gus got down on one knee and was

rewarded with a face full of snuffling and tongue—which he did not seem to mind. After some vigorous ruffling of withers, he stood again and asked, "Whatcha here for? I mean...how can I help?"

"I'm actually here to see the sheriff...but it looks like I'll be talking to a detective instead." I shrugged. "Which is fine. I guess."

"Oh. Well, the boss is up to his eyeballs. Wildfires and security at a convention up at the Hilton."

"No problem."

"Well, if there's anything I can do to help, you just let me know." He gave me a long, knowing look filled with a mysterious subtext that I could not read. It made me just a bit uncomfortable.

"Uh, sure, Gus. Thanks. Thanks a lot."

With that he donned his hat again and set off. "Hope to see you soon," he shot over his shoulder.

"Okay," I kind-of agreed.

I looked down at Scout. "That was...weird," I said. She did not disagree.

It didn't take long to find the detective's office. A generic plaque on the door read, "Jeffrey De Marco." The door was open, but I knocked.

De Marco looked up from his desk and squinted at me through thick glasses. He was a swarthy, rotund man, with thick lips and an impressive, almost regal nose. "You the lady with the dog?"

Obviously. Here was the dog. I entered and, unbidden, sat in the only other chair in his tiny office. The walls were glass, so there was no privacy. If one closed the door, I suppose one could speak without being heard.

"You want to file a report?"

"I want to contribute to a case."

"An open case?"

"I don't know. It might not be a case yet."

He rolled his eyes and sighed. He clacked on his keyboard and navigated with his mouse. I assumed he was pulling up a blank form. "Name?" he asked.

"Cassandra Gibbons. Everyone calls me Casey."

"I will call you Ms. Gibbons," De Marco informed me.

"That will be fine," I assured him. "And this is Scout. Scout Gibbons."

"Pleasure to meet you, Scout," De Marco said to Scout. He seemed to actually notice her for the first time, and a brief smile played at his lips. "I used to have a Boxer."

"Did you?"

"Great dogs. Fun dogs."

"They're clowns," I said.

"They sure are." He nodded, still not taking his eyes off of Scout. "She's a beauty."

"Thank you. She's a good dog."

"I'll just bet she is." He looked back at his computer. But then he looked back at Scout. "Uh, is she...pettable?"

"She's totally pettable," I assured him.

He looked at me uncertainly.

"Go on," I encouraged him. He rose and walked around the desk. He knelt next to Scout, who instantly began to give him the Big Sniff. He let her do her own investigations, and then began to scratch her behind the ears. She rubbed her head against his hand, increasing the pressure, and before I knew it, the two were nuzzling one another. It never ceases to amaze me—the uncanny power to disarm people that dogs possess.

Fortunately, the detective rose before the lovefest became awkward. "Uh...thanks," he said, a little embarrassed.

"She enjoyed it too," I pointed out.

He sat again and, in a softer tone now, turned to me. "How can I help?"

No dummy, I took advantage of this unexpected openness. "I'm not sure if you've heard, but Dr. Shelley Capra died a couple of days ago. She was my...I guess she was my best friend." I waited for this to register.

"I heard something about that. I'm sorry," he said. He met my eyes and he sounded genuine.

"Thank you."

"What kind of doctor was she?" he asked.

"She's a veterinarian. We both are. We both work... worked...I still work...never mind. We're at the Gold Valley Animal Hospital."

"Yeah, I know the place. We used to take our corgi there before he..." He coughed and looked away. "But I didn't know Dr. Capra."

"There have been a number of vets there over the years," I offered.

"Sure," he agreed. He did some clacking on his computer. "I got the report here. It was listed as an accident. The autopsy results were—"

"Inconclusive," I finished.

"Right," he said. "Says here that you found the body."

"I did."

He pursed his lips and gave me a concerned look. "I'm sorry. I'm sorry you had to see that."

"Thanks. It was...horrible."

He nodded his agreement.

"I don't think it was an accident," I said.

"Oh?" His eyebrows shot up. He turned back to the screen. "There were no signs of breaking and entering. Nothing was stolen. The field notes say the place looked neat as a whistle. The words they used were 'spooky,' and 'like a model home.'"

"Shelley was a neat freak," I said.

"I guess so. Still, if there was foul play, you'd expect a mess. And the wound is consistent with a fall. The edges of the counter—"

I closed my eyes and shook my head. "There was no blood on the counter."

He pointed at me. "That is true. But that doesn't mean she didn't hit her head on it."

"It tells us that a fall against the counter was unlikely to be the cause of death."

He frowned at me. "Do you have anything else?"

I held up the file folder and placed it on his desk. "I have this."

He turned the folder around to face him and opened it. He began to rifle through its contents. "What am I looking at? And what am I looking for?" he asked.

"Shelly had a column in the county paper, 'The Pet Pages'—which was a stupid name, because it was only a column on a single page."

"Oh, yeah." He snapped his fingers. "That's why her name is familiar. She gives pet advice. It's a good column. I read it... sometimes."

I nodded. "She was working on something...more substantive. An exposé."

His eyes widened and he pointed to the file. I nodded. "Those are her notes."

"She really does not like this Dog Farm...Eureka."

"It's a puppy mill."

"They sell dogs," he said, shrugging. "So? Don't tell me you're one of those lunatic animal rights people who don't think people should have pets."

"Obviously I don't think that." I pointed to Scout with my chin. "But I can certainly tell you what's wrong with puppy mills. First, their only concern is profit. Bitches are bred again and again, with no recovery time. When they can't whelp anymore, they dump them."

His eyes snapped open, as did his mouth.

I went on. "The dogs there live in cages so small they can barely turn around. For months and sometimes years if they don't find a buyer fast enough. They don't have any room to exercise or play. They sleep in their own filth. Their food and water is often contaminated, and their cages are crawling with bugs."

De Marco looked like he was going to be sick.

I continued. "I see dogs from puppy mills every day. Do you know what I see? Dogs with swollen paws, bleeding paws. Injuries from feet getting caught in the cage wires. They have severe tooth decay and ear infections. Sometimes they have lesions on their eyes. They are often dehydrated and malnourished—and those are the lucky ones who get out and get to a vet. Most receive no veterinary care, and in some places they're left to the mercy of the elements. Those dogs often die of exposure."

I leaned over and tapped on the file folder. "Eureka Acres is one of those puppy mills. Shelly was going to expose them."

He turned over the pages again, with a new, horrific look of fascination. "Are you saying that someone from Eureka Acres killed Dr. Capra because she was going to publish an exposé?"

"It sure looks that way to me," I said.

six

The next day dawned grey and drizzly, which seemed appropriate for a funeral. I noticed all kinds of resistance within myself: *There is too much work to do. What good does a funeral do? Shelley is gone. No one will notice if I'm not there.*

But no matter how many excuses I gave, I heard my mother's voice piercing through the haze: "People only die the once." Besides, I was supposed to give the eulogy. Right. I needed to go. I owed Shelley that. But I couldn't go alone. I needed the person closest to me at a time like this. I needed Scout. I knew it was unusual to take a dog to church, but I knew that Shelley would approve.

I pulled up into the parking lot of St. Julian's-in-the-Valley Episcopal Church and shut off the engine. Scout's snout pointed to the door in eager anticipation.

"Don't be so excited—we're just going to church."

But she was excited. It made me wonder what she knew that I didn't. I had never been to an Episcopal church, and did not know what to expect. I had been raised Catholic, but hadn't darkened a church's doorway since before I went away to college. I wouldn't say that I didn't have a religious bone in my body, but if I did, they were very small bones, like the stapes in my ears. That was it—my stapes were religious, but nothing else was.

I held the door for Scout, who scampered in ahead of me. Once inside, I paused and looked around. The scent of some old, exotic incense romanced my nose. Something in me relaxed. Everything here was oddly familiar. There was a font of holy water by the door. My autopilot took over—I dipped my hand in and made the sign of the cross. Spots of bright color illuminated the walls, cast by the stained glass—still brilliant even on a rainy day. Rich green tapestries adorned the walls and altar area of the gothic-looking structure.

About twelve feet in front of the altar, just before the beginning of the aisle, an urn sat on a small table, along with a large black-and-white photo of Shelley. There was a side altar dominated by an enormous stained-glass window depicting a medieval nun holding an orange cat. I smiled at the oddness of it. I didn't know who this St. Julian was, but if cats were important to her I liked her already.

Scout was looking at me, waiting for a signal. I stepped into the left aisle and felt the rumble of the organ in the stone beneath my feet. It was majestic, powerful, confident—all of the things I was not right now.

Looking around, I saw that there was already a handful of people there. I spied Ellie's ponytail, and saw that an assortment of clinic staff had taken over a section of the pews. I made my way to them and sat next to Ellie. She gave me a reassuring smile.

I had expected Scout to curl up at my feet, but she had other ideas. She sat in the pew on the other side of me, straight upright, her head nearly level to my own, and seemed to be intensely interested in everything that was going on. "You are a better parishioner than I am," I told her.

I had made some notes on the eulogy, and I pulled them out of my pocket and reviewed them. The thoughts all flowed together. It was an outline, but they were mostly stories. I didn't relish public speaking, but I didn't anticipate any trouble moving from one story to the next.

Catching movement out of the corner of my eye, I looked over and saw Shelley's parents passing in the aisle. "Wait here," I said to Scout, giving her the hand signal for "stay." I leaped up and followed her folks until they were seated. Then I stepped in front of their pew and offered my hand. "Mr. and Mrs. Capra, I'm so sorry."

"Thank you," her mother said, but without recognition. She was a large woman, white-haired, her back stooped and her fingers knotted with arthritis. Beside her, her husband looked insubstantial by comparison. He was bone-thin, with a smart grey suit straight out of a stylish 1930s film, his thin hair gelled and combed straight back.

"I don't know if you remember me, but I was Shelley's roommate in college. I'm Casey Gibbons."

"Oh, yes!" Her mother's face brightened. "I remember you! The slutty girl. Of course."

My head cocked in much the same way Scout's does when she doesn't understand something. I'm sure I frowned. Mr. Capra patted his wife's hand and pointed to his head with his other hand. *Dementia*, he mouthed.

"Ah," I said, nodding. "Well, Shelley and I have been working together this past year, and..." And what? And I'm as sad as you are? No. There's nothing worse than losing a child.

Once more Mr. Capra came to my rescue. "You...you found her, didn't you?"

"I did." I stopped being conscious of my facial features as

real emotion pierced through whatever protective covering I had unconsciously conjured. I suddenly felt overwhelmed with sorrow.

"It's too bad she became a Protestant," Mrs. Capra said.

"This all looks pretty Catholic to me," I noted. I was surprised by this myself.

"God understands," Mr. Capra said. Conspiratorially, he added under his breath, "No women in the Catholic priesthood...and then the sex abuse scandals. That was the last straw for her."

I nodded. Shelley had never discussed her religion with me, but her father's reasoning was consistent with the Shelley I knew. Her father patted the seat next to him. "Sit for a moment, won't you?"

My eyebrows rose and I did as he asked. He leaned toward me, which made me a little uncomfortable, but it was what he said next that truly shook me. "Shelly left a living trust. The veterinary practice was hers, you know."

"Yes," I said, wondering where this was going.

"The last time we talked, she mentioned that—should anything happen to her—it should pass to you...if you want it."

I blinked. I opened my mouth, but nothing came out.

"You don't need to do anything right now. I'll draw up the paperwork and give you a call."

Somehow I found my tongue. "I don't know what to say."

"Do you want it?" He looked straight at me for the first time since I'd approached him. Did I want it? There was a deep yes in my belly. "Yes," I said. And I knew it was right.

He nodded. "Then it's yours. I'll be in touch."

"Thank you," I somehow managed. The organ swelled and I realized the service was about to begin. Uncertainly, I got to my feet. I grasped at his hand and held it tightly, which did not seem to please his wife. I let go of it and headed back to the pew where Scout was waiting for me. She was still seated like a regular parishioner. All she needed was a bonnet, and no one would suspect she didn't belong there.

I was still in shock as the first hymn began. There was a general rustling as people stood, and somehow I managed to do the same. Scout stood, too, turning a tight circle on the pew.

My head was still spinning due to the magnitude of Shelly's father's gift, but I forced myself to focus. I owed that to Shelley. A small choir followed the processional cross down the aisle, followed by the minister. Was he a priest? A pastor? I wished I knew more about Episcopalians. It was all very familiar, however, which is to say, it was all very Catholic.

Once in place, the minister gave a page number and I scrambled, fumbling with the red prayer book in the pew rack in front of me, and hastily flipped to the required page. This *was* different, but I have always prided myself on being adaptable.

The minister gave a heartfelt welcome. He said a few things about Shelley that made me realize that he had been far from a stranger—he did know her. *Maybe better than I did,* I thought. I studied the minister. He was about my own age, with brown hair parted in the middle that fell to his collar. His cheekbones were high, as if he might have a Native American somewhere in his family tree. His lips were angular; his smile was kind. It was hard to tell what kind of build he had under his robes, but his face was lean. And his voice was appropriately soothing, a strange mix of joyful and mournful. The juxtaposition felt mysterious to me. I noticed I was leaning in, not wanting to miss a word.

After the readings, he gave a sermon that surprised me. He barely mentioned Shelley at all, and it seemed to me more of an Easter sermon—all about the resurrection and the hope of resurrection—which seemed strange to me.

My mind kept wandering, but I looked at the program and realized that I was up soon. After another hymn, I rose and made my way to the lectern to the left of the altar. I removed my notes from the pocket of my blazer and put them on the lectern. That was the last I saw of them.

I cleared my throat and looked out over the congregation. Many more people had entered since Scout and I had come in, and the number surprised me. I saw encouraging smiles from the clinic staff. But Shelley's parents seemed to be almost crumpled in on themselves. I didn't blame them. Scout remained stock still, upright in the pew, her eyes locked on mine.

I had been feeling guilty all morning because I didn't feel what I thought I was supposed to be feeling. I had a vague sense of what someone should feel when a friend dies, and I had been waiting for it to descend upon me. But it had not. I had simply moved through my days, as unfeeling as a robot.

But when I opened my mouth to speak, nothing came out, nothing but a faint croaking sound as my throat swelled shut. There was something about the atmosphere in the church— the candles, the altar clothes, the pageantry—that unlocked what had previously been kept safely hidden away. My eyes flitted to the urn just a few yards away. It seemed impossibly small for the big presence Shelley had been in my life. I lost it.

I looked at my notes, but I couldn't read them through the liquid film of tears suddenly erupting from my eyes. I felt every eye on me. I started to panic. I didn't mind feeling grief—I really didn't. I expected it. I was, I realized, a little disappointed that I had not felt it more strongly. I only wished that it had picked another moment to drag me under the water like a riptide.

To make it worse, I could hear people begin to whisper. I worked my mouth, but my brain seemed frozen, and I could not speak. That was the moment that Scout decided howling was the appropriate liturgical response to my paralysis.

"Scout! Not now!" I shouted, and that exclamation seemed to shake something loose. I still couldn't see my notes, and I had forgotten everything I had hoped to say. Instead, I opened my mouth and stupid things fell out of it. "Shelley was my friend. I loved her. She...she saved me. I am going to miss her... terribly." My head was empty of any other words in English or any other human tongue. In truth, what I felt most like doing was joining Scout in a good howl. "I'm sorry," I managed, and left the lectern.

My legs were shaky as I made my way back to the pew. Scout whined as I sat next to her, and I felt her snuffling at my face, making sure I was okay. I stroked her head and buried my face in her fur, breathing in the sweet and primal smell of comfort.

The rest of the service passed in a blur. There was communion, but I felt immobilized. Besides, I didn't know what the rules were in this strange church that seemed to be almost completely Catholic in all but name. So I sat quietly, feeling wave after wave of emotion play catch up from the past week, grief now joined by the shame of botching my friend's eulogy. Shelley's father was no doubt rethinking his gift. I gritted my teeth, hardly able to wait for the moment I could bolt from the place and be blessedly alone with my feelings and my dog. The recessional seemed to drag, and I wondered if Episcopalians were required by law to sing every plodding goddamn verse in their blue hymnal.

But finally it was over, and relieved as I was, I began plotting my escape so as to encounter as few human beings as possible. Everyone rose and after an initial storm of bustling, I began to head for the rear of the church. I eyed a door just in front of me, to the left of the altar area. I didn't know where it led, but surely I could find my way to an exit. "C'mon," I said to Scout, and made for it.

It led to a hallway, cinderblocks painted an institutional aqua. There was a doorway at the far end of the hall—through its glass I could see the green of trees and the rumbly gray of the sky. I headed for it, Scout trotting beside me. As we passed an open doorway, I heard a quick "Hey!"

I hesitated. Was that "hey" intended for me? And even if it was, was I obligated to stop for a "hey"? The "get-the-hell-out-of-here" impulse was strong. But something held me back. Reluctantly, I moved back toward the open doorway and peered inside.

"There you are. Come in." The minister was disrobing.

That is—he was fully dressed, but was in the act of taking off the white robe, revealing his street clothes—black pleated dockers and a black clerical shirt. The collar was strange, however—instead of the inch of white at his neck, it was a white band that stretched all the way around.

I stepped into the room, but not too far. One never knows when one will need to beat a hasty retreat. Scout had no such hesitation, however. She barged in and headed straight for the man, burying her snout directly in his crotch.

"Well, hi there," he said, laughing, ruffling at her ears. She knew better than to jump up on him, but I knew she was thinking about it. "Is she a service dog?"

"Not officially," I confessed. "But I needed her to be one... today."

"I understand. I'm glad she's here." He hung up his robe and crossed the room, putting out his hand. "I don't think we've met, not formally. I'm Jack Mornington. Folks around here call me Father Jack."

I shook his hand. "Father Jack," I repeated. "I didn't know Protestants used 'father' language."

"Most don't," he shook his head. "Only us Episcopalians."

"So does that mean you're a priest? I mean, as opposed to a pastor or a minister?"

"I suppose I'm all those things," he smiled. It was a warm, lovely smile. The edges of his lips looked sharp enough to open a can of dog food. I tried not to stare at them. "But our church usually uses 'priest' to describe its clergy."

"Well, it was...ah..." I was going to say "a lovely service," except that I had wrecked it.

"Something tells me that your eulogy did not go as planned," he said.

"No," I admitted. I looked at my shoes and crossed my arms.

"I'm sorry," he said. "That kind of thing has happened to me, too. It's embarrassing and humiliating."

I met his eye for the first time. He was utterly sincere. I felt myself relax a bit; I let my arms drop to my sides. "Yeah," was all I could manage.

"Do you want to talk about it?" he gestured to a couple of chairs. It was a small room, cluttered with antique-looking wardrobes and festooned with banners and ribbons and church paraphernalia I didn't recognize hanging on the walls. The chairs seemed just a bit too close together. As if sensing this, he grabbed the back of one of them and pulled it into the middle of the room, creating some distance from the other one.

He sat, and I did too. Scout took the hint and turned a quick circle at my feet before plopping down on the linoleum floor. I felt Father Jack's eyes on me, and when I looked up, his face was compassionate. He waited for me to speak, and the silence quickly became awkward. Yet he did not seem uncomfortable with it. I wondered if that was a clergy thing. I gave myself permission to be okay with the silence, too, and the moment I stopped fighting it, something shifted. The silence itself became delicious, and after some internal adjustment, I let myself soak it in and enjoy it.

Eventually, though, I said, "I miss her so much."

Father Jack nodded. "She told me a lot about you. She was so excited when you came to work with her."

This news surprised me. It had never occurred to me that Shelley would talk to other people about how she felt about me. But of course she would. "It was a good partnership."

"That's what she said, too," he said.

What else did he know? I tried not to feel uncomfortable.

"How are you taking care of yourself?" he asked.

I didn't quite know how to answer such a personal question from a complete stranger. Perhaps the question didn't seem strange to him because it's the kind of thing he says all day?

"I'm okay," I deflected.

"Forgive me, Dr. Gibbons, but you don't seem very 'okay' to me."

"No." I looked down again.

"Do you have anyone to talk to?" he asked.

Once more, he took me by surprise. My mind raced through my list of friends (short) and acquaintances (long). Now that Shelley was gone, who did I have to talk to, really? The clinic staff? We were all grieving in our own way, but not together. Sarge? I didn't really know if he even considered me a friend. "Not really," I heard myself say.

"Well," he leaned in and put his hand on mine, looking me in the eye. "You do now." He leaned back again and pulled a card from his breast pocket. He gave it to me. "Here's my cell number. Call me anytime, morning, noon, night, middle-of-the-night—it doesn't matter."

"I wouldn't—"

"But you *can*," he said, giving me a sad smile. "I'm giving you permission. And I hope you will." He looked toward the room's small stained-glass window, dim from the storm. "Death is a mystery, and we're not made to walk through mysteries alone. Alone, mysteries can beat us down and wound us, because they're just too damned big. But if we have just one person to walk beside us, mysteries can ennoble us, heal us, make us more than we were. The weight of Glory is meant to be shared."

I had no idea what any of that meant, but it sounded comforting, and he obviously meant well. "Well, uh, thanks." I put the card in my pocket. "Maybe I will."

"I hope you do." He leaned back, but didn't say more.

I rose and offered him my hand again. He got up and shook it. "Let yourself grieve deeply," he said. "It's the only way to move through it and heal."

"Uh...thanks," I said again. Without another word I turned on my heel and was relieved to see Scout by my side. *Maybe there is something to having someone walk beside you after all*, I thought. But I had to stop myself from running for the door.

seven

The numbness returned as I drove toward home. Halfway there, I remembered the clinic—my clinic—and made a quick turn to go back there. Once I arrived, I bade Scout wait in the car. The place was quiet when I walked through the door, although it wasn't empty.

"Dr. Gibbons. How are you?" It was Ellie, seated at the reception desk. She had exchanged the black dress she'd worn to the funeral for a comfortable set of cartoon-patterned scrubs. The shock of green dyed into her hair seemed much more in place with the scrubs, I noted, as did her numerous piercings.

"I'm okay," I said.

"That was completely, utterly unconvincing," Ellie pointed out. "Care to try again?"

"No," I said. She had me, and there was no use denying it. Besides, there was no point. Ellie was one of the most empathic people I had ever met. There was no putting one over on her, even if I had wanted to. "Any action?" I asked. Teri, our regular receptionist, had cleared the calendar for today, and I was frankly surprised to find anyone there.

"Tooby Leppert called to let us know that Summer just gave birth. Six healthy pups—two males, four bitches. One of the bitches is a runt, but seems to be doing fine."

"Oh, that's good news."

"Tooby said she tried to stay home as much as she could, but had to go out today. Summer must have popped as soon as she left. She seemed heartbroken that Summer had to go through that alone."

"Bitches have been whelping all by themselves for millennia," I said. "They're tough. She didn't need Tooby's help, no matter how eager she was to give it. And dogs aren't sentimental about things like we are. I'm sure Summer doesn't hold it against her."

"No," Ellie smiled.

"Besides, she's lucky Summer didn't whelp on her couch. Anything else?" I asked.

"Nope. All quiet," she said. "What can I do for you?"

"I came to give Cecil his five o'clock," I said, referring to the cat we were boarding.

"Already done. I hope you don't mind that I gave it at 4:50."

"No, that's fine. Thank you." My shoulders deflated. Giving Cecil his pill had been something to do. The emptiness of the rest of my day opened its craterous maw and showed me all of its huge, pointy teeth.

"I do have this for you, though." She slid a piece of paper in my direction toward the front side of the desk. I closed the distance to the desk and picked it up.

"You said you wanted a list of people who might want to hurt Dr. Capra," she said. "It's not a long list, but it's a list."

I looked it over quickly, and was surprised to see not just

names—four of them, to be exact—but phone numbers, addresses going back ten years, and social security numbers. "Ellie, this is...how did you...?"

"I just did a little digging."

I knew Ellie was good with a computer, but I didn't know she was this good. "Uh...thank you. Is it...you know...legal for me to have all this stuff?"

"I don't know. There's nothing there that isn't on the internet."

"Yeah. Okay. Um...thanks."

Just then my cell phone rang. "Excuse me," I said to Ellie.

She nodded and turned back to her computer screen. I hit the green button on the phone and put it to my ear. I didn't recognize the number, and half expected it to be a nuisance call.

"Dr. Gibbons?" the voice said. I recognized the voice, but it took me a few seconds to place it.

"Yes?"

"This is Detective De Marco, from the county Sheriff's Office."

The penny had dropped before he said his name. "Yes, Detective. How can I help?"

"I just wanted you to know that I reviewed the file you brought by, and I have discussed it with the sheriff. We found it all very interesting, but...we still don't see any evidence of foul play. We have decided not to investigate. I just wanted you to know."

I reached out to one of the chair backs to steady myself. "I – I'm very sorry to hear that," I managed.

"I'm sure you are. And I totally understand. But we have a limited staff here—and a limited budget—and we have to choose our cases carefully."

"I get that," I said. "I just think you made the wrong decision."

"Well, you're entitled to your opinion, of course. Everyone is."

I'm sure he didn't mean that to be as dismissive as it sounded, but it grated on me. I thought, but I couldn't think of a reply.

"Dr. Gibbons, are you there?"

"Yes." I cleared my throat. "I'm here."

"Oh. Okay. Well, I just wanted to pass along that news. You have a good night."

"Sure. You, too," I said, although how sincerely, I'm not sure. I put the phone back in my pocket.

I must have been staring into space for several seconds, because the next thing I knew, Ellie was waving at me from behind the desk. "You okay?"

"Yes. Why does everyone keep asking me that?"

"Um...because your friend just died and you're acting obviously not-okay."

I took a deep breath. Trust Ellie to give it to me straight. The problem was, I didn't always want it straight. I preferred my truth diluted with a bit of grenadine and a spritz of seltzer. But that wasn't Ellie.

"Do you want me to take you home?" she asked.

"No. I can drive."

"Are you sure?"

"Yes," I said.

"Was that bad news?" She pointed to my pocket with the phone.

It wasn't any of her business, but I stopped myself before saying that. She was concerned about me, and that counted for something. It counted for a lot, actually. "Yes. It was the county

Sheriff's Office—one of the detectives. They've decided not to investigate Shelley's death."

She pursed her lips. "I'm so, so sorry."

"Yeah," I said.

"So what are you going to do?"

I thought about Summer, giving birth all on her own, and I knew. "Tough bitches go it alone," I said.

eight

"Mrs. Garrett, you wouldn't happen to be...missing your teeth, would you?"

Marilyn Garrett's eyes snapped open wide and her hand went to her mouth as if to hide it. She was sitting in the chair in Exam Room Three with her Corgi Snowball on the floor beside her. She stroked Snowball's fur with her free hand to calm her. "How did you know?"

I wanted to say, *Aside from the fact that you're gummier than usual this morning...* But I wisely turned the computer screen toward her and pointed to an x-ray I'd just taken of Snowball's abdomen. "I know because I found them. Snowball isn't dyspeptic, her small intestine is being blocked by an intact dental bridge." I moved my pen in a circle around the misplaced prosthesis. There was no doubt about what it was. Her dog's intestinal tract was smiling at us just as brilliantly as Mrs. Garrett ever did on a good day.

"Oh, my," Marilyn said. "What can we do?"

"Well, if it were pennies or rocks, I'd say a good old-fashioned cat laxative would do the trick—but this looks too big. I think it's unlikely that it'll pass on its own." I turned the screen back toward me and opened a new window. "But just to be sure, we'll put her into a comfy crate here in the clinic and we'll take another film in a few hours. If the bridge is still where it is now, we'll need to get Snowball in for surgery tomorrow. In fact, I suggest we schedule it now, just to be sure we don't give someone else the slot. We can always cancel if she...eliminates it on her own."

I heard a snuffle. When I looked up, Mrs. Garrett was burying her face in her dog's fur and making a choking sound. She was crying, I realized. "Hey," I said, placing a tentative hand on her shoulder. "Snowball is going to be fine. I do these kinds of surgeries all the time. She won't be in any pain, and she'll soon be a lot more comfortable than she is now."

A few additional squeaks escaped her throat, then she picked her head up and nodded. Her eyes were red. "It didn't go so well for Champ," she said.

I stopped my data entry and concentrated on *not* rolling my eyes. *Champ again,* I thought. *We're never going to hear the end of that.* "Things do happen, Marilyn, but things like...well, what happened to Champ...are exceedingly rare. It was a one-in-a-hundred-thousand chance. Snowball is going to be fine...and so are you." I gave her my best reassuring smile. Marilyn didn't look so sure.

"Tomorrow at 7am all right?" I asked her.

"Uh...isn't that early?"

"We're overloaded since Shelley was ki—since Shelley died," I said. "We're just trying to fit people in wherever we can. The surgery won't be 'til eight, but we need to get Snow-ball prepped and sedated."

"Oh. Okay."

"Nothing to eat after 6pm tonight, all right?" I warned. "I mean it. Not even water. Close the lids on the toilets."

"Oh. Okay," she said.

"I'll see you in the morning, then," I said. I put my hand on Snowball's fur. "And you, miss, be good. I'll see you bright and early." I ruffed the dog's ears, but Snowball was too uncomfortable to enjoy it.

I exited the room and shook my head. The ghost of Champ wasn't leaving anytime soon, it seemed. I finished entering my notes into the computer in the back room and then handed the file with its charge sheet to Ellie. Then I spun back toward the rack near the exam rooms and picked up the next file.

Entering Room Two, I was met by a smartly dressed middle-aged man in wire-rimmed glasses and pressed khakis. With him was a black standard poodle with a no-nonsense cut.

"Mr...Dalton," I said, glancing at the file. I shook his hand. "This must be Cher."

"Yes. Chas, please. Good to meet you, Doctor."

"Tell me what's happening with Cher." I put my hands into the pockets of my lab coat and surveyed the dog.

"She hasn't been eating. She's been vomiting...in fact, she can't keep anything down. She's drinking a lot—I mean *a lot*. Other than that, she barely moves."

I nodded. The tech had already taken her temperature—she was running a fever. "Can you help me get her on the exam table?" I asked.

"Of course."

He positioned Cher's front paws so they were on the table, and then hoisted her back legs until she was up. She was shaking, back arched, clearly unhappy and unwell. "Shhhh, girl, you're going to be just fine," I said, patting her side. I fitted the earpieces of my stethoscope into my ears and listened to her chest. There didn't appear to be any fluid in the lungs, and her heartbeat seemed strong and regular. I recoiled my scope and put it back in my pocket.

I felt at her belly, examined her genitals, and checked her eyes. "Okay, girl, down you go," I said, anxious to get her back to ground level where she could curl up and feel more comfortable.

"Do you know what's wrong with her?" Dalton asked.

"Dehydrated, fever, nasty vaginal discharge. I need to run some tests, but I have a strong suspicion."

"And that is?"

"You're a breeder," I said. "What is the name of your business?"

"The Royal Poodle," he said. "Our logo is a poodle with a... you know, a crown."

"Right, I've seen that. You've had some champions."

"We have." He looked pleased that I knew about his successes. "Cher was a champion in her prime."

"She's a lovely, lovely dog," I said. "How many litters has she had?"

"Five," he said.

My eyes widened. I checked myself. "Well, Mr. Dalton, if my suspicions are correct, Cher's brood bitch days are over."

"Oh." He looked disappointed. "Um...how did you know she was a brood bitch?"

"Teats don't get that distended by themselves. Besides, a litter is hard on a body. I'd say Cher has held up amazingly well to carry five of them to term."

"So what do you think is the problem with her now?"

"I suspect pyometra—it's an infection of the uterus."

"Is it serious?"

"Untreated, she'll die within a day or two, the way she's presenting now. I'm going to take her in back for some blood work and an ultrasound. That will confirm the diagnosis, but I'm pretty confident. This isn't my first rodeo."

"What's the treatment?"

"Emergency surgery to remove her ovaries and uterus."

"So she really never will be able to..." He looked down at the dog, who was turning circles, but unable to find a place that seemed comfortable enough to lie down.

"No."

"Uh...how much will the treatment be?"

"Let's make sure I'm right, then I'll do an estimate for you."

"Ballpark?"

I moved my head back and forth. "Three thousand dollars. About what you get for one of her pups, I imagine."

I watched his eyes move back and forth. Cher was not a pet, I knew. This was a businessman, and Cher was simply an asset. And now she wasn't an asset at all, but a rather inconvenient liability. It would be a lot cheaper to simply put her down. I met Dalton's eyes, and I knew what he was thinking. I narrowed my eyes to let him know that I knew it, and that he'd better be careful. My heart went out to Cher—a beautiful bitch with many good years of life left...but only if she was part of a pack that loved her.

Dalton stroked Cher's fur. He looked at his hands. "There was a girl I loved...once. Nancy," he said, smiling sadly. "She had an infection, and...well, she couldn't have children after that."

"You didn't marry her?" I asked.

"It was...complicated," he said. He seemed lost in memory, and it was clearly not a happy memory. "But no, we didn't marry." He looked up at me, then, forcing a smile. "I still loved her, though."

"We are all worth more than our ability to simply reproduce," I said. "And that's true for Cher, as well."

He nodded and bit his lip. My heart went out to him. He seemed to be feeling a mixture of emotions that I wasn't able to read. "Well, I'll do anything for my dogs. Cher has been a good brood bitch, and she deserves a cushy retirement," Dalton said, sniffing.

"I'm glad to hear you say that," I said. "You know, she'd clean up really nice. With your connections, I'm sure you can find a good, loving home for her."

"Yes, that's just what we'll do."

I wasn't so sure. "I can connect you with Gold Country Poodle Rescue, if you like. They'll take her off your hands and handle the whole adoption process."

"No. I imagine we can still get a price for her. As you say, she's a pretty dog."

I nodded and, grabbing a lead from a hook on the wall, slipped it around Cher's neck. "C'mon girl, let's do some tests."

"Good to meet you, Doctor," Dalton said.

"You too, Mr. Dalton. It's always good to know there are reputable breeders around."

"We take a lot of pride in our dogs."

"It shows," I said. I led Cher out of the room, relieved that such a fine animal might have a chance to retire to a loving home.

nine

You fall into bad habits when you live alone. When Dennis and I were married, we ate nearly every night at home, and we put some thought into what we'd eat and whether it was healthy. I'm not saying I miss Dennis (or the sizable nest-egg he lost us), but there certainly were things about married life that were good—healthy eating at home being chief among them.

But no, here I was again at Millie's Diner. I'd taken a booth near the door to keep an eye on Scout. Normally I'd sit at the bar and talk to Sarge, but tonight I needed some space—to hear myself think as well as the real estate afforded by one of the larger tables in the place.

I laid out all of the files I had collected so far, and then turned a page to a fresh sheet on a yellow legal pad. But before I could dive in, I detected a shadow in front of me. Without looking, I turned my coffee cup over. "Decaf, please, Sarge."

Instead of pouring the decaf, the shadow snatched the cup from my table and walked off with it. I looked up to see the back end of a man wearing blue jeans and a gray hoodie walking away from me with my cup. I had to admit, he had a very, very nice back end. I blinked and forced myself to look up. The man walked straight to Sarge, who beamed at the sight of him. He lifted the coffee cup and Sarge filled it from the proper orange pot. Then the man, bearing my full cup, turned around. Aaaand that's when I recognized him. My shoulders deflated a bit.

"Father," I said as he set the coffee cup down on the table within my reach. "Sorry, I didn't see that it was you."

"Hey, Casey. How are you?"

I should have looked at his face, but I was afraid I'd stare stupidly at his chiseled, angular, gorgeous lips. "Ah...I'm okay."

"Famous last words," he said. He gestured to the bench opposite mine in the booth. "May I?"

I really, really didn't want to talk with him, partly because I had work to do, and partly because I didn't like the somersaults my stomach turned when I was near him. "Sure," I said, and moved a couple of the files.

"I saw Scout on the way in," he said.

"Did she put her nose in your crotch?" I asked.

"Just like a perfect lady," he said.

I didn't know quite how to respond to that. It seemed slightly naughty, but in a way I really, really liked.

"So...how are you *really*?" he asked.

None of your goddam business, my head replied. Fortunately, my mouth said, "I don't know."

"That sounds like a much more honest answer."

Part of me bristled at that. He hadn't earned the right to speak so familiarly to me. But it occurred to me that saying hard and honest things was as much a part of his job as it was mine. I didn't let the feelings of my clients stop me from being straight with them. It made sense that Father Jack couldn't either. I felt myself soften toward him a bit. "I don't do...diffi-cult emotions well. I mostly just keep busy until they go away."

"And the only problem with that is that then they never completely go away," he said. "It helps in the present, but makes for a much more difficult future."

"And what do you suggest I do instead?" I met his eye for the first time.

"Grieve, of course. Give yourself space and permission to feel all the feelings coming up. Enter into them, name them, acknowledge them, give thanks for them. And then let them go."

"And do they go? After that, I mean?" I asked dubiously.

"They do. Well, that's not exactly right. Let me think about how to say this." He pulled at one of his beautiful lips and I was amazed at how plastic it was. It was actually *soft.* "When you fully feel it, it transforms into something else. If you don't fully feel it, it becomes like a pesky fly that won't leave you alone for years and years and years."

"But if you *do* fully feel it?" I asked.

"Then it becomes a tender and poignant memory that feels holy and sad and joyful all at the same time."

"That makes no sense," I said.

"No. True, though," he said. He seemed *so sure* it put me off a bit.

"What are you working on?" he asked, gesturing toward the file folders.

"Oh, nothi—" I saw his eyebrow rise and realized lying to the priest yielded nothing but diminishing returns. I sighed. "The police have decided not to investigate Shelley's death. So I figure it's up to me."

"You think it wasn't an accident, then?"

"Have you ever known Shelley to be clumsy?" I asked.

"Never," he said. "And I've seen her on church cleanup days."

I blinked, trying to imagine the Shelley I knew cleaning up around a church. It did not compute. It dawned on me again that there were perhaps large pieces of my friend's life that I knew nothing about. That scared me a bit. "Me, neither. I just can't believe she slipped and fell backward like that."

"She does have a three-legged dog."

"Tripod isn't the kind of dog who jumps up on you. He's way too well-trained. Plus...just the one back leg..." I shrugged.

"Right," he said, pulling on his chin. I hadn't noticed his chin before. It was a nice freaking chin. "How is Tripod, anyway?"

"He's living with one of our techs for the time being. He's doing fine."

"That's good. He's a good dog."

"He sure is." I looked up. "Are you a dog person?"

"I like dogs...a lot," he said. "But I don't have one now."

"But you did?"

"Yes. When my wife was...living."

My eyes widened and the voice in my head said, *So, Episcopal priests can get married?* so loudly that I was sure he could hear it.

"We had a dog together," he continued. "A Portuguese Water Dog named Ambrose."

"I have never heard that name before in my life."

"St. Ambrose of Milan baptized St. Augustine."

"So it's a boy's name?" I clarified.

"Yes. He was a great dog. And he lived a good long time—he was fourteen when he passed."

"That's a long life for a dog."

"Yeah, I'm grateful for that. But ever since then, I...I don't know..."

"You had to really feel some feelings before you were ready to get another one?"

He met my eye and smiled a sad smile. "Yeah."

"Are you ready now?"

"I think I am, actually."

"Well, you're in luck. I just met a standard poodle breeder earlier today."

Jack cocked his head.

"I know, I know—they're not Portuguese Water Dogs," I added. "But they are both smart and curly."

He laughed.

"If you want, I can hook you up," I offered.

"Thank you," he said, but he didn't look completely certain about it. "What do you have going here?" he asked.

He was changing the subject, but I let it slide. "Clues, I suppose. Maybe even evidence, if I can put it together."

"You mean clues about who killed Shelley?"

"Yes."

Now he looked intensely interested. "Who's your number one suspect?"

I tapped on one of the folders. Then I handed it to him. "It looks like Shelley was writing an exposé about a puppy mill. Eureka Acres Dog Farm."

"I've read her newspaper column, 'Pet Pages,'" Jack said. "She's a compelling writer. I guess if she decided to go after someone, it could be devastating."

"That's what I think too. I think Eureka Acres got wind of what she was doing and decided to...eliminate the threat."

Jack nodded as he leafed through the file. "This is...pretty damning stuff. The sanitary conditions alone..."

"Yeah," I agreed. "If I were an evil puppy mill owner, that is not information I'd want published."

He set the file aside. "But proving it..."

"I know." I pursed my lips as I thought about how impossible this all sounded.

"Who else have you got?" Jack asked.

I narrowed one eye at him. "You sure you want to hear all this? Don't you have, I don't know, icons to dust or something?"

"You're confusing me with the Orthodox. We like dust on our icons, thank you very much. Gives us the illusion of being a more ancient church than we are." He winked at me.

I blinked, not sure how to interpret that. Truth was, however, I liked being winked at. I immediately began to think about how I could get him to wink at me again. Then I told myself to stop being silly. I cleared my throat. "Well, okay. Then there's Maggie—Margaret Edgerton, I mean. Shelley was doing surgery on her dog Champ, and he died on the table."

"Ouch," Jack said, taking the file from me. He skimmed it. "I'm guessing Maggie is pissed."

I cocked my head. It sounded strange to hear a priest say "pissed," and I decided I liked it. "Pissed" had never sounded so delightfully dangerous. "She was threatening to sue—that was before Shelley died."

"And now?"

"We don't know. We're expecting the clinic to be named in the suit now, but haven't heard anything from her lawyer...and don't know if we will."

"Maybe she got what she was after," Jack said.

"Maybe," I agreed. "Then there are the animal rights lunatics."

"Oh, now, watch out. I donate to our local animal shelter," Jack said.

"So do I. Believe me, I'm a vet because I love animals. I have nothing against other people who love animals. But...there's a limit to everything."

"The extreme of every virtue is a vice," Jack said, picking up the file near him that I pointed to.

"Huh. I've never thought of it like that," I said.

"Sure. You've got to eat. Food is good for you. Healthy eating is virtuous. But what if you eat too much?"

"It's a...vice?"

"Gluttony," he nodded. "And what if you eat too little?"

"Another vice," I said.

"Yep—anorexia. Not one of the classical vices, obviously, but still destructive."

I felt a strange calm come over me. In the quiet of a few moments, I realized that I really liked this man—even if he was a priest. Not only was he disarmingly handsome, but he was geeky in a way that was both weird and appealing. It wasn't my own particular brand of geekiness, but it was still recognizable as geekiness, and I found that almost impossibly attractive. For a brief moment, I wondered if there was something here, and then just as quickly told myself that if there were, I'd probably screw it up.

"What's wrong?" he asked me. "Do I have a booger?"

"No!" I laughed despite myself. The sound of my own laughter sounded strange to me. It was pretty unusual these days for me to laugh. It felt as good as it did odd.

"Tell me about the animal rights people," he suggested.

"Last month, they spray-painted the clinic. 'Killers,' and 'Animals are people too.' We painted over it. They also spray-painted Shelley's windshield. She had to have her car towed to the shop so they could clean it off."

Jack shook his head slowly, looking at the photos in the file. "What's their deal? Don't they know you guys are trying to *help* animals?"

"They don't believe animals should be pets. They consider it slavery. They think pets should have the same legal rights that humans do. And since we don't *own* other humans, we shouldn't own pets, either."

His brows furrowed. "And just what do they think would happen to all the dogs and cats if we simply turned them all out onto the street?"

"Right. Humans and dogs and cats have evolved together, and we're mutually dependent on one another. We would have an easier time living without them than they would living without us."

"For several generations, at least."

"They'd have to go feral again, which would be...well, it's not the kind of life I'd want for Scout—or for any dog or cat I know."

"'Nature, red in tooth and claw...'" Jack quoted.

"Exactly so," I said. I looked at the file in his hand. "They've been stepping up their protests. It used to be postcards. Then it was email blasts to our clients—"

"Wait, how did they get ahold of your clients' emails?" Jack asked. "Because that's a federal offense, I think."

I shrugged. "I don't know. They just did."

His eyes widened. "And then the spray painting."

"Right."

"People murder abortion doctors," Jack said.

"That's exactly what I was thinking about," I said. "I keep thinking that they must see her in the same light."

"Not just her," Jack said. "Both of you."

ten

The next day at work was brutal. From the moment I entered the clinic at 7am until nigh until closing, there was nothing but an endless stream of animal suffering. I was exhausted by noon. Unfortunately, we were already backed up and I had to work straight through lunch. I had snagged a granola bar between cases, which was a band-aid, not a cure. I lost count of how many of the damn things I ate.

When I finally closed the door on the last client, I leaned against the counter near the centrifuge. My shoulders slumped nearly level to my breasts. I wasn't just tired, I was *bone* tired. I pushed off the counter and stumbled to the front desk.

"Long day, Doc," Ellie said, her face looking as tired as I felt.

"If we get one more emergency, just sedate me," I said. "I've got a syringe of ketamine ready to go, just in case."

Ellie laughed and spun in her office chair to face me.

"Tell me you found a vet to hire," I said, sinking into another chair behind the desk.

"I found four—here are their resumés," she said, putting a short stack of papers in front of me. I'm sure she would have preferred to email them, but I'm old school and she humors me. "But you should know—there are way more jobs than there are vets right now, so they're probably fielding a lot of offers."

"We'll need to stand out," I said.

"Yeah."

"Well, we have Gold Country," I said.

"That's a plus. But do we have money?"

I nodded. That was the question. Shelley and I made a modest salary, by veterinary standards. As the senior practitioner, Shelley made more than I did. Seniority suggested that I was now eligible for a higher salary—I was, after all, the senior vet at the practice. But if I did not increase my own salary, it would give us more "fishing" money to find a new vet. I didn't even give it another thought. "What are we offering?"

"That's up to you," Ellie said. "We haven't listed anything yet."

"Okay. Offer Shelley's full compensation."

She frowned. "Are you sure. You—"

"I'm doing just fine," I said. "We'll catch more flies with more honey...or something like that."

"Okay..." Ellie said, but she didn't sound convinced. Then she sat straight upright. "Oh. Almost forgot. There's something you need to see."

"Oh dear. Is this a good 'something I need to see,' or..."

"Not so much." She whirled around and, turning to the computer screen, pulled up a new browser window. A couple of clicks later and we were at the clinic's Facebook page. "Take a look." Ellie swiveled the screen toward me.

Instantly I saw a picture of Maggie Edgerton—her hair bundled up on top of her head the way my mother used to wear it in the 1970s. Next to it was a long post. I sighed as my eyes scanned it.

If you take your pet to the Gold Valley Animal Clinic, beware. My dog Champ was having trouble walking, and the doctors at Gold Valley told me he needed something called a Femoral Head Ostectomy. I love my dog, and so of course I said yes. I took him in for surgery, and that is the last time I saw my precious boy. They either killed him on the operating table, or they just let him die. If you love your pet, steer clear of Gold Valley Animal Clinic. They're deadly.

"Oh, that's just great," I said. "But I can't say I'm surprised. She can't go after Shelley anymore. The only thing she can do is go after the practice."

"Unless she already went after Shelley, and now she's gunning for you," Ellie said.

"Why me, though?" My hand involuntarily went to my chest. "I didn't do anything to her."

"What if she killed Shelley, but it wasn't enough of a catharsis?" she asked.

"Let me guess—you were an English major," I said.

Her spine straightened instantly. "How did you know?"

"Never mind," I said. Then I sighed. "I guess I need to go pay her a visit. Can you print out her address for me?"

"Sure thing, Doc," she said, and began clacking on the keyboard. I finished up some notes and wearily hung up my lab coat. Ellie handed me the paper with Maggie's address on it as I passed the desk for the final time, heading for the door.

"Are you going to Maggie's now?" Ellie called after me.

"I'd better, before this blows up on us," I said. "If we wait any more, she might post a bad Yelp review. Then we're really in trouble."

"For God's sake, Doc, get some rest."

I waved her off, but I knew she was right. Besides, Scout had been home alone all day. I'd swing by and pick her up on my way to Maggie's, I decided. Then she'd at least get a car ride, and that would cover a multitude of sins.

Speaking of sin, I looked up and was surprised to see Jack walking toward me, grinning to beat the band. He had on black chinos and a black, long-sleeved clerical shirt with the wrap-around white collar. Damn, but he was handsome. "Jack," I said. "What are you doing here?"

"Waiting for you," he said.

"So...you've been hanging around in the parking lot waiting for me to get off work?" I narrowed one eye at him.

He stopped and put his hands in the front pockets of his chinos. He pursed those lips of his and looked worried. "It sounds a little creepy when you put it like that."

"How *should* I put it, then?"

"Uh...I didn't want to disturb you at work, and I suspected that you'd be back on the hunt for Shelley's killer as soon as you were off, so...I figured you might need some backup."

"Huh. Okay, it doesn't sound nearly as creepy that way," I admitted. I didn't admit that I'd be grateful for his company, but I thought it.

His shoulders relaxed. "Whew. That felt like a close one. So...where are we going?" He rounded my car and waited by the passenger door.

"Margaret Edgerton's. But first we have to swing by and pick up Scout."

"Sounds like a plan," he said, and let himself in as soon as I'd unlocked the car.

As we sped toward home, it seemed odd to me how comforting and normal it felt riding in the car with him. At first we didn't speak, and I started to get uncomfortable. But when I looked over at Jack, his eyes were closed, and he seemed to be savoring the wind in his hair. He didn't seem to think the silence was awkward at all. *Maybe it's okay to not say anything,* I thought, which sounds stupid, but at the time felt like a bit of a revelation.

I pulled up at the house and set the brake. "I'll be right back," I said.

He smiled a contented smile. "Nice cottage."

"Thanks. I'm just renting it, but...yeah, I kind of love it."

Walking toward the house, I took in the rolling gold hills behind the cottage. They were a fire hazard, sure, but they were also beautiful. Nearby two birds were singing competing arias, and the air smelled sweet and dry. Scout met me at the door with unbridled joy, leaping more than two feet straight up. It occurred to me that she'd totally hold her own in a mosh pit. I clipped a leash to her collar and locked the door again behind us.

At the car, I opened the back door, and Scout bounded in, heading straight for Jack's face, covering it will her slobbery tongue. "Floozy," I said, but I secretly envied her lack of inhibition.

I started up the car again, and within moments we were on the road once more.

"Um...what are you going to say to her? Margaret, I mean?" Jack asked.

"I have no freaking idea," I said. "I do want her to stop posting negative comments."

"Okay. So how are you going to address that?"

I shrugged.

"Oh," he said. "I kind of thought you had a plan."

"I wish."

"Have you ever...you know...done this kind of thing before?" he asked.

"What? Investigate something?"

"Yeah."

"Nope."

His eyebrows rose dramatically. "Huh. 'Cause you kind of act like you know exactly what you're doing."

"I'm bluffing. I do the same in surgery, especially when I haven't a clue."

He just nodded, but his eyes looked a little afraid. Then he burst out laughing. "Oh, this is going to be fun."

"I'm not so sure about that," I said. "I'm kind of dreading it."

"Well, if you don't have a plan, let's make one," he suggested.

"I'm open to any ideas you might have."

"Sure. Why don't we pick up some flowers on the way? You can say something like, 'I didn't say anything before, because you were Shelley's client, and it was none of my business. But now that Shelley's gone, I feel like someone needs to be accountable. I'm so sorry about what happened to your dog. I brought you these flowers. I just want you to know that if you want to talk, or vent, or yell, or...whatever it is you need to say, that I'm ready to hear it, and it's okay.'"

I blinked. "Are you nuts?"

He blinked. "What?" He seemed perplexed. "She's angry, and she's lashing out publicly. Perhaps if she felt heard—really heard, really cared about—she'd not only stop with the attacks, but she might start talking. She might open up to you. She might tell you something valuable about how Shelley died. And if she's responsible, she might just give herself away. But that can only happen if you get her talking. And the best offense is—"

"A good defense?" I asked.

"No," he said. "Just the opposite. The best offense is vulnerability. If you disarm, you have the best chance of getting her to let her guard down too. Think of it as a tactical retreat."

"Is that what you'd do?" I asked.

"That's exactly what I'd do," he answered.

"And that kind of thing works?"

"I walk undefended into tense situations every day." He smiled at me, and I could see the sincerity in his eyes. "It's the only way to walk out again. It's counterintuitive, for sure. But it works."

I had a hard time wrapping my head around it. I was also too angry to roll over and show her my belly. I lost track of time as I thought it through, and before I knew it, I was pulling up in front of the Edgerton home.

"Here goes nothing," I said. "You should wait here, with Scout."

"Oh. You think so, huh?" He looked amused. "How can I provide backup from the car? Uh-uh. You do the talking, but I'm going to stand up there with you. Standing with is a big part of my job."

"So you're on the clock?"

"Not...exactly," he said.

"You know you still have your collar on, don't you?"

"Oh, hell," he said, reaching for his collar. His hands met behind his head and he snapped it free.

"Is that plastic?" I asked.

"Yep." He handed the collar to me. There it was, a ring of cheap plastic with holes for something like a cufflink at either end.

"Now you just look like a hit man, all in black like that. You don't have to kill me, now that I know your secret, do you?"

"Well, there are secrets and there are secrets." He winked at me, and a rush of chemicals flooded my brain, making me momentarily giddy.

I closed my eyes and took a deep breath. "All right. Let's go."

"We didn't get flowers," he pointed out.

"No. We'll have to do without flowers," I said.

He shrugged. "Okay."

I pushed the doorbell. A few moments later, Margaret Edgerton pulled open the door. Instantly her face darkened. "What do you want?" she asked.

"Did you kill my friend?" I asked. "Did you kill Shelley?"

Her mouth opened and her eyes went wide.

Jack pinched the bridge of his nose. "Oh, Lord," he said.

"Because I've seen what you've been posting on Facebook and on <u>Neighbors.net</u>. That's a lot of aggression. Enough aggression to kill someone, I think."

"What? I never!" Her voice was high and hoarse.

"Maybe you'd like to sit down with me and the sheriff and convince us of that."

"You talked with the sheriff?" she asked. The blood drained from her face. She looked away from us and seemed to collect herself. "I did not kill Doctor Capra!" She finally managed. "The nerve! She killed my Champ!"

"That's a lie and you know it. She was trying to help Champ. And some things just happen. They just do. Be real."

She closed her mouth. For some reason, mine kept going. "You're not helping anyone with your smear campaign. The only thing you're doing is setting yourself up for suspicion. Dr. Capra didn't die by accident. Someone killed her. And anyone with a bone to pick with her is a suspect, and right now that means you."

Margaret's mouth moved, but no coherent words were formed.

"Where were you on the afternoon of July 24th? That was last Thursday, in case you need reminding."

I waited patiently, allowing that awkward silence to build up and just stretch out. Being with Jack was teaching me useful things, but I'm not sure he'd agree that I was putting them to good use. Indignation rose in her eyes until I thought one of them might explode. But then she softened. "I was visiting my husband. He's got dementia. He's in elder care at the Fremont Home in Auburn."

"And what time was that?" I asked.

"I signed in at about 3pm. I signed out at 6pm. I had dinner with him there. Then I drove home."

My eyes moved back and forth as I thought. I'd found Shelley at about 7pm. She'd been dead for an hour or perhaps a little more—the blood was still fresh at the back of her head, after all, and rigor had not set in. It would have taken Maggie an hour to drive home from Auburn, which would put her here about the same time as I found Shelley. "Okay," I said. "We'll check that out. Bet on it." With that I turned on my heel and headed back to the car.

Once inside, I waited for Jack to join me. As he closed the passenger door, he said, "Well, that went well."

"It did," I agreed.

He raised one eyebrow.

"How can we check out her story?" I asked. "If we called that elder care place, would they tell us when she signed in and out?"

"No," Jack said. "But I have to visit a parishioner there tomorrow. I have to sign into that same book. I can check it."

I looked over at him, and to my shame, actually saw him for the first time since we'd arrived. "Would you?"

"Of course." He shrugged. "It's a small thing." His face took on a concerned look. "Are you sure you're okay to do this kind of thing? I mean, that was pretty...aggressive."

"We got what we needed."

"And if she's not our killer? Was the way you just talked to her justified? This is a woman who has experienced a lot of loss."

"So have I," I reminded him.

"No doubt, which reinforces my question. Is this something you are really...I don't know...fit to pursue right now?"

"Fit to pursue?" I asked him, my hackles rising.

"That came out wrong," he admitted. "What I'm saying is... are you too raw to do this kind of...investigation...without inflicting more damage on people? I mean, hasn't there been enough hurt already?"

The question hung on the air. The only other sound was Scout panting in my ear.

"Fair question," I decided. "Besides, I'm..."

"Overtired and overstressed and undergrieved." He smiled. It was all compassion.

"Will you stop being so goddam good?" I asked. "It's irritating."

"I'm not being good," he said. "I'm trying to find what's just. Isn't that what you want?"

I had to think about that.

"Or do you just want to smash something?" he added.

I felt emotion thicken my throat. Water rose unbidden to my eyes. I blinked it back. Then I felt his hand on my arm. "It's okay to feel it, Casey. You need to."

Then it came, busting out of me like a fire hose. I bashed my head against the steering wheel and sobbed. A wail escaped my throat. Scout howled.

When the sobbing subsided, I discovered my head was resting on Jack's shoulder and he was hugging me tightly to him. His hand rubbed the back of my head, and he was making soft shushing sounds. I drew away and wiped a trail of snot on my sleeve.

"That was good," he said.

"That was humiliating," I countered.

"You need to do more of that," he said.

"I need four fingers of whiskey," I said.

"Whiskey is also good," he agreed.

eleven

It was not how I wanted to spend my lunch period, but I was intrigued to get the text message.

> Can we talk? Gold Country Herald Expositor.
> Leslie Braun. 12:30?

I was tempted to say I didn't have time, but it just wasn't true. I typically got an hour and a half for lunch. Some days we ran late, and I only got an hour, but the stars aligned today, against all odds.

I swung by the cottage first and picked up Scout, who was all perky ears and sniffs as we sped toward nearby Utah City where the Herald Expositor's offices were located.

As we entered the building, I was grateful for the air conditioning. Scout turned heads, as she always did, because she was such a stunningly beautiful dog. The problem was, I suspected she knew it.

I found a directory on the wall near the elevators and figured out where I was supposed to go without too much difficulty. Time is never my friend, but this day I arrived only five minutes late—early by my standards.

"Dr. Casey Gibbons to see Leslie Braun," I told the woman at the reception desk.

She didn't even look at me, just nodded and picked up the phone. "Your 12:30 is here." She hung up, and still not looking at me, she turned and pointed down the hall. "Big office at the end. You can't miss it." Then she answered a ringing phone.

"C'mon, Scout," I said, and headed down the hallway. Sure enough, at the end was a large office. There were window panels on either side of the door, and I saw a large, middle-aged man with greasy black hair biting down on the end of an unlit cigar. I'm not proud of this, but I instantly disliked him. He looked exactly like the kind of bigoted, chauvinistic jerk I've encountered so often I've developed a six sense—and those antennae were definitely quivering. If my Spidey-senses were right, I didn't want to write for him no matter how much it paid.

Nevertheless, I was here, and the grown-up somewhere in the deep recesses of my subconscious reminded me to give him the benefit of a doubt. I knocked.

Leslie Braun squinted at me, and then waved me in. I turned the knob and Scout bounded in ahead of me. I gave her a gentle warning tug on her leash.

"You brought your ghost writer, I see," he said.

"This is Scout," I said. "I'm Dr. Gibbons."

"Thank you for clarifying. I suspect that the dog doesn't type."

"Scout might surprise you," I said.

Scout surprised me by jumping up onto the faux leather couch and sitting at attention, ears pointed straight toward the ceiling.

"He's eerily intelligent," Mr. Braun said.

"Yes. *She* is."

"*She*. Sorry."

See? the voice in my head said. *Chauvinistic.* I forced myself to be polite. "It's okay. I make the same mistake myself all the time. There's something inherently masculine about all dogs, just as there's something inherently feminine about all cats."

"You see there?" He pointed at me. "That's exactly the kind of thing I'm talking about."

"It is?" I asked, not following him at all.

"Are you just going to stand here?" he asked. He shooed me toward the couch with a flick of his chubby fingers.

I sat, my head almost level with Scout's. *We could be visiting a couple's counselor*, I thought, and smiled.

"Your friend wrote one of our most popular columns," he said, holding his cigar stub between two knuckles of his left hand.

I know I was supposed to be listening to him, but my eyes were glued to his gross cigar stub. My father had died of lip cancer. He'd started smoking at thirteen. "You know, just chewing on that will give you lip cancer," I said.

He ignored me. "I didn't say I liked her columns," he said. "I just said they were popular."

"It's not the tobacco that causes cancer, by the way," I noted. "Most people are surprised to hear that."

"She got on my nerves, because she was always overreaching. We asked for a feel-good advice column, you know?" He leaned back in his chair and rested one foot on a partially open drawer.

"It's actually the artificial fertilizer," I told him. "It breaks down into radioactive isotopes."

"She kept getting on her soapbox about this or that. One week it was a tirade against people who don't get their dogs neutered—or spayed, or whatever it's called. The next week she was all on her high horse about dog maulings being the fault of the owners, not the fault of the dog—which is total BS."

"People think it's the tobacco that's the problem, when really it's good old-fashioned radioactivity. It's the real danger," I finished.

He narrowed one eye at me. "I got a business to run here."

I narrowed one back at him. "I have a calling to uphold."

"Your job is pets, not people."

"My job is health, and I specialize."

"You're irritating in a very unusual and fascinating way," he said, pointing his cigar at me.

"I aim to please," I said. I shook my head to clear it—of my fixation on his cigar, of the ghost of my father. Then I shuddered.

"What just happened there?" he asked, "Because that was a little weird."

"Did you say why I'm here?" I asked him. "Because if I'm supposed to read between the lines, I have to level with you: I suck at that. I prefer to be straight with people, and I prefer that they're straight with me."

"Jesus, lady, you ever hear of foreplay?"

"Is that what this is?" I don't know whether it was the cigar or remembering my dad, or Braun's pushy demeanor, but the numbness I'd felt earlier was dissipating fast. I was suddenly aware of a lot of feelings—conflicting, strong, painful. I felt claustrophobic. I just wanted to get out of there.

"I don't know what this is. In fact, I'd like to start over. Maybe we can set some ground rules. Here's what I'd like to see happen. You come through the door, introduce yourself, and tell me the gender of your dog. Then we'll make pleasant small talk for a few minutes until we've established some rapport. Then I'll get down to business."

"I only have time for half of that," I said, pointing to my Snoopy watch. "So why don't we just skip to the 'getting down to business' part?"

He rolled his eyes and said "Jesus" again. "All right. Your former partner—God rest her soul—wrote a very popular column for us."

"'Pet Pages,'" I said. "That's a stupid name, by the way."

He scowled at me. "I came up with that."

"Knock me over with a feather," I said.

"Your friend, Dr. Capra, she thought it was stupid too."

"That's because Shelley was *not* stupid."

"You are coming dangerously close to being insulting. I don't like being insulted in my own office. In my office, I do the insulting."

"Got it," I said. "I'm socially dyslexic." In fact, I was just barely holding it together. Intellectually, I knew that grief was unpredictable. I'd heard people say that it came and went with no discernible pattern, but now that I was actually experiencing it, it was nothing like what I had expected.

For several moments, we sat in silence. This was not Jack's easy silence, this was tension-you-could-slice-like-a-peach silence. The voice in my head told me that I was blowing this for no discernible reason, and I forced myself to relax. Then, to my surprise, Braun laughed. "You really know how to pile it on," he said, gesturing at me with his cheroot. "Look, I asked you here to get to know you, and to ask you if maybe you'd consider taking over the column."

"Can I change the title?" I asked.

His face went slack and his eyebrows rose comically with surprise. "Does that mean you'll do it?" he asked.

I didn't know. I hovered between making a commitment and just cutting and running as fast as my feet could take me.

"I...uh...I have to think about it," I said. "But the title is a nonstarter."

"Okay, what if you keep the title for six months, just to establish your rapport with the readers, then you can change it to something...mutually agreeable?"

I had to admit that this was a fair compromise. "What's the compensation?"

"Compensation?" he asked.

"You didn't pay Shelley for the work she did for you?"

"She considered it community outreach, I think. It was free marketing for your clinic, you know."

"Ah. So you're asking me to provide free labor out of the kindness of your heart."

"Why do you have to make everything sound so ugly?"

I was breathing more deeply now, and was relieved that the feelings seemed to be subsiding. It was easier to focus on what Braun was saying and my usual sarcasm kicked in. "I'm pointing out the preexisting ugly. I'm just wiping the cream-cheese frosting off it."

"Okay, okay. 2¢ per word."

"And that works out to, what? Two dollars per column?" I asked.

He shrugged. "It's pay."

"It doesn't even pay for the coffee required to write the damn thing," I countered.

"Fine. 20¢ a word."

"Twenty dollars a column?" I asked. "I'll put an hour's work into that, easy. You want the column, you'll pay my hourly rate for it."

"Which is?"

"$150 per hour."

"You want me to pay you $150 for each column?"

"I want you to agree to that before I'll think about it," I clarified.

"You drive a harder bargain than my Uncle Morty," he told me. "But okay, let's say we strike a bargain. *If* I offer you your outrageous sum—"

I glared at him.

"—I'd like you to take the column in a new direction."

"I thought readers liked the column the way it was."

"The readers did. But I didn't. And the advertisers didn't."

"Which advertisers?" I asked.

"That's not important," he said. "What's important is that this needs to be a fluffy-puppy kind of column. Feel-good, you know."

"You. Want me. To write a feel-good 'fluffy-puppy' column?" I asked.

"Yeah. Something sweet. Something...inoffensive."

"Have you *met* me?" I asked.

twelve

It's a good thing that Scout has a mind of her own, because I was so lost in thought leaving Braun's office that I didn't notice whether she was with me or not. Fortunately, when I came to in the elevator, she was dutifully sitting by my feet—in fact, leaning against my leg.

"Oh! Dr. Gibbons!" I had barely noticed my dog, but had not at all noticed that there was someone else in the elevator. That's embarrassing, but I forced a quick smile and whiplashed my brain trying to place the face and voice.

She was a bit taller than I, but a lot younger. And she did look familiar...

My struggle must have been evident, because she very kindly made the connection for me. "I'm Tracy Chaconas. I brought my cat Pinky to see you a couple of weeks ago."

The penny dropped, and I shook my head. "Tracy, of course. I'm so sorry. I'm...pretty distracted at the moment."

"I bet. I heard about Dr. Capra. I'm so sorry."

"Thank you. How is Pinky?"

"Much better, thank you!"

I didn't recall what had plagued Pinky, but I figured I could bluff. "I'm so glad," I said.

"What are you doing here—oh! I'll bet the big guy asked you to take over Dr. Capra's column."

"He did."

"How did it go?" She looked genuinely worried. The elevator stopped at the ground floor, but something told me to stay. So I watched the doors open and close. A glance at the control panel revealed that Tracy had selected the third floor, apparently opting to go down to go up. *What the hell*, I thought. *It's a nice day for a ride.*

"Uh...it was...interesting."

"Did he rip you a new one? You know, like he did Dr. Capra?"

"No," I said, suddenly alert all over. "Did he rip Dr. Capra a new one?"

"It was famously loud. I don't think there's a person in the building who couldn't hear it."

"What was it about?" I asked.

"Well," she leaned in closer and dropped her voice to a whisper, even though there were only the three of us in the elevator. "It started out being about advertising, but it ended up being about sex...I think."

"Sex?"

"Yeah. Something about someone named Muscle Man...at least, that's all I could hear."

"Muscle Man?" I asked. "That sounds like an action figure."

She shrugged. "Look, I'm just glad he didn't yell at you. You should be careful with him. He's got a temper."

"How much of a temper?" I asked.

The elevator reached the third floor, but Tracy didn't go out. I hit the button for the ground floor again. The image of a yo-yo flashed through my mind. "He's punched reporters before," she nodded gravely, her eyes boring into mine. "I've seen it."

"So he's violent?" I asked.

She nodded. "Everyone's terrified of him. And there's a rumor that he's...you know...connected."

"Connected to whom?" I asked.

"To the mob. The Reno mob, or so I hear."

Reno, Nevada was a little more than an hour's drive due East.

"Tracy, thank you. Do you mind if I contact you later, in case I think of any questions you might help me with?"

"Sure. Here's my card." She handed me a plain, neatly printed business card with the Herald Expositor's logo at the top.

"Thank you," I said. The doors opened, and this time, Scout and I headed out.

I held the door for Scout, who exited with her head held proud and high, pointy ears erect. The sunlight flashed on her brindle coat. In dim light, the colors seemed to muddle together, but the dazzling sun made her bronze and black stripes shine out in brilliant contrast. I gave myself permission to pause and admire her beauty. She wasn't having any of it, however, and gave a tug on her leash in the direction of the car.

My brain began to swirl again with the new information. Could Braun really be a suspect? If this was a mob hit...

Scout barked. I snapped out of my reverie and looked at her. She was sniffing around my car, and was clearly unhappy about something. That's when I noticed the odd shape of the tires. They were flat—every single one of them. I knelt by the driver's-side rear tire and scowled. A neat line had been cut about half an inch from where the tire met the rim. "Goddam it," I breathed. It had been slashed. They all had.

I put my hands on my hips and let out a growl that even

Scout would have been proud of. Had Braun sent a goon out to do this as I was meeting with him? It seemed unlikely. I looked around. I saw people going about their merry ways. No one seemed to be paying any attention to Scout or me. I looked back at the tires. "Well, shit," I said out loud.

That's when I saw the note. It was a piece of notebook paper held in place by the driver's-side windshield wiper. The wind whipped at either side of it as I slid it out from under the wiper. In large block letters, it read

YOUR NEXT

And underneath, in very small type: "Animal Liberation Army."

thirteen

I stuffed the paper into my pocket. "C'mon, Scout," I said, and headed off for the Utah City police department. Fortunately, they were well staffed. I was able to make a report on the vandalism promptly. Walking back to my car, I dialed AAA, and told them my situation. They told me it would be a thirty-minute wait until the tow truck arrived. They lied. It was forty-five minutes.

While I waited, I called the clinic and explained my situation. Then I called my mechanic and told him to be expecting a large package. Fortunately, my mechanic had some tires on hand, but wouldn't be able to replace them until tomorrow. I told him that would be fine. I was just grateful he had a set of tires that would work.

When the tow truck arrived, Scout and I stood out of the way. I waved as it drove off. I put my hands on my hips and turned to face my dog. "Now what?" I asked.

Scout's ears perked up, which was not an answer. We were on foot in downtown Utah City, a good ten miles from the clinic, where I was due to scrub for surgery half an hour ago. If we were in a city of any size, I'd just call for a Ryder driver from the app. But this was Utah City, population 1,300 during the high season. The Ryder app was as deserted of cars as Mackinac Island.

"We could hitchhike," I said to Scout. She seemed eager, but I knew it was a bad idea. I reviewed my options. I could call the clinic and ask if anyone could come and pick me up. That would have me there in a half hour, at the most, but it would take clinic staff away from their work. Of course, without me there, there was only so much they could do.

Another thought tickled at my brain. I could call Jack. The notion seemed fraught with danger. I was amazed at how excited I felt at the prospect, and it made me worry a bit about myself. Plus, he was at work, doing...whatever it was priests did. I decided I ought to get some clarity on that. It seemed a pretty cushy job, only really working one day a week, but I realized there was probably more to it than that.

But it felt awfully forward. It was something you asked your boyfriend to do, not someone you had a crush on but hadn't even had a date with. Date? I shook my head. What was I thinking? My hormones were getting out ahead of me, and my brain did not approve. No, I couldn't call Jack.

On the other hand, he'd been very supportive of my investigation, and I had just had my tires slashed. It was something he would want to know about. It was something I would want to tell him.

Before I thought better of it, I retrieved his card from my pocket and dialed him. To my amazement he picked up on the second ring.

"Jack here," he said.

"Jack, hi, it's Casey."

"Casey! I'm so glad to hear from you!" He sounded eager as a puppy. An adolescent part of me found that thrilling.

"Yeah, listen, Jack, I just had all four tires slashed—"

"Holy cow," Jack said. "Are you all right?"

Did he just really say "holy cow"? Who says "holy cow"? "Uh...yeah, I'm fine. Scout's fine."

"Do you have any idea who—"

"Yeah. Those animal rights crazies who vandalized the clinic, the ones that were threatening Shelley."

"Now they're coming after you," Jack breathed.

"Yeah. And there was a note. It said, 'your next,' without the apostrophe."

"Holy cow," Jack said again. "So not only are they threatening, they suck at grammar."

"Either that or I'm misreading it. I mean, maybe it's not supposed to be a contraction. Maybe it's supposed to be the possessive 'your,' in which case 'your next' what? Your next vacation? Your next goat? Your next eggplant?"

"You're overthinking this. It's just a typo. It's a threat, plain and simple."

"You're right. I know you're right."

"What's happening with your car?" he asked.

"Just had it towed. That's...kind of why I'm calling."

"Oh. You need a ride?"

"Yeah. Can you?"

"Gee, I wish I could, Casey, but...I have a client coming in about five minutes."

"A client?"

"Yeah. A spiritual direction client. Do you want me...should I cancel and come get you?"

I could tell he was struggling with what to do. "No. No, don't. I'll call the clinic."

"You sure? I hate to think of you out there—"

"I'm in downtown Utah City. The worst thing that could

happen to me here is a sugar coma from the fudge shop. I'll be fine. Please...keep your appointment."

"Okay. If you're sure."

"I'm sure."

"Uh...hey, Casey. I found out some stuff. Do you think maybe we could...I don't know, meet up for dinner?"

I blinked. Was he asking me on a date? No. It was more business. Still, I tried not to sound too eager. "Uh...okay. Can you swing by the clinic about 6:30? We can go to Millie's."

"Perfect. And that gets you a ride home too. Ope! There's my client. I'll see you tonight." There was a click and he was gone.

What the hell is a spiritual direction client? I wondered. There was a lot about Father Jack I wanted to know more about, that was for sure. If only he wasn't religious. I was about to phone the clinic when I noticed a chugging sound near me. Looking over, I saw an old-fashioned pickup truck which had once been a bright cobalt blue, with several patches of gray from the Bondo. A dark face peered at me through the passenger-side window.

"Sarge?" I asked. I walked over to the window. He was in the driver's seat, which was why I couldn't see him clearly. But it was him, with Prince, his Cavalier King Charles Spaniel by his side. He gave me a big grin. Prince barked at me.

"You hoofing it?" he asked.

"My car was vandalized," I said.

The grin on his face faded fast. "By who?"

"Some animal rights group."

His face became cloudy with trouble. "Oh, Case, I'm so sorry to hear that. You and Scout need a ride?"

"Are you headed back to Gold Valley?"

"Going right now. Get Scout up in back, and let's get you home."

I lowered the tailgate and bade Scout jump up. She easily cleared the four feet into the truck bed. Then I fixed her leash to her collar and attached it to a convenient hook near the sliding window facing into the cab. I cinched up the leash so that Scout couldn't get near the edges of the truck and told her to be good. I then climbed into the cab, settling next to Prince, who instantly proceeded to give my face a bath, whether it needed it or not.

"You okay?"

"I'm fine. Just...late for surgery."

"Well, hold on to your hat, then and let's get you to the clinic."

"Thank you so much, Sarge," I said.

He could have gunned it, but fortunately was mindful of Scout in back. He accelerated gently and a few moments later we were merging onto the highway.

"What's the special tonight, by the way?" I asked him.

"Chicken marsala with a Zinfandel reduction."

"You're pulling my leg, right?" I asked.

"I am not. I'm trying to up my game. Boiled corned beef just doesn't turn out the crowds like it used to."

I laughed. It felt good.

"We gonna see you for dinner, then?" he asked.

"Yeah, you'll see us."

"Us? You wouldn't be referring to that cute Episcopal priest guy, would you?"

"Cute?" Did Sarge just say "cute"? My eyes were attracted by motion, and for the first time I noticed a large fuzzy die hanging from Sarge's rearview mirror. Only there were no dots on this die. It was a large, cubical version of a rainbow flag. I cocked my head the same way Scout does. I looked at Sarge. I looked at the die. I looked back at Sarge. "Sarge," I asked. "Are you...gay?"

He laughed then, a big belly laugh. "Your gaydar is worse than my grandmama's. She was always wondering when that Liberace was going to find himself a good woman."

I laughed then. It was like a huge part of Sarge's life had just opened up to me. And he had trusted me with it. I felt both honored and relieved. Whatever sexual tension I might ever have felt toward him just melted away, and I felt closer to him than I ever had. "Thank you for telling me that," I said.

"Ain't no secret," he said. "I mean, after all, have you seen my dog?"

fourteen

I was exhausted by the time six-thirty rolled around. What I wanted more than anything was a hot bath and a bottle of Pinot Grigio. But I didn't want to disappoint Jack. I put on a good face when he arrived. He was too cheery by half, and it was a little bit irritating. We swung by the cottage to pick up Scout. Even though she'd just sit patiently outside the restaurant, it was at least a change of scenery, and I knew she'd appreciate that.

Once at Millie's, I bade Scout to lie down and stay. She dutifully obeyed, putting her muzzle on her front paws with a resignation that didn't seem *too* resentful. Inside, I was about to look for a table when Sarge waved us over to the counter.

"We're dead as a doornail tonight, and I'd be glad for the company," he entreated. I was touched. It was the first overtly social gesture Sarge had made, and I wondered if perhaps we'd bonded a bit on our drive that afternoon. I glanced at Jack and he shrugged. "Anywhere is good for me," he said.

His eyes showed a slight disappointment, however, that he would not have me all to himself. That made me feel good, but not good enough to reject Sarge's overture. So, basking in masculine camaraderie, I sat down where I could keep an easy eye on Scout, setting a stack of file folders on the counter with a satisfying smack. Jack took the stool nearest me.

"You look like you need alcohol," Sarge said to me.

"Is it that obvious?" I asked.

Jack nodded his agreement. "Oh, yeah."

"Do you still have some of that Frog's Leap cab?" I asked.

"Three more bottles," Sarge said, already turning to find his stash.

"Now you're down to two," I said. Within what seemed like only moments, Sarge had poured three glasses and left the cork off to breathe.

"On the house," he said.

"That's awfully sweet of you," I said.

"I like to help the poor and needy," Sarge said.

"I don't know about poor, but I'll cop to being a little needy," I said with a sigh.

"You're not too needy," Jack assured me. "Just needy enough."

I play-slugged his arm.

"I'm so sorry about your tires," Jack said. "Did you make a police report?"

"Yeah. Before I called you, even," I said. "I don't expect anything to come of it."

"You don't think much of our local law enforcement, do you?" Sarge asked.

"When they do something about...anything...I'll commend them," I said.

"That seems fair," Sarge conceded.

"I have news," Jack said. "I went to the Fremont Home today, to visit a parishioner—"

"Where is that?" Sarge asked.

"Auburn," Jack said.

"That's a bit of a drive, just for a visit," Sarge said.

"Well, visiting is the most important part of my job," Jack said. "It's what I spend most of my time doing. When people are sick or aren't mobile anymore, they need to be reminded that people love them, that we're thinking of them and praying for them, that they're still a part of us."

I had wondered what Jack did with his time. Now I knew. And I was touched by it. Who was this wonderful man who spent the bulk of his time actively loving people? And why did I find that so sexy? I cleared my throat. "So what did you find out?"

"There wasn't anyone at the desk when I got there, so after I signed in, I turned back a page or two and took a picture with my phone."

"What did you find?" I asked, a bit surprised that Jack had actually remembered. I'm not sure I would have.

"Maggie said that, at the time Shelley was killed, she was visiting her husband at the Fremont Home. But there was no Margaret Edgerton signed in at that time. But a Tess Barker was. I did a google search, and look at what I found."

His thumbs flashed over his phone, which he then held facing halfway between Sarge and me. We leaned in to see, and there, plain as day, was a photo of Maggie Edgerton, beehive hairdo and all.

"Wait, Maggie Edgerton is not her real name?" I asked.

"I don't know what her real name is," Jack said. "She might have a number of aliases. I only know that two of the names she goes by are Margaret Edgerton and Tess Barker."

"So what do we know about Tess Barker?" Sarge asked.

Jack pointed at Sarge. "Exactly what I wondered. So I did a bit more digging. Turns out, Tess Barker has been convicted of serial fraud and extortion."

Sarge whistled.

"She was threatening to sue Shelley," I explained to Sarge. "Her dog died inexplicably during surgery."

"Oh, God," Jack said.

"What?" I asked.

"I just had a terrible thought," he said.

"The thing about terrible thoughts is that they demand to be shared," I said.

"How long has Maggie—or Tess, or whatever her name is—been bringing her dog, uh—"

"Champ," I supplied.

"Right, Champ. How long as she been bringing Champ to the clinic?"

I tugged the file folder containing Maggie's clinic records out of the stack and opened it up. I scanned it. "The surgery was her second visit."

"So, she brought Champ in for the first visit when?"

"The week before. That's when Shelley diagnosed Champ's disintegrated acetabulum—that's a hip socket. It can get really painful. Champ was having trouble moving without pain. Shelley suggested a Femoral Head Ostectomy, which is exactly what I would have done. There's a ball at the end of the femur that fits into the socket of the hip. The Femoral Head Ostectomy just cuts that ball off. The muscles of the leg hold things together well enough, and the dog is usually out of pain pretty quickly."

"But something went wrong," Jack said.

"Yeah, Champ died on the table."

"Do you know why?"

I shook my head. "His blood pressure just plummeted, and within a few minutes he was gone."

"No explanation?" Jack asked.

I knew there wasn't, but I looked over the file again. "No," I said.

Sarge was biting his lip. "Uh, Casey, I'm guessing Shelley used a general anesthesia for that surgery?"

"Yes," I said. "Isoflurane."

"Are there any drugs that are contraindicated for Isoflurane?" Sarge asked.

"Sure, lots," I said, and I rattled off a few.

"Did you—or Shelley—do an autopsy?" Sarge continued. "Did you check for any of those drugs?"

"Are you suggesting that Maggie Edgerton drugged her own dog in order to make him die on the table?" Jack asked. "Why would she do that?"

"So that she could sue Shelley," I breathed. I met Jack's widening eyes. "Serial fraud and extortion."

"But who would be so cruel as to kill their own dog?"

"I'm gonna bet Ms. Edgerton didn't have that dog for long," Sarge opined. "In fact, I'll lay odds that she scoured the rescue places looking specifically for a dog with a bad hip."

I felt a cold chill run down my spine, so cold I even shivered.

"You okay?" Jack asked.

"Yeah, just...creeped out," I admitted. "But if Shelley was her ticket to the easy train, why kill her?"

"Maybe Shelley was on to her," Jack offered. "Is there any evidence of that?"

"No, but..." I trailed off for a moment. "I haven't really searched Shelley's office. I grabbed some files, but..."

"There might be a lot more information just waiting to be discovered," Sarge said.

Suddenly I felt like bolting, grabbing my dog, and heading for Shelley's. But then I remembered that Jack was my ride. I told myself to calm down. Besides, if I was going to search

Shelley's office, I wanted to do it when I was rested and had the leisure to really pore over it.

"Okay," I said, setting Champ's file aside. "That bears more investigation for sure. But Maggie isn't our only suspect." I grabbed another file. I pulled out the flyer that I'd found on my car earlier that day. "The nut jobs. I'm pretty sure they're the ones who slashed my tires today."

"Them animal rights people?" Sarge asked.

"Yes. The Animal Liberation Army," I said.

"That's not their real name," Jack said, incredulous.

"It is. See? Right there. Next to the copyright symbol." I pointed to the paper. Jack squinted at the 7-point type.

"Have you googled them?" he asked.

"Yes," I said, pulling some more sheets from the folder. I passed them to him. "Their basic ideology is that all domesticated animals ought to be returned to the wild. They see themselves as liberators from 'the human colonial domination of nature.'"

"I think they need to be liberated from human colonial delusion," Sarge said. "If you turned Prince out into the forest, he'd be breakfast for an owl before sunup."

"Exactly," I said. "These people are vegans—"

"Not that there's anything wrong with that," Jack interjected.

"Fine. They're *militant* vegans," I corrected myself. "They don't eat meat or any animal-derived products and think that anyone who does ought to be put to death."

"Jesus," Sarge said. "That's harsh punishment for a quiche."

"There are those who say quiche deserves punishment just for being quiche," I said, "but yeah. Their whole manifesto is pretty brutal."

"So do you think they...what? Put Shelley to death?" Jack asked. "Why single her out?"

"She's the head veterinarian in the Valley," I said. "There are other practices in nearby towns, but in Gold Valley, our practice is *it*."

"But why single out a veterinarian?" Jack asked. "I mean, you help, you heal—"

"And you perpetuate the status quo," Sarge said, pointing at me.

"Yeah. We're the authority figures," I agreed. "Individual pet owners are the culprits, as far as they are concerned, but we're the ringleaders."

"What about clubs?" Jack asked. "You know, dog show-type clubs."

"Oh, yeah, there's a King Charles Springer Spaniel club in Auburn," Sarge nodded, crossing his arms. "I been thinking of checking that out."

"There's a greyhound club," I said. "I'll give them a call and see if they've been harassed." I made a note on the yellow legal pad.

"Just who are these people?" Jack asked.

"That's a very good question," I said, nodding. "I have no clue."

"We could narrow it down to people who don't have pets or domesticated farm animals," Sarge said. "In a small town like this, it wouldn't be a long list."

"Yeah, but a list like that doesn't exist," I said.

"You could check the tax records against your database at the clinic," Sarge said. "I mean, some folks will take their pets to other vets nearby, but you'll narrow it down by a lot."

"That's a lot like work," I shook my head. "I'm not sure I have the bandwidth for that. In fact, I'm sure I don't."

"What about Ellie?" Sarge asked.

"You know Ellie?" I asked.

Sarge raised one eyebrow. "Where else she gonna eat in this town?"

"Oh. Yeah. Okay." I shook my head. "I can't ask Ellie to do that. It's...it's too much."

"She loved Shelley too," Sarge said. "She might jump at the chance to do something to help."

She might at that. I decided to set the question aside for the moment. Maybe if the time was right, I'd float the idea by her...but something about it just didn't sit right.

I set the folder aside and picked up another one. "Then there's Leslie Braun."

"The newspaper guy?" Sarge asked.

"Yeah. He summoned me to his office and rudely informed me that I would be taking over Shelley's column."

"Oh, yeah," Sarge said. "'Pet Pages.' I love that column. I didn't even think about the fact that it won't be there anymore."

"Well, if Braun has his way, I'll be writing it," I said. "I haven't said yes yet, but I haven't said no, either. What troubles me is that one of the newspaper employees—one of our clients at the clinic—told me that Shelley and Braun had had a pretty major blowout. Lots of yelling on both sides, apparently."

"Did he hear anything?" Jack asked, reaching for a toothpick.

"She," I corrected him.

"I'm sorry," Sarge said. "Ya'll hungry?" He leaned forward, eager to help us.

"Yeah," I admitted, "but my stomach's too tied up in knots to eat. Let's finish talking this through, and then we'll see."

"Good enough," Sarge said, leaning back against his counter again.

"Did she hear what they were yelling about?" Jack tried again.

"Yeah. Something about 'Muscle Man.' She didn't know what it meant."

"Oh, God," Sarge said.

"Does that mean something to you?" I asked.

"Could she have meant Massaman?" he asked.

"No, she definitely said 'Muscle Man,' but I can totally see how she might have heard 'Massaman' and interpreted it as 'Muscle Man," I said, my eyes moving back and forth as I thought. "So what is 'Massaman'?"

Sarge looked uncomfortable. "Ah...well, it's a kind of curry in Thai cooking. It's also the nickname of a guy from Thailand, lives not too far from here. He's uh...connected."

"As in 'the mob' connected?" I asked.

"Yeah." Sarge rubbed the back of his neck with one hand.

"Well, Tracy did say that Braun was running with the mob," I recalled. "Could this Massaman be...I don't know... some kind of hit man?"

"Didn't I say that?" Sarge said, starting to pace back and forth, still rubbing his neck. "I thought I just said that."

"No," I said. "Being connected and being a hit man are two different things."

"Seems like a matter of degree more than a matter of kind," Jack pointed out.

I narrowed my eyes at Sarge. "Uh...Sarge, you're weirding me out a bit. Ever since I mentioned 'Muscle Man,' you've been jumpier than a flea. What's wrong?"

"Ah, well, y'see, me and Massaman got some history," he said.

"He was your lover?" I asked, my eyes going wide.

"No!" Sarge protested.

Jack's eyebrows shot up. He said nothing, but he was suddenly more alert than Scout waiting for a Milk Bone.

"Nothing like that," Sarge continued. "I...when I bought Millie's, I couldn't quite raise the cash. Massaman offered me the balance of what I needed for a ten-percent cut the first two years." He shook his head and looked at his shoes. "It was the only way I could swing it."

"What happened when you paid it off?" I asked, "Because that was, what, five years ago or something?"

"Yeah. I gave him his ten percent cut for twenty-four months exactly. And then he shook hands and tipped his little bowler hat, and that was it. Except for the occasional Hawaiian Spam burger—on the house—I don't really see him."

I shook my head. "Do you feel like you dodged a bullet?"

"Every damn day," Sarge said. "Those whole two years, I lived in constant paranoia. What was gonna happen at the end of it all? Would they say, 'Okay, now you owe us 5% for the rest of our life'? Or would they ask me to do something...something I wouldn't ordinarily do...you know, to pay a debt of gratitude or something?"

"But nothing like that?" I asked.

He shook his head. "No, thank you Jesus." He glanced at Jack. "No offense, padre."

Jack raised his hands. "I'm all about thanking Jesus," he said. "No need to apologize on my account."

"But why would a newspaper editor sic a hit man on Shelley?" I asked. "I know they had...creative differences...when it came to the column, but that's hardly worthy of a whacking, don't you think?"

"Maybe it wasn't about 'creative differences,'" Jack noted.

"What else could it be about?" I asked.

"What it's always about," Sarge said. "Either love or money —and it doesn't seem to be about love."

"Sure," I agreed. "But how? Why?" I needed to go over Shelley's files. I needed to tear her office apart. I felt the urgency rising, and for a brief moment was glad the police had not taken her case seriously. If they had, Shelley's house would be sealed and there would be no way for me to examine her things.

"What was she working on?" Jack asked. "Didn't you say she was working on a big story?"

"Yeah," I said, tugging at the last folder in the stack. "Eureka Acres Dog Farm. She was working on an exposé, and for some reason, I get the sense that Braun was none too happy about it."

"But why...?" Jack asked.

"I don't know," I sighed. "You'd think an editor would jump at a local exposé like this. Maybe it's as simple as Shelley not staying in her lane."

"Not a killable offense." Sarge shook his head.

"No," I agreed. "If there's anything there, it has to be something else."

"These folks had their livelihood on the line," Jack pointed at the folder.

"Yes," I said, opening it slowly.

"Have you talked to them yet?" Sarge asked.

"I...I'm afraid to," I said. "Dog farms are often 'shoot first, ask questions later' kinds of places, not unlike pot farms."

"Time to pack up and break camp, then, soldier," Sarge said.

"Yeah," I said, my shoulders deflating. A little cloud of doom hovered over my head. I'm amazed I didn't actually feel rain from it.

"You can do it, Case," Jack said. "I'll go with you."

"You will?" I asked, and instantly felt a bit stupid.

"Of course. How else are you going to get there?"

I frowned. "I am expecting to get my car back tomorrow."

"Oh." Jack looked momentarily troubled. Then he brightened. "Okay. So you drive."

fifteen

The next day was a brutal barrage of sick pets. I usually go home for lunch to give Scout some relief, but there just wasn't time. I worked straight through lunch, and in the ten minutes I might have had to myself, I sent emails to a few of the candidates for the vet position. And every time I turned around, it seemed, I was haunted by the same thought: what else was waiting for me in Shelley's office? I didn't relish the tedium of going through it all, but I also knew that, somewhere in there, I would probably find clues that might lead us to her killer.

I was just hanging up my lab coat at the end of the day when Ellie poked her head around the corner. "Someone here to see you..." She waggled her eyebrows up and down.

"What?" I asked. I was bone-tired and my feet hurt.

When I walked into the waiting room, Jack was flipping through a copy of *Dog Fancy*. His collar was off, but the top button of his black clergy shirt was still fastened. He glanced up, saw me, and setting the magazine aside, jumped to his feet. "Ready?" He flashed that smile.

"Um..." I said, uncertain.

"Eureka Acres," he said, his face falling a bit. "I thought we had a date—er, I mean, that we were going to, you know, go... check it out." He coughed and scratched the back of his head. It was cute. I'm not sure confronting evil puppy mills constituted a date in anyone's book, but I was open to it. And Jack definitely wanted to be here.

"Oh. Yeah. I guess I kind of blocked that out," I said, realizing that Shelley's files would need to wait until another day.

"You are really dreading this, aren't you?" he asked.

"Oh, yeah." As sharp as my tongue can be, I don't actually like conflict. In fact, I pretty much do anything I can to avoid it.

"What are you afraid of?"

It was a good question. There wasn't a concrete scenario I was hoping to avoid, but a looming feeling of dread descended on me whenever I thought about it. My shoulders sagged and I sighed.

"Do they even know that Shelley was working on the exposé?" Jack asked.

"I don't know. I assume so...if they did it, I mean."

"Well, that's something," Jack said. "Let's find out if they even knew. If not...that kind of rules them out, don't you think?"

I nodded, but I must not have looked convinced, because Jack asked, "Do you...want to put it off?"

I looked down at my blistering feet. "No. No, let's get this over with."

"Does it help that we're doing it together?" he asked. "I mean, it's kind of like opposite and balancing stimuli. It's not something you want to do, but you get to hang out with me."

That was sweet, and I almost smiled. "Yeah...that doesn't really balance it out, sorry."

"Damn." For a brief moment he looked genuinely hurt.

Then, like flipping a switch, he was back to his normal, aggravating level of cheer.

I looked back at Ellie and opened my mouth to say goodbye, but, out of sight of Jack, she shook her head and silently mouthed, *Are you crazy?*

Maybe I was. Then again, maybe I was just exhausted. Or, as Jack had predicted, perhaps I was profoundly undergrieved. Whichever it was, I was definitely occupying an altered plane of reality, one that I was not enjoying one little bit.

As we walked out to the parking lot, Jack asked, "Did you get your car?"

"Yes, the shop sent a driver up to me at 7am, if you can believe it, and I drove it straight here. Do you mind if we pick up Scout on the way?"

"Not at all. I love Scout," he said.

Love. This man *loved* my dog. Perhaps that was hyperbole. And perhaps it wasn't. But loving Scout was definitely a nonnegotiable for any possible romantic partner. Jack had already cleared a huge hurdle.

I told myself to stop thinking silly thoughts and pulled my Civic onto the road. Once more, Jack seemed content to ride together in silence. After a couple of minutes, however, I was starting to crawl out of my skin. "Are you lonely?" I asked.

I have no idea where that question came from. I hadn't intended to ask it. It was way too personal, and it was none of my business. I just opened my mouth, and it fell out. Perhaps it was because Jack looked a little wistful as he watched the trees go by out the passenger window. Or maybe I was just projecting.

But the question didn't seem to faze him. "Oh, yeah."

I was horrified at myself for even asking the question, but

before I could do any real interior bludgeoning over my stupidity, he went on.

"I think most clergy people are," he confessed. "People are afraid of us, so we don't have many friends. And a lot of us are workaholics, spending all of our time tending to our parishioners. But we're not allowed to be friends with our parishioners—"

"You're not?" I asked.

"Well, it happens, but it's discouraged. Professional boundaries, you know. I'm sure it's the same for you."

It was. We were warned against getting too close to our clients or their pets. And like Jack said, it happens, but it isn't encouraged.

"I...I had no idea. That's sad."

"Yeah, it can be. I had friends back in Chicago, but since I moved here...it's hard to make new friends when you're our age."

I knew the truth of that.

"I've asked many of the other pastors out for lunch, and the Methodist pastor and I meet up for a game of chess once a month or so. We don't have a lot in common, but we both play, so..." He shrugged.

I pulled into the drive at the cottage, and put a gentle hand on his forearm. "I'll be right back," I said. He nodded, and I speed walked to the house. A few moments later, Scout bounded to the car and actually jumped through the driver's window, covering Jack with snuffles and licks.

"I'm sorry," I said. "She's a terrible flirt."

But Jack was loving every minute of it. "Are you kidding? I'm going to take all the affection I can get." I wondered if that was a hint as he pressed his forehead against hers, and rubbed it back and forth as her tail ticktocked like a metronome about to achieve flight.

I entered the address into my maps app and fixed my phone into its holder atop the dashboard. A few moments later we were wending our way along backroads lined with dry brush, oaks, and California laurels.

"So what do you know about this puppy mill?" Jack asked.

"I know they're defrauding the public—breeding mutts, then giving them a fancy name and charging out the wazoo for them."

"Oh. Like labradoodles?"

"Exactly. Not. A. Breed." I rolled my eyes and shook my head.

"A damn fine mutt though," Jack said.

I couldn't argue with that. Mutts had a better chance of being healthy than purebreds, simply because of the genodiversity.

I turned left at a dead end and drove under a canopy of walnut trees stretched out on both sides of the road, their branches intertwining above us.

"Lovely," Jack said, with a sigh. "What else?"

"Their neighbors have been complaining. They've been slewing dog sewage into a creek..."

"Yikes," Jack said. "Let me guess, the creek passes onto the neighbor's property, and their livestock drink from it."

"Yep. Four cases of bovine paratyphoid, according to the article I found in Shelley's office."

"Have you gotten over to Shelley's office again for a closer look?" Jack asked.

"When?" I shook my head.

"Right."

"Plus, they're breeding with total disregard for the safety of their animals. I can't tell you how many puppies we've seen with congenital heart conditions."

"A reputable breeder would screen for that," Jack surmised.

"Exactly," I agreed. "If you find that your stud or brood bitch has a heart condition, you just don't breed them. Period. At least, that's the responsible thing to do."

"And what happens to *those* dogs?" Jack asked. "The ones who can't breed?"

"Funny, I just had one of those. Fortunately, it was from a reputable breeder. He said he was going to find her a good home." I looked over at Jack. "Standard poodle. Maybe you should check her out."

He gave me a sad smile, but then turned his head and looked out the passenger window. I was beginning to realize that, for all his talk of healthy grieving and recovery, Jack was hiding a pretty deep well of sadness all his own. I wanted to put my hand on his arm, maybe even hold his hand, but it seemed too forward. It was too much, too soon. The slow revelation of his complexities didn't make him less intriguing, but more.

"What's the gist of Shelley's article—the one she was working on?" Jack asked, still looking out the window.

"The exposé?"

"Yeah."

"Well, the sewage thing was old news, but the heart condition thing is not. Shelley had documented about fifteen cases from our practice alone. She was gathering permissions from owners so that she could go public. I found signed consent forms from eleven of them."

"She was being careful," Jack said.

"That was Shelley. No 'i' undotted, no 't' uncrossed."

"It sure was," he agreed. "She was junior warden for a couple of years, and that was the only time the vestry has run like clockwork."

"I have absolutely no idea what half of those words mean," I confessed.

"Arrived," the GPS app announced.

I turned into a gravel drive and began a long, slow ascent up a hill dotted with mad tangles of trees swimming in a rolling ocean of brown grasses. Eventually, a farmhouse came into sight, along with a barn and several squat cinderblock buildings I recognized as kennels.

As I rolled to a stop, a beefy man in overalls emerged from the barn, wiping his hands on a rag. He put the rag into his back pocket as he walked down the drive toward us. He had on a wide-brimmed hat and sported a long salt-and-pepper beard that hung halfway down his chest like a gnarly bib.

His face gave nothing away as he approached the driver's-side window. He leaned down and said, "Hey, now, what can I do for you?"

"Is this Eureka Acres Dog Farm?" I asked. There had been no signage, which I thought was a little bit odd.

"Who's asking'?" His eyes flitted back and forth between me and Jack.

I opened my mouth to speak, but Jack interjected—"I'm thinking about getting a dog."

"Are ya?" he asked, taking Jack's measure. "I got dogs. What kind of dog were you looking for?"

"What kind of dogs do you got?" Jack asked.

"We specialize in designer breeds," the man said. "We got Cockapoos, Maltipoos, Labradoodles, Puggles, and Morkies."

"No standard poodles, huh?" Jack asked.

"Nossir, not what we do here."

Jack nodded and got out of the car. "Well, in that case, can I see what a Labradoodle looks like?"

I decided the ruse had gone on long enough. I opened my door and the man with the beard stepped back. I offered my hand. "Hi, I'm Dr. Casey Gibbons. You sold one of my clients a Morkie with Patent Ductus Arteriosus recently."

"You a vet?" he asked, his eyes narrowing.

"Yes. I'm—I *was*—Dr. Shelley Capra's partner."

He hocked and spat. Then without another word, he turned on his heel and went back to the barn.

"Was it something I said?" I asked.

"Maybe you should dial back the charm," Jack said.

"I didn't know I had any," I confessed.

"It's a charming kind of anti-charm," Jack said, "which is hard to explain."

"Huh." I put my hands on my hips, wondering what to do now.

"You know, you might have just played along, pretending we were interested in a puppy, and asked some probing questions."

"You're really stuck on this 'having a plan' thing, aren't you?" I asked.

"I'm not sure the plan-averse method is really working out."

I wasn't either, if I was honest. But I didn't need to say that. Just then the proprietor reemerged from the barn. This time he was holding a shotgun.

"Holy crap," I said.

Jack's hands instantly went into the air. "Don't shoot," he said. "I'm a priest."

The man looked confused for a second, but then he focused on me.

"Don't shoot, I'm a priest?" I said to Jack. "That's the best you can do?"

He shrugged.

As the proprietor got closer, my own hands went up. I decided this was the time for fast talking. "Mr.—I'm sorry, what's your name?"

"Clementine," he said. "Make sure you get that right in

your newspaper story, little lady. Harry J. Clementine."

"Oh, I think you misunderstand me, Mr. Clementine. I'm not working on a newspaper story."

He faltered and the gun wavered. "You're not?"

"No. That was my friend, Shelley. But now she's dead."

I scanned his face to see his response. At first he looked bewildered, his eyes moving back and forth quickly. Then he looked relieved. "That article she was working on..."

"It died with her. It won't be published," I said. I didn't know if it was true—hell, I might finish the damn thing myself. But I had no plans to do so, so it seemed true enough.

"How did she die?" he asked, the shotgun slipping from his shoulder a bit.

"She was killed," I said. "Murdered."

He narrowed his eyes. "By who?"

"Whom," Jack corrected.

"Are you a grammar Nazi?" Clementine turned the shotgun on Jack. "'Cause I hate grammar Nazis."

"'Who' it is, then," Jack said. "Anglicans are big fans of the vernacular."

"That's why we're here," I said. "I was hoping we might be able to...rule you out."

"You sayin' I killed her?" The shotgun resumed its place tight against his shoulder.

"I think you had reason to kill her," I said. "But I think a lot of other people did too. I'd like to rule you out, if you'd be kind enough to talk to us."

"I didn't kill that bitchhound," he said. "She was trying to shut me down!"

"She was trying to shame you into complying with ethical breeding practices and norms," I countered. "That's not the same thing."

"Last I checked this was a free country," he said, turning the shotgun back on me.

"That doesn't mean you're free to defraud people," I said. "You're selling mutts under the guise of 'specialty breeds'—"

"Ain't nothing illegal about that," he said.

"And you're breeding dogs that you know have heart disease—conditions you are passing along to the puppies you produce."

"Ain't nothing illegal about that, neither," he said.

"Either," Jack corrected.

The gun swung back to Jack. "I had about enough of you," Clementine said.

"'I have had,'" Jack corrected, "Or use the contraction, 'I've.'"

"Jack, what are you doing?"

"Sorry. It's a bit of a compulsion."

So Jack *did* have faults. Fortunately, my grammar is impeccable, so I doubted I'd find it too annoying. Clementine, however, was growing visibly annoyed. "Jack," I said, "why don't you just take note of the...logodiversity...and give me a rundown when we're back in the car?"

"Shut up, in other words," he said.

"Yes," I said.

"I like 'logodiversity,' though," he said. "Clever neologism."

"Thank you," I said. "I can be funny under fire."

"You two through yet?" Clementine asked.

"We can be," I said. "But I still want an answer from you. Where were you on the afternoon of July 24th?"

"I am holding the gun," Clementine said.

"I see that," I responded. "And I'm trying to find out who murdered my friend."

"Any enemy of Dr. Capra is a friend of mine," the old man concluded.

"Where were you?" I asked.

"Right here," he said.

"You don't need to consult a calendar?" I asked.

"Nope. Don't go nowhere, not usually. Not in weeks. Wife does the shopping."

I was amazed that he was married, but perhaps I shouldn't have been. It takes all kinds. "Can anyone vouch for that?" I asked.

"My wife can," he said.

"Can we speak to her?" Jack asked.

"You cannot," he said.

"Because..."

"Because she's...not well."

"That's a little convenient," I noted.

"Don't care what it is to you. Ya'll get back in your car and get out of here."

"We'll be back with the sheriff," Jack promised.

"You do that," he said.

"No we won't," I said. Jack was a newbie at this kind of thing. As a surgeon, I knew where to stick the knife. "We'll be back with the county health inspector."

I watched color drain from his face. Now he looked worried. "Now see here..." He began to close on me, the shotgun trained on my head.

"Not another step!" Jack shouted and sprang past the front of the car, diving between me and the approaching breeder. That's when Clementine tripped on a rock. The shotgun erupted with an explosion that echoed through the hills.

Jack stumbled to his knees.

sixteen

We were lucky to get cell reception this far out in the boonies. I pressed a handkerchief—helpfully provided by Mr. Clementine—to Jack's wound to staunch the bleeding until the ambulance arrived. I wanted to ride with him, but I had Scout to think about. In moments Jack was swept onto a gurney, fixed with an IV bag, and loaded into the back of the ambulance. And then he was gone.

Driving home, I chewed my nails down so far that one of them started bleeding. *It's all my fault*, I thought. *If I hadn't dragged him out there...* Wave after wave of guilt washed through me, and in spite of the fact that I don't believe in God, I uttered what I supposed was my first prayer in decades. "I don't know who you are—or *that* you are—but...if you care, please let him be okay."

It seems incredible even now, but for some reason as soon as I'd uttered those words, I felt calmer. I tried not to think about it—which was easy, because all I could do was worry about Jack.

I dropped Scout off at home again and drove far too fast to

the emergency room. I needn't have hurried, because as soon as I arrived there was nothing to do but wait.

I was alone, sitting by myself in the waiting room. And I'm not sure what I was waiting for. I wasn't a relative. The doctors wouldn't tell me anything. They probably didn't even know I was there. I went to the nurses' station and waved to get someone's attention. HIPAA rules being what they were, I wasn't sure what they could tell me and what they couldn't, but at least they would know I was there.

"Yes?" one of the nurses said, a little curtly. I knew she was busy, so I tried to be brief.

"My friend—Jack Mornington—he was shot, and...an ambulance brought him in, and..." And what? She cocked her hands, but her eyes were not without compassion. I felt my throat thicken and my eyes well up. *Do not cry, goddam it,* I told myself, but it was no use. "Will he be...is he alive?"

"Are you a relative?"

"No, but..." I opened my mouth to say, *I'm his girlfriend,* but I wasn't sure it was true and it made me sound like a teenager, besides. "We're dating."

She nodded. "Give me just a minute."

I nodded back and searched my molars with my tongue, trying to master my emotions. I wiped at my eyes with my wrist and then found myself pacing in tight, fast circles in front of the desk.

It might only have been a minute or two before she returned, but it felt like forever. I searched her face for a clue. "He's alive," she said. "I can't give you more than that, other than he's in surgery now."

"Thank you. Thank you," I said. "I'm just going to be...over there." I pointed. "If anything...if there's any news...or anything you can tell me..." I didn't have to finish.

"I'll come find you. I promise." She gave me a grave smile

and turned back to her duties. I took a deep breath and forced myself to stop pacing and sit.

In my imagination I replayed what had happened again and again. Jack's back was to me when the shotgun went off, so I didn't actually see it happen. I saw him fall. I saw where the buckshot had entered—upper right chest. It's possible that it missed the lungs, and possible that it didn't. Probably his shoulder had taken the worst hit, and the biggest danger had been shock and loss of blood. I focused on that, but somehow it was small comfort.

It had been a long time since I felt genuinely attracted to someone. My ex disgusted me by the time we split—not for any hygiene reasons, but simply for being an untrustworthy toad. I had steered clear of relationships since—save for the occasional whiskey-induced one-night stands. I can count those incidents on two shameful fingers.

I still wasn't sure Jack and I had enough in common to make a successful couple, but I was intrigued enough to want to find out. The religion thing bothered me, but I had been touched by his honesty about people being afraid of him. I wasn't afraid of him, was I? He seemed just the right sort of goofy, which translates to sexy in my book. And he didn't seem to be the crazy kind of religious person. In fact, I hadn't yet figured out just how religious he was. I imagine you have to be pretty religious to be a priest, but did he possess a sufficiently annoying degree of religiosity to keep anything from develop-ing? I didn't know.

I hoped I'd still get a chance to find out. *Don't think like that,* I warned myself. *He's going to be fine.* I find my own attempts at comfort utterly unconvincing, no matter how sure I am of the outcome.

I must have nodded off, because someone was shaking me. Not hard, just enough to bring me to consciousness. I squinted up, into the light, into the face of Deputy Gus Tucker.

"Hey, sleepyhead," he said. I must have been very groggy, because it seemed like he was looking at me with affection, maybe even a bit moonfaced.

"What?" I croaked.

"What are you doing out here?" he asked.

"How is he?" I asked. "Mornington. Jack. Father." I said his name exactly backwards. There are times when I do not understand myself. This was one of those times.

"Oh," Gus looked surprised and a little bit hurt. "Are you here...with him?"

"I was with him when he got shot," I said.

"Oh," he looked relieved. "That's good."

"It is?" I scratched at my hair. I imagined that it must have been a nightmare tangle by now. That was all right. I could only see me and Gus here.

"Uh...I'm here to take his statement, actually."

"Is he conscious?" I asked.

"Yes, but they want him to sleep."

"Screw that," I said and stood, a little wobbly.

"Maybe you better sit down," he suggested.

Blood had rushed from my head and I did feel dizzy. I plopped back down.

"If you were there, I'd like to get a statement from you."

"Okay," I said. "Can we do it later?" I really, really wanted to see Jack.

He must have read my face, because Gus said, "They won't let you see him right now. He needs to *sleep*." He emphasized "sleep" because apparently I had not gotten the clue the first time. I had heard him. I'm just one of those people who thinks the rules don't apply to them. Yes, I can be annoying.

But as my brain fog parted, I realized he was probably

right. I sighed. "Okay." I waited until he'd pulled out his mole-skin and pen. Then I told him all that I could remember, in as much detail as I could muster.

Tucker wrote everything down. When I was finished, he closed the notebook and asked. "So you're investigating your friend's death?"

"You guys aren't doing it," I said, with more acid in my voice than I'd intended.

"De Marco isn't going to be happy about that," he said.

"Don't give two flying figs what De Marco likes and doesn't like," I said. I stood up.

"Can I take you home?" he asked.

"I have my car," I answered.

"Maybe I can follow you," he said, "just to be safe."

"That's a bit stalker-y for my taste," I said. "I'll be fine."

"You're sure?" he asked.

"I release you to go protect and serve...somebody else," I said, with a dramatic flourish. It wasn't characteristic of me.

"Are you drunk?" he asked.

I considered. Had I had anything to drink? I didn't think I had. "No, just punchy."

"You sure you can drive?"

"Absolutely."

He nodded and stood. "Well, take care, and let me know if you need anything."

"I'll send up a smoke signal," I said.

He gave me a pained smile and walked toward the door. Just shy of it he turned around and walked back to me. He pulled a business card from his wallet. "It...uh...takes me a few minutes to get a joke sometimes." He handed me the card. "No smoke signals necessary. Just...call my cell phone...if you need anything."

"Okay," I said.

"I mean *anything*," he repeated.

"Okay," I repeated.

"You need soup, or-or-or groceries—"

"I'll give you a ring," I gave him a pained smile of my own.

"Or you just want to talk. Or, you know, want someone to walk with....maybe with your dog."

What the hell was he going on about? I wondered. "Will do, deputy. Got the card right here." I put it in the pocket of my scrub shirt and patted it.

"Okay," he said.

"Okay," I said.

"See you later," he said.

"Maybe so," I said.

"Bye then," he said.

I was about to throw a shoe at him when he finally exited through the sliding glass doors. If Scout had been there, I would have said, "That was weird," but as it was, I only thought it.

I turned and headed for the nurses' station. There was a different nurse behind the desk, now. Her red frizzy hair almost obscured her face. "Yes?" she said at last, placing the phone in its cradle.

"I'd like to see Jack Mornington, please." I gave her my best professional smile. Then my smile faltered as I realized that Jack was probably a nickname. "Um...that's probably actually John Mornington...or Jonathan."

"So...not a relative?" she asked. I sighed inwardly. Whatever headway I'd made with the other nurse, this one wasn't having any of it.

"No. I'm...a friend."

"Not a very close friend." She narrowed one eye at me.

I swallowed hard. "Not yet," I said, and instantly felt weird about it. "I *am* a veterinarian." I was pretty sure that didn't count for much here, but it was the only thing I could think of to say.

"Well, I'm sorry, but John Mornington is not permitted visitors right now. He's resting." She gave me a disarmingly compassionate look. It clearly gave her no joy to deny me, and I wasn't expecting that.

"I see," I said.

"Why don't you call tomorrow, and I can let you know before you come down?" She grabbed a business card that was general to the hospital as a whole from a holder on the counter between us and scrawled a suffix to the phone number. "This extension will get you directly to this desk."

"Thank you," I said, pocketing the card. "That's very kind of you."

I turned to go, but before I got very far, she called out, "Uh...Miss?"

I turned.

"Your friend...he's going to be fine. They got all the buckshot out, and it didn't hit any arteries or vital organs. But...you didn't hear it from me."

I felt another sudden swell of emotion and blinked back tears. I nodded. "Thank you." And then, before I could humiliate myself, I left.

seventeen

When I got home, Scout greeted me by bouncing up and down in a display that would have made Tigger jealous. "I'm sorry, little girl. I've been a bit busier than usual." Scout's stub of a tail turned in quick circles in her excitement. I felt momentarily guilty for not being just as excited to see her. Truth was, though, I was exhausted. I sank to one knee and hugged her to my chest.

She was too wound up for any snuggling action, however. She ran directly to her bowl and, with a deft flick of the paw, flipped it onto its back with a loud clatter.

"Yes, I get it. It's way past dinner time." I picked up her bowl and filled it with kibble, then added a dollop or two of wet food to spice it up. I put it on the floor and watched as she tore into it.

I noticed that my hands were shaking. The reasonable part of my brain told me that I should eat something too, but the lizard brain was in almost complete control, and it was a lush. I opened a cabinet and retrieved a bottle of Booker's Bourbon. I poured three fingers of it and gulped half of it in one go.

Over the next several minutes, I gloried in relief as the warm tendrils of the whiskey cascaded over my brain, relaxing my muscles and bathing my anxiety in its golden balm. It was late, and I had a full slate of clients the next day. As soon as Scout was done eating, I headed for bed.

Despite the ministry of the whiskey, I simply couldn't get my brain to shut off. Scout was out like a light, nipples up with all four feet in the air, snoring louder than a garbage truck.

After an hour of turning and tossing, I finally gave up. I couldn't stop worrying about Jack. I briefly wondered if it would help to pray. And then I briefly wondered if the priest was turning out to be a bad influence on me. I felt like I needed to do something, anything. I could sit by his bedside, I thought. But it was the middle of the night, and I was not family. There's no way they would let me in.

In fact, I realized there was very little I could do—about Jack *or* Shelley—at this hour, and that made me even crazier. I couldn't shake the look on Clementine's face when I'd told him about Shelley's death. If the news didn't surprise him, he was a better actor than anyone that grammatically challenged had a right to be. I wondered if I had missed something in Shelley's research on Eureka Acres. I had been wanting to go through her files again, and between work and Jack getting shot, simply hadn't had the bandwidth to get over there. But giving Shelley's office another search was something I *could* do without waking anyone up or getting myself arrested for harassment. "And I've got all night," I said out loud. That apparently woke Scout, and she opened one lazy eye, glancing around until she found me. "You wanna go for a ride?" I asked.

"Ride" was a word she knew. She leaped from the bed and began to run in circles. "That's too extroverted by half," I told her. "It's late." She was not deterred.

Ten minutes later, Scout and I were sitting in Shelley's

office, a single desk lamp illuminating her desktop. I grabbed her research on Eureka acres, and also pulled her personal files for the past three months for good measure—as always, Shelley was well organized. I also grabbed her "important docs" file. "Never know what you're going to find," I breathed.

I leafed through the Eureka files again, but didn't see anything new. I kept expecting some odd fact to leap out at me, like in a Hallmark Channel mystery-romance. But I found no epiphanies. I sighed and closed that file. I turned to Shelley's personal files, but these were unremarkable—receipts and miscellany pertaining to everything except work. I lost all sense of time as I poured over each scrap of paper. In the end, however, nothing raised any kind of alarm. I set those files aside and opened the "important docs" folder.

The punning part of my brain wondered if it might contain bios of famous doctors—Albert Schweitzer, Dr. Phil, Doctor Doolittle, perhaps—but no, it was just what you'd expect. There was the original of her license to practice veterinary medicine—a copy hung on the wall in one of our examination rooms at the clinic. There was some information about investment accounts, a life insurance policy—

I paused. "A life insurance policy?" I said out loud. I saw Scout's ears prick up at the sound of my voice. Pulling it out of the file, I scanned it. When I saw who the beneficiary was, I felt a shiver. "Stephen Thomas Capra," I said. Shelley's ex.

I didn't know Stephen Thomas well—he was a part of Shelley's life when the two of us lived in different parts of the country and weren't in regular contact. But I had met him several times. I had not been impressed. He seemed like a bit of a sad sack, one of those people who never get a break, and he knew it. He walked around with a black cloud overhead, and I always got the sense that he was seeding that cloud when no one was looking. He had lost job after job, and I think Shelley finally just got tired of him leeching off of her. I looked to see who had initiated the policy. In the back of my mind I knew that if Shelley had the paperwork, she had probably taken out the policy...and indeed, a quick glance at the opening paragraph affirmed it. I sighed, "Oh, Shelley." She was a good person. She often complained that he asked her for money. And she usually gave it to him. It occurred to me that this policy was a way for her to help Stephen Thomas one more time in case anything happened to her. What I didn't know was whether Stephen Thomas knew about the policy or not. If he did...it might just be the payday he had waited his entire life for.

I booted up Shelley's computer, and found a phone number for Stephen Thomas in her contacts. I jotted it down on a Post-it and put it in my pocket.

"Scout, are you ready?" Instantly Scout was on her feet and ready for adventure. Sleep, however, was beginning to catch up with me, and adventure was far from my mind. There was probably more to find in Shelley's files, but it could wait. My gut told me that I had just found a significant clue, and I was eager to follow up on it.

In the morning.

eighteen

T he next morning, as I headed into the break room to put my lunch in the fridge, Ellie stopped and cocked her head, just like a confused hound. I was running on about four hours of sleep and definitely functioning (if you want to call it that) in an altered state. "Oh, dear," she said. "The bags under your eyes have bags."

"Yeah," I said. "I didn't get a lot of sleep."

"Are you okay? Why were you at the hospital?" she asked.

I narrowed one eye at her. "How did you know I was at the hospital?"

Her head lowered into her shoulders and she bit her lip. "Uh...I have an app on my phone called 'Find My Friends,' and I...uh...put in your number."

I blinked for a few seconds while my brain caught up with this fact. "That seems like...I don't know...a bit of an invasion of privacy, don't you think?"

She looked like she wanted to crawl under a rock. "Well... ordinarily, sure, but...you see, your phone is owned and paid for by the clinic, so if anything should happen to it—like, if you lost it or it got stolen, you know—that way we'd know where it is."

"That is a very pretty rationalization," I said. "Did you practice that?"

"I did, yeah," she confessed.

I sighed. "Okay, I concede the point about the clinic needing to keep track of its phones. But where I go is my own business. So unless and until I inform you that I have somehow lost my phone—you're not going to look me up on that app of yours. Promise?"

She didn't meet my eyes. I waved my hands in front of her face and she jumped a bit. I drew my hand to my own face until she was looking at me. "Promise?" I asked again.

"Okay. I promise," she said, a bit defeated.

"Good enough," I said. "Now who's up first?"

"I still want to know why you were at the hospital."

That was fair. And so I told her everything. Her hands went to her mouth as I described Harry Clementine shooting Jack. "Is he okay?" she breathed.

"Caught him in the shoulder," I said. "He's going to be fine. But he'll need to mend."

"Is he your boyfriend?" she asked.

"No," I answered, a little too quickly. "He's just a friend...for now."

She nodded, getting it. "Do you want me to call the hospital for updates throughout the day?"

I was moved at the offer. "Well, that would be lovely, except that they won't tell you anything. HIPAA rules, you know," I said, referring to the guidelines laid out in the Health Insurance Portability and Accountability Act of 1996.

"Oh. Right," she said. "Sorry."

"It was a sweet thought," I said, placing my hand on her arm. "Thank you." After a pause, I repeated, "What's up first?"

"Your only surgery for the day cancelled," she said. I breathed a sigh of relief. That brought the probability of doing any permanent damage down dramatically. "But we've still got a full schedule. "Mrs. Wessen is here with George to hear about the results of his tests."

"Right, thank you," I said, and headed over to the rack to snag George's folder. I wasn't sure I was ready for a full day, but ready or not, it was coming. I wondered just how long I could continue at this pace. I realized it was going to be this way until we got another vet, and that was not something I could pass off to someone else. It was something I would have to do myself, but I was damned if I knew when.

In between seeing clients and their ailing animals, I huddled in back and furiously entered my notes. I figured if I entered my notes quicker, I might buy a few precious minutes to do my vet search—and maybe to follow up on the animal rights terrorists or that insurance policy I'd found.

First things first, though—I pulled up one of the files Ellie had sent me. Dr. Ajeet Singh was two years out of vet school— a handsome fellow sporting a full beard and what looked like a gold lamé turban. *Is he Muslim?* I wondered. I had never heard of a Muslim vet. And yet, why not? I briefly wondered if Jack would have any wisdom on the subject.

I quickly read through Singh's file. For such a short career, he'd accomplished a lot. After graduating, he stuck around and spent a year doing research. He'd already published four papers in peer-reviewed journals. I scrolled through the titles: "The Efficacy of Acupuncture on Feline Encephalopathy," "Alternative Anxiolytics and the Pregnant Bitch," "Tickborne Disease Interventions in New England Chipmunk Populations," and the strangely titled, "Speculations on a Field Mouse's Psychedelic Experience in Three Acts."

"Holy cow," I thought. "He's doing some out-there stuff." It was cool stuff, however. I wondered if the good people of Gold Valley really needed cat acupuncture or psilocybin micro-dosing for their gerbils. Then I remembered that this was Gold Valley we were talking about. Of course they did.

It would be stupid to act on a hunch on the first name I'd pulled up, but there was nothing wrong with scheduling an interview with the guy. I shot him a quick email and headed in to see my next client.

After removing 27 porcupine quills from a schnauzer's very tender nose and muzzle, I raced for the back to once more hastily enter my notes. I glanced at my watch—I had four minutes before I had to see the next client. "One for the clinic, and now one for me," I whispered to myself. I quickly googled the contact info for the Gold Valley Greyhound Club, called, and was relieved when a kindly voice answered.

"Yello," a woman's voice said.

"Hi. This is Doctor Casey Gibbons down at Gold Valley Veterinary Clinic—"

"Oh, yes! Dr. Gibbons, so nice to hear from you. It's a shame what happened to Shelley. She was Mumu's doctor. I guess we'll be coming to see you, now."

"I guess you will. I'm sorry, what is your name?"

"Oh! Silly me. Bettina Cantwell, but you can call me Betty."

"Ms. Cantwell, so nice to meet you." I took a breath and dove in. "Listen, we've been getting a lot of heat here at the clinic from an animal rights group calling themselves the Animal Liberation Army."

"I'm so sorry to hear that. What kind of heat?"

"Well...nothing too bad, nothing I can prove anyway. Some vandalism of the clinic. They slashed the tires of my car—"

"That's terrible!" Betty proclaimed.

"Anyway, I was wondering if you—or any of your club members—had experienced any harassment, as well?"

There was a long silence. I glanced at my watch. Two minutes.

"What's it worth to you?" she asked.

I blinked. "What?"

"You heard me, Doctor. That's probably some important information to you, otherwise you wouldn't be calling me. If it's important, it can be monetized. So what's it worth to you?"

I opened my mouth, but my brain was frozen in at least three places. I finally coughed out, "Well—uh, what do you want?"

"We get rescue greyhounds through here every so often— every couple of months or so. Sometimes they're in rough shape. You have no idea what the racing world does to them."

I did know, but there was no use arguing the point. "Yes. And? So?"

"We rescue these noble beasts out of the kindness of our hearts, pro-bono-like. I'd like to trade this information for some pro-bono work of your own. Say...checkups and initial treatments for two rescue greyhounds?"

I held the phone handset away from my ear and stared at it. Was she serious? I put the phone to my ear again. "Ms. Cantwell, I can't—" There was a click, followed by a dial tone.

"What the actual f—" I stopped myself. There were impressionable young techs around, after all.

I replaced the handset in its cradle and held on to the counter as a wave of disorientation rolled through me. *Did that just happen?* I wondered. I didn't have time to contemplate it further, because my next client was waiting. I grabbed the folder and headed in.

"Mr. Bell, is it?" Dennis Bell sat with his feet together, a bow tie at his puffy neck, and a cat transporter on his lap.

"Call me Dennis," he said.

I stuck out my hand. "That's fine, Dennis. You can call me Dr. Casey."

He smiled an anxious smile.

"You must have been one of Shelley's clients," I said. I knew that was true, it was in the file, after all, but it was a way into the conversation.

"Yes. She was a good doctor. She knew how to keep a secret."

I cocked my head and glanced at his file again. That's when I noticed something odd. Shelley used a name—Cannoli—but nowhere in the file did it actually say what kind of animal Cannoli was.

"Ah, well, client confidentiality is important to us. So long as it's nothing illegal—"

"Maybe I better go," Mr. Bell said. He was sweating now, and his eyes darted back and forth like he was watching hummingbirds.

"Woah, woah," I said, holding my hands up and making soft patting gestures. "There's nothing Shelley would have done for you that I won't. I trust her. And I think you can trust me."

His hackles were up, I could see that. He stood motionless and I could almost smell the gears burning in his head as he thought. Finally, though, he sat down again, and hugged the carrier to his chest. I noticed that his socks matched his bow tie. Snazzy.

"Why don't you tell me a bit about Cannoli, starting with just what kind of animal he—or she—is."

"He. He's a ferret." His neck disappeared as he sunk down.

Suddenly I understood. Ferrets were illegal in California, for some arcane reason that I didn't remember. "Relax, Dennis," I said, sitting in the other chair in the room. "No one is going to report you for having a ferret. Our only goal here is to make sure that Cannoli is as fit and happy a little weasel as he can be."

Suddenly, he looked like he was about to cry.

"Okay," I said, "Let's get Cannoli out of the carrier and up onto the examining table where I can—"

Suddenly, Ellie stuck her head in the door. "Everyone out into the parking lot. I can't explain. We just have to do it— wait, is that a ferret?"

"Ellie, what are you—?"

"That's too cute!" Her eyes were wide with wonder. Then she glanced back at me. "Parking lot." Then she slammed the door.

"What's going on?" Mr. Bell asked.

"I don't know, but I'm sure we'll find out soon enough. Maybe it's a fire." Wildfires in California were becoming quite a problem, especially in dry Gold Country. "Can you get Cannoli back in?"

Bell proved to be an adept ferret-wrangler, and within moments we were out the door and crossing the lobby, headed for the front. In a few more moments we were in the parking lot, with all of the other clients and their pets. The sun was hot above us. I smelled wet dog and tar from the warm blacktop, but I didn't smell any smoke.

Finally, Ellie stepped through the door and walkout out across the blacktop toward me. "We've had a bomb threat," she said.

nineteen

I must have stumbled a bit, because Ellie took my arm to steady me. "A bomb?" I asked. "Here?"

Ellie nodded. "I picked up the phone, and there was this voice, just like on TV, very low and electronically distorted—you know the kind? Like on reality crime shows when they want to disguise someone's identity."

I had never watched a reality crime show in my life—not one that I'd admit to, anyway—but I did know what she was talking about. "And what did it say?"

"Just, 'We have planted a bomb in your clinic. Stop enslaving animals. Set them free.' I said, 'Who is this?' and they said, 'The Animal Liberation Army.' And then they hung up."

Whoever was behind the Animal Liberation Army, I could see that they were escalating, and fast. "Do you think it's a hoax?" I asked. "You know, just trying to disrupt our business? They could see that as a win."

"They could," Ellie agreed, biting her lip. "But then we got this." She handed me a sheet of paper.

"What's that?" I asked.

"A list of their demands," she said.

Just then I heard the sirens. I looked up to see the flashing lights of police cars tearing down the county road toward us. "Thank you for calling the police," I said, scanning the paper.

"Of course. First, get everyone moving out to the parking lot, then dial 911."

"At personal risk to yourself," I admonished her. "You should have left the building immediately and called from your cell phone."

I heard nothing back from her and looked up from my paper. She was looking at her shoes and her lip was trembling. "Oh, hey," I said, putting my hand on her elbow. "Ellie, I'm sorry. I didn't mean for it to sound like that. I just meant that...I don't want to see you hurt, especially because of some kind of heroics. You did just the right things—as always. I'm not upset with you, I'm just...panicked and scared for you...because I care about you."

I saw her feeling at her molars with the tip of her tongue, which meant she was trying not to cry. She nodded. I pressed my forehead against hers—which was not easy because she was taller than I was. But she took pity on my feeble attempt at solidarity and leaned down a bit.

The police cars screeched to a stop. A gaggle of deputies emerged in their tan uniforms and Smokey the Bear hats. One of them strode straight up to me, and I was relieved to see that it was Gus. I let go of Ellie and turned to face him. He tipped his hat.

"Casey, I'm so sorry," he said.

"Thanks, Gus."

"Is everyone out?"

I looked at Ellie, who nodded. "All except the Allens' cat who's in the oxygen cage. I couldn't get the cage out without turning it off, which would make it useless. And the cat won't survive long outside it, so..."

I nodded. "That cat is not long for this earth, no matter what," I said. It was the truth, but I still felt bad as I said it. "You're not going in, are you?" I asked Gus.

"No," he shook his head. "We're here to establish a perimeter. Ya'll need to get a bit more distance from the clinic. Excuse me."

He turned and raised his voice. "We need a quarter-mile distance from the clinic. If you have cars, go to them now, and leave as quickly as you can. If you're staff, we'll escort you to a safe distance. Let's get moving, folks!"

People scattered then, most racing for their cars. Gus turned back to us. "You want to ride or walk?" he asked.

"Where should we go?" I asked.

"Just up the road a bit, I guess," he said. "There's a truck stop about the right distance if we go south, so let's head there."

"Okay," I said. "I prefer to walk, I think."

"Me too," Ellie said.

"All right. Mind if I walk with you?" Gus asked.

I was surprised that I didn't. For all of Gus' awkwardness— and the obvious and uncomfortable fact that he seemed to have a crush on me—I felt comforted by his presence. He suddenly seemed assured and calm—which was exactly what I was not.

We walked toward the truck stop—a grimy place I had made the mistake of eating lunch at exactly once. But their driveway was wide, and upon reaching it, we turned and looked back at the clinic. Gus started asking questions—were there questionable clients that day? Anything out of the ordinary or suspicious? Anyone come in without an animal?

We answered "no" to all of his questions, which didn't help

much. As we talked, I noticed a tightening in my gut that hadn't been there before. I realized I was angry. And since I'm not good at processing silently, I didn't hide it. "So, Gus, does all this mean you're going to take Shelley's death more seriously?"

Gus blinked, his face a blank slate of incomprehension. I pressed on. "Honestly, do you think this is all unconnected? Is a bomb scare enough to get the sheriff's attention, or will you just sweep it all under the rug again once the bomb squad leaves?"

Gus' face twitched, and his mouth opened, but nothing comprehensible came out.

"I'm serious, Gus," I said. "I'm pissed about the fact that you all just declared Shelley's death an accident and wiped your hands of it, despite a mountain of evidence to the contrary." I pointed at the clinic. "Case in point, deputy."

Gus finally seemed to find his tongue, but he obviously wasn't comfortable. "Uh...Casey, I'm sorry. It wasn't my call. I understand...I really do."

"Then do something about it," I said.

"I don't make the decisions," Gus said. His eyes were almost pleading. "And we don't know that they are connected. But I promise you that we are taking the vandalism to your car and this bomb threat seriously...very seriously."

"You just don't think it's connected to Shelley," I said, not quite a question.

Sadly, he shook his head. I gritted my teeth and fumed. I glanced at Ellie and saw that she was almost tweaking from the anxiety generated by this little confrontation. I sighed. "Okay, Gus. I get it. There's a chain of command. There are rules."

He nodded, but he looked like a hound that had just been

yelled at. "We have a situation on our hands right now, Casey. I really need to—"

"Yeah, yeah," I said, not able to look at him.

Gus cleared his throat. "Um...bomb squad is coming up from Sacramento—they'll be here in about..." He glanced at his watch. "...about 45 minutes now. But...you don't need to wait here. If you want to go home, I can call you once we check the place out."

"I'll stay," I said, with a finality that brooked no argument. Gus nodded. I turned to Ellie. "You should—"

"Stay right here with you," she said, with equal finality.

"Okay, then," I said. I closed my eyes for a brief moment and tried to collect myself. *Reset*, I thought. I took a deep breath and opened my eyes again. "What will the bomb squad do when they get here?"

"They'll do an infrared sweep to check for electronics." His head snapped up as if he'd just remembered something. "You know, it's a good thing you're going to stay, because we really need to know where you have equipment already—computers, printers, the machines that go 'bing!', you know."

Despite all the tension in the air—or perhaps because of it—I laughed at the Monty Python reference. But before I could speak, Ellie said, "If you can bring me some paper, I'll draw you a map of the layout of the entire office, and where all the electronics are—right down to the surge protectors."

"That would be great," Gus said, and he set off at a trot toward the clinic again, presumably toward some paper and a pen.

As he jogged, a midnight blue sedan pulled up to the clinic, but was waved away by a sheriff's deputy. It slowly rolled down the shoulder toward us, on the wrong side of the road. It stopped just shy of us. Ellie and I watched as a young man got out, his hair gelled into an almost surfable wave, smacking his chewing gum. He slung a leather document bag over his shoulder and walked over the hot gravel toward us. He squinted at me, then at Ellie, then back at me. "You Doctor Gibbons?"

"Yes, but the clinic is closed—"

He fished a yellow envelope out of his bag and handed it to me. Reflexively, I took it.

"You've been served," he said.

twenty

I poked my head around the corner, but didn't open my eyes. "Are you decent? Is it safe?"

I heard Jack laugh and then groan. "Don't make me laugh. It hurts too much."

"Is it safe?" I asked again.

"Yes, yes, I'm dressed and everything." I opened my eyes and entered the hospital room.

"You call this dressed?" I said, indicating his gown.

"You can't see the back of it, so I'm decent. And this is as close to dressed as I get in here," he said.

If I didn't already know he'd taken a shoulder full of buckshot, I wouldn't know it just by looking at him. He was sitting upright, reading the morning paper. Even his perfect hair was combed.

I sat down in the chair nearest the bed. I was dying to tell him about the bomb scare, about being served, about the insurance policy—but I controlled myself. This time needed to be all about him. "How are you?" I asked. "I mean, how are you *really*?" Before he could answer, I added, "And I'll know if you're lying. I'm a doctor, and I'm used to patients who can't talk to me. So I *know* things."

"Fair enough," he smiled. "My whole chest hurts when I move. Otherwise, I feel okay."

I nodded. "Are you on painkillers still?"

"No. Weaned off yesterday," he answered. "Dammit."

I laughed. "As long as you enjoyed them while you had them."

"Oh, I did." He winked. Then he sighed. "It's so good to see you."

His voice was sincere, and I realized I felt the same. *How strange,* I thought. *A week ago, we didn't even know each other.* But I didn't know how to answer him. So I didn't. "When will you be going home?"

"Tomorrow, hopefully."

"You want a ride?" I asked.

"Aren't you working?"

"Well, yes, but if you can arrange to be released at noon..."

"Nothing happens according to *my* schedule here," he said. "I've already asked Susan—our church secretary—if she'll come and get me when they finally withdraw their talons. I'll be fine."

Despite myself, I felt a stab of jealousy. Who was this Susan, and how close was she with Jack? He must have seen the distress in my eyes, because he said, "Wait until you meet Susan. She's about eighty years old, strong as an ox, and fiercely lesbian. She's got a buzz cut just like Sarge." He tried to point to his hair, but it apparently hurt too much and he lowered his arm with a wince.

"Oh," I said. I'm sure my cheeks flushed. I was ashamed of myself...but not too much. "I'd love to meet her."

"Oh, you will. She bosses me around the parish. Not even God crosses her."

I laughed.

"So what's happened while I was down for the count?" he asked. I hesitated, but he *had* asked. It felt okay, so I told him about finding the life insurance policy, and the process server, and the bomb scare. He whistled. "You're not in the habit of gathering moss, are you?"

"I am a rolling freaking stone," I answered.

"So what did the bomb squad find?" he asked.

"Not a thing," I said. "False alarm. The way Ellie and I figure it, they wanted to disrupt our business, and they did just that."

"Damn, Casey, I'm sorry."

"I also wasn't paying attention, and I hurt Ellie's feelings, and now I feel like a total jerk."

"Oh, yeah, I know that feeling. Happens to me on a nearly daily basis."

"Being consecrated doesn't make you any more perfect, then?"

He moaned. "Not by a long shot. By the way, only bishops are consecrated. Priests are ordained."

"Geek," I said.

"Church geek," he corrected. "What happened to that puppy mill guy? The one who shot me."

"Gus says he's being held pending the investigation. Have they interviewed you yet?"

"Yeah, but they wouldn't tell me anything."

"Figures," I said. "Apparently, he couldn't make bail, so he's sitting there."

"Makes you think, though, doesn't it?" he asked.

"Think what?"

"Well, he didn't hesitate to shoot me. The man is obviously...not adept at moderating his emotions. Makes it even more likely that he came after Shelley, don't you think?"

He had a point. I was instantly angry at myself for not having had that thought earlier. I mean, it's true that things had been flying at me pretty fast, but still...I should have clued in on that. "I'm utterly clueless," I confessed.

His brows knit together in confusion. "Where did that come from?"

"Never mind." I waved it away.

"You're *really* hard on yourself, aren't you?" he asked.

That was true, but I didn't need him to confirm it.

"How are you taking care of yourself?" Jack asked.

There was that question again. "I'm going to take a bubble bath and get my nails done."

His eyes narrowed. "It's cruel to mock an injured man."

"So ask better questions."

"Whiskey and a massage?" he asked.

"Now you're talking," I said. "But who has time for that?"

He grunted, obviously not pleased. Here he was, newly emptied of buckshot, and he was worried about *me*. It was cute. Touching, even. Adorable.

"So what are you going to do next?" he asked. "I mean, about the Shelley thing."

I paused. There were so many threads, so many leads, so many suspects. But my animus against Jack's shooter won out. "I need to stop putting off that puppy mill."

His eyes widened. "But—"

"He's in jail, remember? And I'm betting his wife isn't half the shot that he is."

twenty-one

There was no time for dinner, so I picked up a frozen burrito at the EZ Mart. While it was in the microwave, I bit my fingernails and thought about Jack. Then I heard a dinging sound that made me jump. *It can't be the microwave*, I thought, *I just set the damn thing.* A quick glance around the store revealed an old-fashioned pinball machine, a relic from the early sixties, by the look of it. While radiation made my burrito pop and sizzle, I wandered over to the machine. The player looked like a logger, his green baseball cap on backwards, a greasy towel hanging from his back pocket. I kept a respectful distance and watched the ball pinging from bumper to bumper.

That's me, I thought, *bouncing from one thing to the next*. The next thought I had was, *I'm being played*, and I felt a shiver run through me. Deep down, I knew it was true, but I didn't rationally know *how* it was true.

The next ding was from the microwave, and I grabbed my way-too-hot-to-eat burrito and headed out the door. Back on the road, I opened the window, hoping the burrito would cool off faster. I had left Scout at home—I didn't know what awaited me at Eureka Acres, and I didn't want to take the chance of hurting someone else that I cared about.

I pulled up the long drive to the puppy mill with a growing sense of dread. I didn't know how much Harry Clementine's wife knew. Hell, I didn't even know what I was going to ask her. *If Jack were here, he would ask me about my plan,* I thought. *Well, good thing he isn't here, then,* another part of my brain responded, *because we haven't got a clue.*

I set the emergency brake and got out of the car. I walked past the barn and saw the cinderblock and chain-link kennels to my right. The farmhouse was straight ahead—two stories, its weather-beaten paint chipped and in sore need of attention. I paused on the porch and cleared my throat. Then I knocked.

Several minutes passed without any sign of life. Then I heard a thump. The door cracked just a bit and a sliver of wan face became visible. A red, swollen eye looked me up and down, then looked behind me. Finally, the door opened wider to reveal a woman in late middle age. Her hair was straight and stringy, her face ashen and tight. Her eyes were obviously irritated by something. It could have been allergies, but from the way she held herself, I suspected that she'd been crying.

And why not? Her husband was in jail. *And it's your fault,* the unhelpful voice in my head accused.

"Who are you?" she asked. Before I could answer, she added, "What do you want?"

Pity moved me more than propriety in the moment. "Are you okay?" I asked. "What's wrong?"

"The puppies," she said, her voice rising against an onrush of tears.

"What's wrong with the puppies?" I asked.

"They're dying," she said. Her lower lip trembled.

"I'm a veterinarian," I said. "Show them to me."

She looked at me uncertainly, but then she nodded and swung the door open even wider, turning into the house. I followed her, my nose twitching at the acrid stench of mold and pipe tobacco.

The house was cluttered. Everywhere I looked there were stacks of newspapers and old books. The stacks were neat, arranged at right angles to everything else in the room, but they left little room to navigate. I was terrified I would bump into one and start a chain reaction that would bring down their glorious collection of library materials.

The kitchen was not clean, I noted, but perhaps Mrs. Clementine was in the middle of cooking something? It didn't appear so. I noticed a huge bottle out on the counter, next to an open cupboard. I looked at my host, who had already disappeared into the next room. I leaped to the counter and leaned in for a closer look at the bottle. "Trimethoprim sulfa," I read, and I'm sure my eyebrows must have shot up. It was a common treatment for intestinal parasites.

I hopped back to the doorway and hurried after the breeder's wife, catching up with her without her noticing my detour, or so I hoped. She led me out the back door and down a short path to a cinderblock kennel complex. She opened the chain-link gate, and I followed her in.

She turned on an overhead fluorescent light, which buzzed and flickered its protest at having its rest disturbed. Mrs. Clementine pointed. Despite the overhead light, I had to squint. I pulled my phone out and hit the flashlight button. I opened another chain-link gate and entered, squatting as I shone the flashlight around.

The place reeked, and I quickly saw why. Eight puppies huddled in the darkness, surrounded by their own waste. Two wadded blankets were covered in filth. Most of the puppies lay in a pile, but a couple tried to stand. It was clear that something was wrong with them, however. Their legs were stiff, and their movements were uncoordinated—even for a puppy. None of them seemed to be able to pick their heads up—even the ones who could move. It was a parasite, all right.

"They're showing signs of hypermetria and cercival hyperesthesia," I said, squatting down to get a closer look at the puppies.

"Is that treatable?" asked Mrs. Clementine.

"Those are symptoms, not a disease. They've got a parasite," I said. "Why is it so filthy in there? Puppies need a clean environment."

"Harry keeps them clean—my husband, Harry."

"And Harry's in jail," I said.

"How did you..." Her voice trailed off. "Oh. You're *her*."

"The one and only," I said, standing up again. I held my hand out to her. "Dr. Casey Gibbons. Nice to make your acquaintance."

She shook my hand, but with some reluctance. "You can call me Nancy."

"Nancy," I said with a nod. "Can you show me the bitch?"

"What bitch?"

"The bitch what born them," I said, affecting a hillbilly accent for some reason. Then, realizing she might think I was mocking her, I tried a different tack. "The momma-dog."

"Oh. She's sick too. We're keeping her over here, away from the puppies—although I don't see what good it's doing."

She pointed to a nearby kennel. I opened the gate and stepped in. She was a sizable standard poodle—obviously the "poo" and "doo" parts of the cockapoo, doodles, and whatever other designer mutts they turned out here.

The poor girl was flat out on her side, and didn't even twitch an ear as I got closer. Bad sign. I held one of her lids open with one hand while I waved my phone flashlight back and forth slowly. Then I checked the other one. "Jesus," I swore.

"What?" Nancy asked.

"Your momma-dog here has nystagmus and anisocoria, and I haven't even got past her eyes."

"Are those symptoms too?"

"Yes. It means that her pupils are different sizes and her eyes are twitching in different directions of their own accord."

"Maybe she's dreaming," the woman said.

"No. She's awake," I said. "She's just very, very sick."

I stood up and walked back out of the kennel. "Let's talk," I said to her.

Looking cowed, she turned and led me back to the kitchen.

"Would you like some tea?" she asked.

"Sure, thanks," I said, and sat heavily in one of the chairs at the table.

Nancy put the kettle on and I watched as she shakily pulled two teabags from their sleeves and draped the strings with their tabs over the sides of two mugs.

The water must have been warm already, as the kettle began to moan in no time at all. She poured the water and set the mugs on the table.

She didn't offer sugar or milk, but that was all right—I didn't take either.

"How bad is it?" she asked.

"I need to run a blood test to be absolutely sure, but I'd bet a week's wages your dogs have neosporosis. It's rare, but I've seen it before."

"Is that bad?" she asked.

"Does it *look* bad?" I asked.

"Yes," she admitted.

"Yes, it's bad."

"How did it happen?" she asked.

"Usually, it happens when owners feed dogs diseased meat. Any beef from sick cows come through here?"

Her face blanched. I had my answer. "Just too good a deal to pass up, huh?"

"What should we do?" she asked.

I sighed. "I'm going to go back to the clinic and get what I need to draw some blood. And, because I'm pretty sure I'm right and we can't waste any time at all, I'm going to start your momma-dog on subcutaneous Clindamycin. She'll need a new IV bag every eight hours, so I'm going to teach you how to stick her in the back of the neck with a needle. Are you okay with that?"

Her eyes went wide, and she swallowed. "I guess I have to be," she said.

"Good girl," I said. That probably sounded condescending or patronizing or something, but I was angry and I didn't care. "I'm going to give Clindamycin to the pups too, but you can give that to them orally, in an eyedropper, straight into their mouths. You have to get all of them, so you'll need to devise some system for making sure you don't miss anyone or accidentally give someone a double dose."

"They're not very active," Nancy said.

"No, but if we get them in time, they soon will be."

"Okay."

"While I'm gone, you need to get those puppies cleaned up. Give them baths, but don't just turn the hose on them. Be gentle with them—they're in rough shape. Have some compassion."

She looked down, which I took to be an indicator of shame.

Well, good, I thought. *She should be ashamed.* "Then scrub out their pen—with bleach, and rinse it well."

"Me?" Nancy's hand went to her chest.

"I don't see anyone else, and I've got my hands full. It's all-hands-on-deck time, if you want to save your livestock."

Her face grew dark, and I realized I was about to have a revolt on my hands. I decided to nip it in the bud. Before she could speak, I said, "Look, either you can do it, or I will call animal control, and they will take the whole situation off your hands—permanently. They'll also shut this place down."

She made an unqualified retreat. "Oh. Okay." Her eyes darted back and forth as she thought. "So...how long will they need to be on the...Clinda...Clinda—"

"Clindamycin. Eight weeks. Plus Trimethoprim. You've got a big bottle of that in the kitchen. I don't know how you got it —and I don't want to know—but you can't give that to the puppies, or to their mother right now. They'll both need liquid forms, at least until your momma-dog is strong enough to be pilled. Ever pill a dog?"

"No," she said.

"You don't do much around here, do you?"

Her eyes flashed and I realized I'd overstepped. "My husband looks after the dogs. I do *everything else*."

I was unapologetic. "Well, now you'll have to do it all."

She opened her mouth to protest, but then seemed to think better of it. She looked down at her tea with pained resignation and nodded silently.

"It's going to be a long night for both of us," I said. "So before we're both tired and cranky, I need you to answer something for me."

"Okay. Does this have to do with—?"

"Where was your husband in the late afternoon on July 24th?"

She pursed her lips and her eyes moved back and forth. She rose and went over to a drug store calendar hanging on the wall. She flipped back to the previous month and studied the blue scrawls in the little box. "He was here. The man came out to repair the well-thingy."

"Well-thingy?"

"A pipe broke. When Harry was mowing. He clipped the... the part of the well that is above ground, to let the air out, you know."

I was clueless as to the vagaries of rural wells, but I nodded just the same. "Okay. Can you give me the number of the well-repair service so I can confirm that?"

She looked like she was going to protest, but once more she mastered herself. She went to the requisite junk door and pulled a pencil and a Post-it pad from it. Leaning in to read the calendar again, she jotted down the number and handed a yellow Post-it note to me.

"Jefferson and Sons," I read. "Sounds redundant."

It was apparently a joke not worth acknowledging, as Nancy sat heavily. "So...if your husband didn't kill Dr. Capra, why did he shoot Jack?"

"Who's Jack?" Nancy asked.

"Jack Mornington, the Episcopal priest," I said, then I nearly choked as I added, "my friend."

She must have noticed because she met my eyes for the first time, and there was something new in them. Caring. I instantly felt naked. I took a deep breath to fortify myself.

"He doesn't like trespassers, or meddlers, or...people accusing him of doing something he didn't do."

"No," I agreed. "No one does."

Nancy crossed her arms and hugged herself. A faraway look came into her eyes. "Do you ever wonder...how different your life would be if...well, if you had made a different choice?"

I blinked. "Different choice?" I asked. "What choice are you talking about?"

"A long time ago, two boys loved me. I never thought anyone could...would have me. And then there were two..."

I frowned, trying to make the connection. Then the penny dropped. "Oh..." I said, and I felt myself softening toward her. "You're wondering...maybe you married the wrong man." It wasn't a question, but she answered it anyway.

"Yes. I never thought I'd be married to someone...in jail."

I nodded. "I'm divorced, so...I've wondered the same thing myself. A lot. Obsessively. An unhealthy, god-awful amount."

"How do you deal with it?" she asked.

"With what? The regret?" I asked.

She nodded, her eyes fixed on mine.

I sighed. "If I knew the answer to that, I'd...I suppose I'd like myself more."

She looked down, continuing to nod.

I stood up and put a hand on her arm. "I'll...I'll be back just as soon as I can, maybe an hour. You might want to put on some coffee—it's going to be a long night."

"Thank you, doctor," she said, not looking at me.

twenty-two

The sun was up before I headed home. I needed to shower and change before heading into work, but I worried about passing the parasite onto Scout as I did so. She was loose inside the house, and she had access to the back yard. She was also well trained. I decided on a plan of action.

As soon as I parked the car, I walked to the back yard fence and called her. No doubt she had heard the car and was waiting by the front door. But she heard my voice and within moments was through the dog door and bounding across the deck toward me. She leaped off the wooden deck and almost ploughed into the fence. I stood back a couple of yards.

"What a good girl!" I praised her. "Now, Scout, sit."

She obeyed. I held my hand up, like a traffic cop indicating "stop." "Scout, stay." I put extra gravity in my voice so she would know it wasn't just a game. Then I turned and headed for the front of the house. Before turning the corner, I looked back and was relieved to see Scout in exactly the same place. I knew she would be, but I had to check—too much was on the line.

As soon as I was inside, I closed the dog door, trapping Scout outside for the time being. Then I stripped, throwing my clothes directly into the washing machine. I set it for "heavy duty" and "hot" water. Then I went to immerse myself in hot water too.

Newly disinfected and dressed, I almost felt human. I had a slight headache coming on, which I ascribed to exhaustion. More coffee than usual was the prescription for both the headache and the fatigue. I started the coffee maker and then let Scout into the house. I waited for her to stop leaping about before grabbing a yogurt cup for breakfast. By the time I finished it, the blessed coffee was done.

I put Scout in the car and headed for work. I don't normally take Scout to work, but I didn't feel right about leaving her home any longer. She was a good girl, and would not likely act out, but I didn't want to try her patience. Dogs are intensely social creatures, and it's not healthy for them to be alone for long periods. Once at work, I put her in one of the spare kennels where she could see the techs and other animals. If I got a spare moment, I'd walk her. Until then, we were all company for her, and she seemed content.

I wished I was. The lack of sleep had put me in an altered state. I felt stoned, and realized that the danger that I would make a mistake or miss something had risen substantially. I would need to be extra careful, extra mindful, at least until I could get a good night's sleep.

Fortunately, I didn't have any surgeries scheduled, and that lowered the risk considerably. Now if only I could avoid stupid mathematical errors when figuring out medicine dosages based on an animal's weight. Normally I was pretty good at doing math in my head, but right now "five times two equals kumquat" sounded like a perfectly legitimate sum.

Also a plus, the morning's work was far from routine. One

woman brought in not one but two potbellied pigs needing hoof trimmings. I grabbed my diagonal-cut mini pliers and got to work.

At lunch, I took Scout out for a trot. We followed the road north until we found a food truck parked by the local cannabis dispensary—location is everything, and whoever thought of putting a food truck in a cannabis dispensary parking lot was nothing short of brilliant. I passed on the weed, but loaded up on the pulled pork. There was no way I could eat the whole sandwich, but Scout selflessly offered to help. She's such a giving dog.

We got back to the clinic with ten minutes to spare before my next client. Ellie caught my eye and waved me over. I held up my index finger and put Scout in the kennel first. "What's up?" I asked, sidling up to where she was seated at her computer.

"I have some good news for you," she said.

"Do tell. I could use some of that."

She looked up and actually saw me for the first time. "You look like hell."

"Thanks. I feel like it too."

"Did you paint those bags under your eyes, or are you naturally endowed?"

"Good news? Focus," I said, pointing at her screen.

"Oh yeah." She ran her fingers through her green hair and took a deep breath. "You are going to be very very happy with me."

"I have had zero sleep, and I have a hair-trigger temper at the moment," I warned her.

"All right, all right. I tracked the bomb scare email to an IP address, and after some sweet talking and a little hacking—"

"Don't ask, don't tell," I warned her.

"Right. So, I traced the IP to a street address. And guess what? It's in Utah City." She handed me a Post-it note.

"Really?" I asked, taking the note.

"Really." She beamed at me, looking for all the world like the impish pixie she was.

"Who lives there?"

"D. Travers. That's all I know."

I pursed my lips and read the address over and over. Then I put it in the pocket of my lab coat. "Good work, El. Really, really good work."

twenty-three

I had intended to make dinner for Jack and take it over to him. But nothing went as it was supposed to. Besides, I was so tired my eyelids were threatening foreclosure. I thought about asking for a raincheck, but I just couldn't do it. For one thing, Jack had been shot—because, and only because, he had been with me. I owed it to him to check in on him. For another thing, for me, dates were rarer than a chihuahua without a cute sweater. I needed to take them when I could get them, even if I was in danger of falling over in a narcoleptic fit.

Thus it was that Scout and I found ourselves opening a black wrought-iron gate behind St. Julian's-in-the Valley. An ornate brick path, overgrown with grass, led through a copse of gnarled trees toward a house that looked like it had been plucked straight out of a fairy tale by the Brothers Grimm. I recognized the architectural style as mock-Tudor, with dark wooden beams set into white plaster walls rising to a dramatic peak over the porch.

The sun had still been up when we parked, but the trees

surrounded the house on all sides, creating a permanent state of woodsy gloom. I rang the doorbell, but it didn't seem to work. After a few minutes, I pounded on the ancient-looking carved wood door.

That worked well enough. A few moments later, Jack swung open the door and seemed his regular, chipper self. He was wearing gray sweatpants and a checked red-flannel shirt. His hair was mussed and there was a dab of shaving cream just under his jaw. I stifled a desire to wipe it off.

"Hey," I said. "I was half expecting Lurch to answer the door."

Jack laughed. "The Munsters have a haunted mansion. I just have a haunted cottage."

I gave him an exaggerated frown. "Lurch is from the Addams Family. Get your 1960s pop references straight." I handed him the brown-paper shopping bag I'd picked up on the way over. "I brought you some dinner."

"You shouldn't have," he said, beaming.

"You're right. I *should* have cooked, but it's been a hell of a day," I said.

"A rotisserie chicken, potato salad, chips, four cans of brown ale—what more could a fellow ask for?" He looked me in the eyes and smiled. "Thank you." Then he knelt down and nuzzled Scout. "And how's my favorite Boxer?"

Until that moment, Scout had been a perfectly behaved lady. No more. She leaped on him, and Jack emitted a pained groan. "Off!" I commanded, and Scout, looking chagrined, hung her head below her shoulders and returned to my side. "Sorry. 'Don't jump on people who have been shot' isn't in her vocabulary. We're working on it."

"It's okay," Jack said, getting to his feet with a groan. "Come in."

I hadn't been to Jack's house before, and I have to admit I was curious. Inside, it was just as Fantasyland as the outside, but instead of giving the impression of ancient decrepitude, the cottage glowed with warmth. Candles adorned a stone fireplace, where a log was burning—or was that a propane insert? I saw that it was. No matter—it was still homey.

The artwork on the walls was religious, mostly, but not sentimental. I saw icons of people I did not know staring from the walls, bearing witness to...what? I was intrigued to find out. The furniture was in the arts-and-crafts style; it looked like it might be several decades old.

Scout instantly jumped up on the couch and made herself at home. "Sorry about that," I said. "Do you want her down?"

"No, she's fine," Jack said. "Can I get you a glass of wine? Or a sherry? Or—"

"How about a whiskey?" I asked.

His eyebrows shot up. "Ohhhhkayyyy." A broad grin broke out over his face. "American, Canadian, Scottish, or Irish?"

Oh, it was going to be like that, was it? I narrowed my eyes and wondered just how comprehensive this exploration could possibly be. "Northeast Scottish single malts?" I asked.

"Old Pulteney, Ballblair, Glenmorangie, or Dalmore?" he asked.

I called his bluff. "Ballblair."

"Damn," he said. "That's the one I don't have. You did have to pick that one. How about the Old Pulteney? It's peaty as hell."

"That will do nicely," I said. To be honest, I preferred a good old-fashioned American sour mash, but I had been intending to broaden my whisky horizons anyway. He went to a cabinet that was indeed impressively stocked, poured a couple of fingers into a tumbler and handed it to me. I waved the glass under my nose, closed my eyes, and breathed in deep. I smelled butterscotch and caramel. I took a sip, and a rich smokey flavor sent wave after wave of pleasure over my tongue. "Okay," I almost choked, "that's good."

"It is indeed." He took a sip himself. "Have a seat." He indicated a chair near the fire and sat himself on the couch next to Scout, who instantly began giving his face a bath. I silently envied my dog, not for the first time.

"How are you feeling?" I asked. "You seem a bit too up-and-about."

"Well, to be honest, I've been in bed most of the day," he said. "But my energy is coming back. And just lying there is driving me nuts. I'm halfway through the second season of *Downton Abbey*, and it's only been two days."

I smiled. *Downton Abbey* seemed like just the sort of thing Jack *would* watch, and I guessed that it wasn't his first time bingeing the show. I only wished I'd watched it so that I could make an intelligent comment on it. "Do you mind if I take a look?" I asked.

"At what?"

"At your shoulder. I *am* a doctor, you know."

"Oh. Well. Sure." He started to unbutton his shirt. His motions were slow, and I realized that raising his right arm was painful. But he managed the buttons all right and I helped him draw the shirt off. I might have taken more delight in the striptease had he not obviously been in pain. Spots of blood poked through the white gauze bandages. Gently, I pulled the tape away from his arm and lifted the bandage up and away from the wound. I was relieved to see that there was no sign of infection. The holes left by the buckshot were still visible, but were closing up. It looked as good as one might possibly hope for. I carefully replaced the bandage and helped him on again with his shirt.

After it was on, and Jack sat back on the couch again, I noticed that he was sweating. "I'm sorry, I didn't realize that would be so challenging," I said. "Next time just tell me 'no.'"

"You don't strike me as the kind of person who takes 'no' for an answer." He smiled.

"You get to push back," I said. "And I hope you will." I meant it. I didn't know what this thing between me and Jack actually was, but if it was going to be anything, I wanted a partner, not a supplicant.

"All right. You asked for it," he said.

"Good." My eyes went to the fireplace and something in me relaxed. Maybe it was the whisky, maybe it was just the coziness of the setting. Whatever it was, it felt good. Scout was splayed out over most of the couch, using Jack's leg as a pillow. She had started to snore.

"So...does the church give you this house?"

"The church gives me use of it. It's considered part of my compensation. But I don't own it. It's part of the church properties."

I nodded. "What made you want to become a minister?"

He rolled his eyes and hooted. "That is a long story. The short version is I didn't want to become a minister at all."

"So how did you end up here?" I asked.

"Well...you like dogs. Have you ever heard that poem, 'The Hound of Heaven'? Francis Thompson?"

"That sounds familiar, but I don't know it, no." I took another sip of the excellent scotch. If all single malts were this complex and wonderful, Jack might just make a convert of me.

"*I fled Him, down the nights and down the days; I fled Him, down the arches of the years; I fled Him, down the labyrinthine ways of my own mind; and in the mist of tears...*" he quoted.

"Are you saying God tracked you like a hound?"

He sighed. "Exactly."

"Do you know how crazy that sounds?" I asked.

"If you don't believe in God, or if you think God is just some energy field or a pocket of celestial gas...yes, that sounds crazy. But if you think God is a person who loves and hopes and grieves, then I don't think it's crazy at all."

"This is going to take some time for me to get used to. I'm... not religious."

"That has crossed my mind," he said, sounding pained. "Think of it this way: people are composed of three fundamental parts—body, mind, and soul. You are a doctor for the animal nature, the body. Psychologists are doctors for the psychological nature, the mind. I am a doctor for the spiritual nature, the soul. We have different specialties, but we're both healers."

I blinked, and just like that, my world made a one-quarter turn, and everything looked a little bit different. "Okay," I said. "I can buy that."

"We both use diagnostic tools, and we both write prescriptions," he went on. "And sometimes people get better...and sometimes they don't. For both of us, I think, there's an element of mystery."

I nodded. Maybe Jack and I had a lot more in common than I originally thought.

Just then Scout whimpered and turned nipples-up, all four feet in the air. She was apparently running in her dream, and one of her front paws nearly clawed at Jack's face. He leaned back to avoid the flopping appendage and laughed.

"You're really good with her," I said.

"She's a great dog," he said. "So much so that...I don't know. I've been thinking that maybe it's time to get a dog of my own."

I sat up at attention. "Oh? What kind?"

"I don't know," he said. "Maybe you can help me. I'd like a

dog who's smart, loving, not too high-maintenance. And I want to give an older dog a good home, a dog that most people wouldn't want."

If I ever had any doubts about Jack Mornington, they were gone now. He might as well have been whispering sweet nothings in my ear. I checked to see if I was drooling. Fortunately, my dignity was intact. I cleared my throat. "Uh...that's lovely, Jack. I think you should look into a standard poodle."

He frowned. "A poodle? Isn't that the definition of high-maintenance?"

"Sure, if you have a show dog. But you can also give a poodle a no-nonsense haircut that's easy to maintain. They're easy to care for, they have the most marvelous personalities, plus they can do long division faster than you can."

"That smart, eh?"

"God's honest truth," I said, holding my fingers up in the girl-scout salute.

"Huh."

"In fact, I know about a breeder who has a lovely brood bitch who's looking for a home. Her name is Cher. Why don't we go meet her?"

"Cher?" His eyebrows rose. "Not high-maintenance, huh?"

"Just meet her," I said. "I'll call and make us an appointment. What do you think?"

He looked at the fire for a moment. Then he nodded. "Sure. Okay. Let's do it."

A warm feeling flooded through me. It was partly the whisky, but also excitement at the prospect of bringing some joy into Jack's life.

"How goes the investigation?" Jack asked. His eyes shone in the firelight.

"I went to see Mrs. Clementine. Her husband is still in jail. They weren't able to make bail."

"Oh...I'd like to say I'm sorry to hear that, but I think it may actually be safer for the world if he is where he is."

"I certainly understand that," I said.

"What did she say?"

"Well, not much. Let's just say that as soon as I got there, I realized we had a medical emergency on our hands. I was there all night."

"Is that why you look like you're about to drop off to sleep at any moment?"

I shrugged. "The whisky isn't helping."

"Or it is," he said. "Did you glean anything?"

"She gives her husband an alibi for the time Shelley died. Says he was home. She even showed me an appointment on the calendar when a guy from the well company came out."

"You should be able to check that," he said.

"I did. I called in between clients today. It checks out."

"Huh," Jack said. "There goes your number one suspect."

"Yep," I said, pursing my lips. "But that's good, isn't it? Aren't we that much closer to knowing who did it, having eliminated someone who didn't?"

"That's what I like about you," he said, pointing his tumbler at me, "You are relentlessly glass-half-full."

I burst out with a laugh that was a little too loud. "That is funny only because it is not even remotely true."

He laughed, and I knew he knew that. He was ribbing me. It felt good. "And then there's the bomb thing," I said.

"What's up with that?" he asked, leaning forward.

"Ellie tracked the...internet protocol thingy...whatchamacallit—"

"IP address?" Jack asked.

I snapped my fingers. "That's it. Anyway, she traced it to a house...or at least an address...in Utah City."

"Did you go?" Jack asked.

"No, not yet. I'm...I guess I'm getting psyched up to go."

Jack stood. "Well, what are we waiting for?"

"It's 7:30 at night."

"The evening is young. No one is in bed yet. No one over five, that is."

"Jack, the last time you went with me to interview someone you got shot."

"I am painfully aware of that fact," he said. "Statistically, the odds are against it happening again. At least, so soon."

"I don't have that kind of faith in statistics," I said.

"I'm the faith guy," he said, "you're the science gal."

"I'm the 'science gal'?" I shook my head.

"What? Did I say something wrong?" he asked.

I shook my head and chuckled. "No. I'm just giving you a hard time."

"Well?" he said, heading for the door. "Are we going to go?"

"No," I said. "I'll go tomorrow. I promise."

He looked disappointed.

"And you, young man," I said, "are under doctor's orders to rest."

"How do you know?" he asked.

I narrowed one eye at him. He sighed. "Only stands to reason."

"Damn straight," I agreed.

"Well, then. Dinner?" he asked.

"Sure," I said. "Let's finish our drinks first."

He nodded and sat. We both stared at the fire for a bit. The silence might have been awkward except that somehow it never seemed awkward with Jack. It was weird.

I cleared my throat. "Um...you mentioned that you were married...you know, before...well, before she died." It sounded stupid even as I said it. I felt like crawling out of my skin.

"It's okay," he said. "People die."

I am an idiot, I thought. Apparently I never learn, because I hastened on. "So was that *before* you became a priest?"

He cocked his head, apparently trying to make sense of my question. Finally, he said, "We were married while I was in seminary."

"Oh." I pursed my lips, confused. "So...it's okay for you to have...you know...lady friends?"

"Are you tap dancing around the celibacy question?" he asked, a sly grin spreading over his face.

"I guess I am," I said.

"I like to think of us as 'the sensible Catholics,'" he said. "Episcopal priests are not celibate."

"None of them?"

"Well, I'm sure there are *some,* just as there are in the general population. I'm just saying we're not required to be celibate. In fact, we're encouraged not to be."

"Really? How does that work?"

"No! Nothing like that. I just mean, we're encouraged to be married."

"Oh." I felt heat rising to my face. Again, it might have been the whisky, but I'm sure part of it was good old-fashioned embarrassment. "And to get married, you have to date."

"Quite," he said.

"And how about sex...I mean, before marriage?" Okay, that was the whisky talking. I cringed and instantly regretted being so forward—but I still wanted to hear the answer.

"There are conservative Christians and liberal Christians," he said. "Conservative Christians are very concerned with...let us say, personal morality. Liberal Christians are much more concerned with social morality—structures of oppression, and so forth. So conservative Christians are very concerned about people having sex who shouldn't be."

"And liberal Christians?" I asked.

"We don't care who you're sleeping with, just so long as you're not oppressing migrant workers."

I laughed out loud. "Is that true?"

"Every bit of it," he said.

"It better be," I said.

twenty-four

The next day was another tornado at work. I was bustling between exam rooms with hardly a chance to catch my breath in between. Only at lunch did I have a chance to breathe, and even it was shortened from an hour and a half to forty-five minutes because we were backed up.

I stuffed the corner of a sandwich into my mouth as I googled the Royal Poodle and hit the phone icon. A moment later, a woman's voice answered with a professional greeting.

"Hi. I'm Dr. Casey Gibbons. A few days ago your owner, Mr. Dalton, brought one of your brood bitches in—Cher? Oh, good, you know who I mean. Yes, well, Mr. Dalton said he'd be looking for a good home for Cher, and I just wanted to know if she was still available? I have a friend looking to adopt, and I'd love for him to come and meet her."

The woman asked me to hold. I put my phone on speaker and turned back to my sandwich. A minute or two later, I heard her voice again. "Dr. Gibbons? I'm sorry, I'm afraid Cher has been placed."

"Oh. I'm happy to hear that...and sad," I confessed.

"We have a couple of other retired bitches and studs, if you'd like to come up and meet them."

"Oh. Sure. That would be lovely." I pulled up my calendar and made an appointment. I figured Jack's schedule was probably pretty free—because buckshot—but I'd check with him later about it.

After I hung up, I looked at the time. I had twenty minutes left. What I really wanted was to take a quick stroll in the sunshine to clear my head. But the burden of Shelley's death weighed on me. If I didn't avenge her, no one would. I phoned her ex-husband.

Stephen Thomas had always been an odd fellow. He liked people to use both names, and I obliged. He was one of those people who attracts bad luck like a magnet. Only when Shelley got free of him did her life stop being a nonstop roller-coaster of drama. Being around Stephen Thomas was exhausting at the best of times, and I steeled myself for whatever ride I was about to send myself on.

But instead of speaking to Stephen Thomas, a robotic voice informed me that his voicemail was full and could "take no more messages. Goodbye."

"Hm..." I said. I wracked my brain for the name of the place Stephen Thomas worked. I drew a blank at first, but then pulled on a vague thread. Then the name popped into my head like a neon sign. I googled Rutgers Cement in Auburn and hit the phone icon.

"Rutgers," the voice on the other end announced. "We deliver, you pour."

"Hi there," I said. "My name is Dr. Casey Gibbons. I'm looking for Stephen Thomas Capra. His ex-wife was...has died, and I want to make sure he's been informed."

"Oh. Geez. I'm sorry to hear that. Shelley?"

"Yeah," I said, surprised by the sudden lump in my throat.

"Oh, God. Shelley was a star."

"Yes. Yes, she was. Who is this?"

"Oh, sorry. I'm Benny Collins, day shift manager here. And, apparently, I handle phones because *someone is doing her nails!*" He raised his voice at this last bit.

"They're almost dry, Benny," a young female voice with a Brooklyn accent said somewhere in the distance.

"Anyway, that's tough news."

"Is Stephen Thomas around?"

"I wish I could say he was, but...no. We had to fire his ass."

"Oh. That's terrible. Uh...when?"

"About a month ago."

"Could I ask why?" It was none of my business, but I so wanted to know.

"Yeah. Embezzlement. Or should I say, *attempted* embezzlement. Some people are just too stupid to attempt crime."

"Ah. I'm sorry to hear that," I said. "Well, bad news all around."

"It sure seems that way," Collins agreed.

"You wouldn't happen to have any forwarding contact info, would you?"

"Yeah. He's got a house. I had to call it up on google earth once—I don't remember why. But it's a ramshackle place, looks like a crack house. You want the address?"

"Please," I said.

He put me on speaker and hummed a tuneless tune until he found it. I wrote it down. "Hey, it's too bad about Steve Tom," Collins said. "He's a nice guy when he's not stealing from you."

I scrawled the name on a Post-it. "Thank you, Mr. Collins. I'm so grateful for your help."

"You bet. You take care." He hung up.

"How the mighty are fallen," I said, instantly realizing that quoting the Bible was more Jack's thing than mine. Still, it fit. Stephen Thomas had been a banking guy...until he wasn't. The guy had a PhD in messing up. If he had been so hard up as to try to embezzle, and then had lost his job...he could be desperate indeed. Desperate enough to kill for the insurance money, though? I didn't want to think so. Stephen Thomas might be a loser, but I couldn't picture him as a killer. Still... desperate people did desperate things.

After work, I swung by Jack's place. Don't ask me why. First, he shouldn't be up and about. Second, he'd already literally taken a bullet—or at least a round of buckshot—for me. It didn't seem fair to put him in the line of fire again. But he had been insistent. And for some reason I can't explain, I really really wanted him with me.

He was waiting on the street outside the church when I pulled up. "Wow, you're eager," I said as he climbed in.

"If I don't get out of that house, I'm going to go nuts," he said, shutting the car door.

"That's a bit dramatic, don't you think? It's only been a couple of days." I looked in my mirror and pulled onto the street.

"I need to escape over-eager parishioners loading up my freezer with casseroles. I'm in danger of being love-bombed to death."

I giggled.

"Plus, I have a bit of ADHD," he confessed. I could see he was serious. "Hope that's not a deal-breaker. It does make doing a lot of nothing my own peculiar brand of torture."

"So how do you sit still for church services?"

"I don't!" he laughed. "I picked the one job where I get to be at church and, alone among the entire congregation, don't have to sit still for a minute of it!" He looked over at me. "Please be impressed. It was quite a coup."

I laughed. "Okay, I can see that," I said. "But why not just avoid church altogether?"

"You might as well ask, 'Why not avoid life?'" he said.

"I haven't been to church since before I went to college, and I never felt impoverished," I said.

"It would be a terrible loss for me," he said.

I respected that, and I *wanted* to respect that. I didn't understand it, though. I always considered myself a "spiritual but not religious" sort of person, although if pressed, I would have to come clean and confess that I wasn't even all that spiritual. So why my attraction to Jack? It had to be more than the lips.

I changed the subject. "How are you feeling?"

"A little better every day. I've got more energy than yesterday."

"Glad to hear it," I said. "Oh, I made you an appointment to look at a poodle."

"Oh, yes? Good. When is it?" I told him as he fished out his cell phone and checked his calendar. "That will work fine." Out of the corner of my eye I watched as his thumbs flashed, entering the date.

"They don't have Cher anymore, though. She's been placed."

"Oh, too bad. I was warming up to the name. I was going to hang a disco ball over her dog bed."

I laughed. That was one reason I liked Jack. He really did make me laugh.

"I've been thinking about Maggie Edgerton," he said, putting his phone back in his pocket. "I think you can rule her out as a suspect."

"Why do you think that?" I asked.

"Because Shelley was her golden goose. If Maggie killed her dog in order to set Shelley up for a lawsuit—"

"Which I think is very likely," I interjected.

"—then she would have nothing to gain by killing Shelley. Suing Shelley was her meal ticket. And it's not like she was really angry at Shelley for killing her dog—she probably did that herself, so that takes the 'crime of passion' element out of it."

I nodded. "She's still moving ahead with the lawsuit. I got served, after all."

"Did you?" His eyebrows shot up.

"Yeah. Didn't I tell you about that? Sorry," I said.

He waved the apology away. "It's not like you don't have a lot on your plate."

"True," I agreed.

"But even so, her case is weaker with Shelley out of the picture," Jack reasoned.

I suspected that was true. "So she's a scam artist and a nuisance, but not so much a killer," I tried it on for size.

"That's my opinion," Jack said.

I wasn't ready to give Maggie a total pass, but I mentally moved her from the "definitely a suspect" category to the "maybe a suspect" category. I ticked off the options in my head once more. "So that leaves the animal rights terrorists as our top suspects," I noted.

"I guess it does," Jack agreed. "Unless there's something else you're not telling me."

"Is this how it's going to be?" I asked.

"I'm teasing," he said. "Uh...so what are you hoping to learn here?"

"I don't know. I guess I'm just...information gathering."

As I drove, I had been following the GPS map to Utah City with the sound down. It led us to a plain, small yellow house with what looked like a dead tree in the yard. A birdhouse hung from the tree, looking cheerless—a failed attempt at ornamentation. A couple of bicycles littered the yard, fallen where they had been dropped, but clearly not abandoned.

"You sure you're up for this?" I asked. "Maybe you should sit in the car."

"I am not staying in the car, Mom," Jack said.

"Ouch. Little early to play the 'mom' card, dontcha think?" I asked.

"Sorry." His brows knit together. "That didn't come out the way I intended."

I narrowed one eye at him. "Watch yourself, buddy," I said.

"Roger wilco," he said. We got out of the car and walked together to the porch.

"You got a plan?" he asked.

"Yep," I pressed the doorbell.

"Does it involve blurting out an accusation?" he asked.

"Pretty much," I said.

"Maybe you should let me handle one of these," he said.

"Yeah?" I asked.

"Yeah," he said.

"Okay. Take it away," I said.

"I haven't had time to make a plan!" he protested.

The door swung open. A woman in early middle age stood behind the screen door, looking us up and down. "Yes?"

"Hi," I said, as Jack clearly wasn't ready. "My name is Dr. Casey Gibbons. This is Father Jack Mornington."

The woman's eyes widened. She glanced back and forth at us uncertainly. "Is this a religious thing?"

"No," I said. "We'd just like to ask you a question or two. May we?"

"What is this about?"

"It's about some...well, some terrorist activity," I said.

She looked instantly concerned. "Terrorist activity?" she asked.

"Yes," I said. "Would you consider yourself an animal rights activist?"

"No..." She shook her head as she said it, but something flashed in her eyes.

"What about your husband...or partner?" I asked.

"No, my husband is not an activist either," she said. "Why?"

"Do you know of anyone who might have used your internet to promote animal rights activities?" I asked.

Her eyes narrowed. "What's this really about?"

I sighed. "I'm a veterinarian. Our clinic got a bomb scare. We traced the warning email here." The trace was probably illegal, if I knew Ellie, so she didn't need to know any more than that.

"Oh, dear. That's terrible," she said. "But...no, I didn't send it. My husband didn't, I'm sure. He's a hunter."

"Well, thank you for your time," I said. I held a business card out to her. She pushed open the screen door about two inches and took it. "If you think of anyone else who might have had anything to do with this, can you give me a call?"

"Of course."

We turned to go, but Jack suddenly turned back. "Oh, do you have wifi?" he asked.

"Yes," she said.

"Is it password protected?" he asked.

"No," she said.

He nodded. "Okay. Thank you."

He was quiet as we walked back to the car. "Thoughts?" I asked him. We got in and shut our doors.

"If Ellie is right, and the email did come from this address," he said, "it could be that whoever sent it parked out on the road here and piggybacked on their wifi signal to send it out."

I nodded. "Try it. See if you can do it."

He pulled out his phone and I watched as his thumbs moved quickly around the screen. He held the phone up to me. Wile E. Coyote plummeted off a cliff and the Roadrunner sped off. "How's that for a signal?"

"Why not put a password on it?" I asked.

He shrugged. "Some people just don't have the patience for it."

I got that. There was a lot about the technological world I didn't have patience for, such as any form of social media—a total waste of time, in my opinion. "How would anyone know that there's an unprotected signal here?" I asked.

"There are apps that are specifically designed to find them. Someone could just drive down the street until they found one."

"So anyone could have just parked here and sent that message from the wifi at this house?"

"Yep," he said.

I sighed. "So that leads us absolutely nowhere."

twenty-five

I brought Scout to work the next day. I didn't know if she'd rather be home alone or in one of the runs at the clinic—honestly, it's a toss-up of suboptimal choices—but I was feeling needy that morning and wanted her close. Just knowing I could pop my head in to see her wagging her stubby tail made me feel better.

I wanted to call Jack to find out how he was feeling after his bigger-adventure-than-his-doctor-would-have-approved-of the previous night, but once more, there was no time. I glanced at the white board to see who my next client was. It said only "Carhart, Room Two." I scanned the folder bin on the back of the door to Room Two, but it was empty. "Ellie?" I asked, sticking my head around the corner. "There's no folder."

She was on the phone, and held her index finger up in my direction. After a few moments, she looked up at me and mouthed, "Nope." I blinked. *Okay, then,* I thought. *We're in new territory.* Even if Room Two contained a new client, someone at the front desk would have created a folder for them.

I entered the room and saw only a woman in smart business attire. She was about ten years older than I, trim, and serious. Her blond hair hung in a bob to her shoulders, and her eyes were lit up by oversized red glasses. It was perfect.

But she had no animal. That was strange indeed. She stood, and obviously noting my confusion, she stuck out her hand. "Fuchsia Carhart," she said. "I'm your lawyer. Well, actually, I'm the lawyer for the clinic."

"Oh," I said. "What a surprise."

"This is work stuff, so it ought to be done during work hours," she explained, sitting back down. "But your assistants said you're too busy to be bothered during work hours. So one of them set me up with an appointment. Which means we have a half hour. Which means we should probably get down to business."

"Oh. Right. Okay, then. Sorry, I just wasn't prepared for this." I sat in the other chair in the small room.

"Sorry to ambush you," she said. She opened her briefcase and took out a folder. She opened it and I saw a page of lined yellow legal paper filled with chicken scratches. "What can you tell me about Margaret Edgerton?"

"Other than that she's suing us?"

"I wouldn't be here otherwise. So yes. Other than that."

"I don't really know much about her," I confessed. Just then I heard Scout howl—a high, mournful note that wavered with sorrow. Without thinking, I turned my chin to the ceiling and answered with a soulful howl of my own.

"That was unexpected," Carhart said, her pencil-thin painted-on eyebrows high on her forehead.

"We have a thing," I explained. "But about Maggie Edgerton: she was Shelley's client. I've never seen her professionally."

"Can you tell me about the procedure that ended the life of her dog?"

"Of course." I explained the ins-and-outs of a Femoral Head Ostectomy. "It was major surgery," I finished, "but it was also fairly routine, and patients rarely die."

"But this one did," she said.

"Yes."

"Was there an autopsy?"

"You mean a necropsy," I corrected her. "No, there wasn't."

"Is that normal?"

"We usually do a necropsy only if the client requests it."

"You mean the animal's owner?"

"Yes."

"Why do you think Ms. Edgerton didn't request one?"

I shrugged. "For the same reason most people don't. They're expensive. If the dog is already dead, why spend another thousand dollars to find out exactly why? It doesn't make sense to most people."

She was furiously scrawling as I talked to the top of her head.

I continued. "Unlike human medicine, veterinary medicine tends toward being practical."

"Practical?"

"If you have to pay for everything out of your own pocket, you are not likely to order unnecessary tests...or necropsies."

"Oh." She wrote a few more notes, then looked up at me. It wasn't a hopeful look. "Well, I hate to be the bearer of bad news, but without Dr. Capra here to give a fuller account, we're on our back foot here. Our case doesn't look good. My recommendation is that you try to keep this out of court. I think you should offer a settlement."

"How much money are we talking about?" I asked.

"Well, they're suing for $500,000," she said.

I knew that much. What was news to me is that they actually might get it. "What do you think we should offer?" I asked.

"I think you should offer $250,000. I also think you should call it a bargain."

"We have insurance that will cover that, right?"

"Maybe," she said. "You pay for insurance, but they'll want to do their own investigation. Again, Dr. Capra being out of the picture complicates things. If the insurance company can find a way to wriggle out of it, they will. My guess is that they will."

"Egad," I said. I hadn't had a chance to dig deep into the practice's financial affairs yet, but I suspected it could mean an end to us. I took a deep breath and narrowed my eyes. "But... what if we suspect foul play?"

"What?" The lawyer reared back in her chair. She obviously hadn't expected that any more than she had expected me to howl.

Just then Ellie knocked, and without waiting for my response, she poked her head in the door. "She's kind of insistent," she said, and opening the door a bit wider, allowed Scout passage. Scout was wagging so fiercely that her back paws lost their purchase on the floor, causing her to slide about on the slick linoleum. Ellie closed the door again.

"My dog, Scout," I explained. "The howler."

"Hello there, Scout," the lawyer said, not moving toward the dog.

"Scout, sit," I commanded. I didn't want her to be a nuisance, just in case the lawyer was not a dog person. Scout obeyed.

"Foul play how?" Carhart asked.

"I've been doing some investigation of my own," I explained. "Maggie Edgerton's real name is Tess Barker. She's a conman—conwoman, whatever. Anyway, she seems to make her living bringing nuisance lawsuits."

"Really?" Carhart began to take notes on the yellow legal page in her folder.

"Really. We think she acquired the dog solely for the purpose of killing it and blaming Shelley."

"Wait, who's 'we'?"

"Uh...me and...my...uh, priest. Friend. Priest-friend. Jack."

"Huh. Well, you're just full of surprises. So this was a new dog?"

"Well, Maggie was a new client. I can't say how long she had the dog, but she only came to us for the one appointment where Shelley evaluated Champ—and then the surgery itself, of course."

"How do you imagine she...Ms. Edgerton...accomplished this?"

"There are lots of drugs that are contraindicated for the anesthetic we use. We didn't think to check for them before the body was cremated, but...that's my guess."

"So you can't prove it," Carhart said, still writing.

"No," I admitted.

"That doesn't leave us much better off than we were before," Ms. Carhart said, sounding as tired as I felt.

"Maybe not," I said. "But I'll bet this isn't the first time she's pulled this particular scam."

"I'll bet you're right," Carhart said. She put her notes back in her briefcase and stood up. "Okay, it's a lead. It's not a good lead, but it's a lead. The only thing I need from you is permission to pursue it. Remember, we charge by the hour."

"And just how much, if you don't mind my asking, do you charge by the hour?" I asked.

"$400," she said.

"I am in the wrong business," I said. "So how much do you think it will cost us if you investigate this more?"

"A lot less than $250,000," she said.

twenty-six

At lunch, I took Scout outside and shared my sandwich with her. Normally she is not a mustard fan, but she didn't turn her nose up at it today. What a good girl.

After I finished the sandwich I looked at my snoopy watch and discovered I had about a half hour. How best to use the time? I ticked through all the leads in my head, but the one that rose to the top was Shelley's ex, Stephen Thomas. I'd gotten his address from his former employer, but it wasn't like I could just nip 'round—he lived in San Jose, which was about a three-hour drive south-southwest. Suddenly, I hit upon an idea. I pulled up my Ryde app. For the point of departure, I picked a place not far away—I didn't want to pay much if I didn't have to, and I hoped the driver could get there quickly. I picked the main public library. Then I entered Stephen Thomas' address as the destination. Fortunately, San Jose is lousy with ride-sharing drivers. In a few short breaths, Ryde had paired me with a driver—Talmage, driving a blue Geo. I called the number, and the driver picked up instantly.

"I don't see you," he said. The app was no doubt displaying my picture, just as it was supposed to.

"That's because I'm not there," I said.

"I don't have time for—"

"This is not a game, this is deadly serious. I'm not there, but I need you to drive to the destination and knock on the door. That's it."

"Look, lady—"

"Hey, my...friend isn't answering his phone. He's been fired, and I...I'm afraid something bad has happened to him. I'm over three hours away. Would you please just drive to his house, knock on the door, and call me back to tell me if he was there?"

A few seconds of silence passed. Finally, he sighed. "Yeah, that sounds okay," he said.

"Thank you. Thank you so much. His name is Stephen Thomas. I'll be waiting to hear from you."

I hung up, hoping against hope that I *would* hear from him.

To pass the time, I walked Scout up the County Route to the gas station and back. I was just putting her back in the run when my phone rang. "Hello?" I asked.

"This is Talmage, from Ryde."

"Talmage, hi. What happened?"

"Your guy wasn't there."

"There was no one home?" I asked.

"Oh, no. There was someone home. Your Stephen Thomas guy wasn't there."

"Who was at home? Did they know where he was?"

"Not a clue. Apparently they just bought the house. No idea where your guy is."

"Damn." I bit my lip. Then I sighed. "Well, thanks a lot, Talmage. That's a great help."

"Doesn't sound like it."

"No, it was. At least I know where he isn't."

"Well, good luck with this...whatever it is...your manhunt."

I laughed, as "manhunt" sounded so serious. Well, wasn't what I was doing serious? I didn't know how to feel about that. Talmage hung up and I put the phone back into my pocket.

I snagged the file from the back of the exam room door and spun into the room, only one minute late. "Hello, Mr...Saetang. And who do we have here?"

A large, beefy man smiled up at me. He nearly covered the chair he sat on. His muscles threatened to burst out of his t-shirt. On his lap was a tiny pink hairless cat. "This is Jok." His accent was clipped, and I wondered where he was from—one of the Pacific Islands, perhaps? He was certainly built like a Tongan or a Fijian.

"Jok looks like a pretty happy cat. What are we seeing him for today?"

"Oh, nothing. Jok is fine."

"Oh. A checkup, then?"

"You could say that." His eyes told me that there was a hidden meaning to his words. I felt a chill run through me.

"Well, Mr...uh..." I opened his file again to glance at his name.

"Saetang," he supplied. "But you can call me Massaman."

I froze. Massaman. Muscle Man. It turned out both names were accurate. But what did he want with me? Deliberately, I put the file down on the metal examination table and sat opposite the large man in the other chair.

"I know your name," I said, crossing my legs, leaning back, and trying to affect a calm poise.

"Good. Then I will not need to waste time on introductions."

An introduction would be a good idea, I thought. I remembered that Tracy Chaconas at the newspaper had said that

Shelley and Leslie Braun had argued about him, and that Sarge had borrowed money from him and had gotten an ulcer in the bargain. Sarge had said he was connected to the mob somehow and was from Thailand—but that was all I knew. I decided listening was my best bet. "How can I help you?"

"I made a deal with your former partner, Dr. Capra."

"You knew Shelley?"

"Of course. Don't be coy, please."

I nodded. "Shelley didn't tell me anything about you. So if you want me to know what this is about, you'll need to explain it."

"I can tell from your face that you know more than that," he said.

"But not much more," I confessed.

He must have sensed the truth of that, because he nodded gravely. Then he said, "Dr. Capra borrowed $20,000 from me."

I sat up straight. "What? Why?"

"You know that shiny new digital x-ray machine?" He smiled.

It wasn't that new—Shelley had bought it about a year ago, or so she had said. It was absolutely essential to our practice. "She borrowed money...from you...to buy our x-ray machine?"

He nodded, briefly closing his eyes. His left hand stroked the cat on his lap.

"And how much does she...or, I guess, me now. How much do I still owe?"

"She made significant progress. She paid off $10,000."

"So there's only $10,000 more to go," I said.

"Then there's the interest—20%," he said.

"So I still owe...what? $14,000?"

He nodded again, slowly and serenely.

I did a quick calculation in my head. "It sounds like Shelley was paying you $500 a month?"

"That's right. I have come to collect."

"And you expect me to just believe you about all this? For all I know you're a scam artist who walked in off the street and decided to demand payment for a machine that's already paid for."

He chuckled and shook his head. "That would be very ballsy indeed. And a worthy scheme. But no. The debt is legit."

He leaned forward and looked me in the eye. He lowered his voice and in a hoarse whisper said, "I was sorry to hear that Dr. Capra met with an...accident."

I shuddered involuntarily. Slowly, his lips drew back in a malevolent smile. It was a threat. I knew it, and he knew that I knew it.

I looked at my feet to break the spell. "Okay, but I haven't got that kind of cash on me. I assume you want cash."

"That is the only way. Nothing traceable."

"Can you give me until tomorrow?" I asked.

"I'll send one of my boys by tomorrow. Just give him an envelope with the cash in it. Unmarked bills, please. And we do check."

I nodded. "Okay." I was far from okay with it, but I needed time to think, and paying him $500 would buy me a month to do just that.

He rose and, cradling his cat, he headed for the door out to the waiting room. "Thank you, Doctor. I hope we shall never need to see one another again."

I wanted to say that I hoped the same, but instead I said, "Did you kill her? Shelley, I mean. Did you kill her?"

He didn't answer. Instead he looked at me with something approaching pity. Then he opened the door. "Goodbye, Doctor."

twenty-seven

My hands were still shaking as I sat down at the counter at Millie's. Sarge noticed. "You okay?"

"Yeah. No. I don't know."

"You want to talk about it?" he asked.

"Yes and no," I said.

"You got that ambivalence thing down," Sarge said. "Here, go give this to Scout." He handed me a plate with a piece of fried Canadian bacon.

"Wow, that's generous," I said.

"I suspect Scout hasn't been getting the quality time with you she's accustomed to," he said. "She's got to get her love somewhere."

I nodded sadly and carried the plate to the door. I set it down in front of her, and she wolfed it down in seconds. I gave her head a scratch, told her to sit and stay, and wandered back to my perch at the counter.

"This don't have to do with that cute preacher, does it?" he asked.

"No," I assured him.

"Because that guy is head-over-heels for you."

I gave Sarge a pained look. "Do you think so?"

"Are you blind, doctor?"

"I do think he likes me."

"And what about you? Do you like him?"

I wagged my head back and forth, teetering toward one shoulder, then toward the other.

"Uh-huh." He picked up a spatula and pointed it at me. "You've got to give him some hope, girlfriend. I mean, if you want him to stick around."

"What do you mean, hope?"

"You know, some encouragement."

"Sarge, we haven't even been on a date."

"Define 'date,'" he said, narrowing one eye.

Is that what we've been doing, with Jack accompanying me on my investigation? Were we dating? It seemed to me that if we were, we'd both need to be explicit about it. But maybe I was wrong. "Do you think that *Jack* thinks we're dating?"

"Why don't you ask him?"

I pursed my lips and frowned.

"Have you even kissed him yet?"

"No!" I said, a little too forcefully.

Sarge shook his head. "I will never understand straight people. I would have had that priest in bed already. It's part of the finding-out-if-this-is-right process. If you wait until you know it's right, and then you have terrible sex, where does that leave you?"

"Will you please not talk about sex?" I asked. "That's like soooo far down the road. We're at the very beginning."

"Straight people are just weird," Sarge said. "Sex is a good thing, you know."

"I'm not anti-sex!" I said, a little too loudly. I looked around. Sure enough, several of the other patrons were looking at me. I lowered my voice to a whisper. "Can we just please talk about something else?"

"You know, that deputy's kind of sweet on you too," Sarge wagged his eyebrows.

"Please. Gus?" I asked. "He's a goof."

"He's goofy with love," Sarge said.

I knew he was right, and I felt myself blushing. I didn't find Gus attractive—or at least not *very* attractive—but knowing that he found me attractive made me feel good. I had begun to doubt that I was lovable. Gus and Jack were proving me wrong.

Almost as if my thoughts had summoned him, Sarge straightened up and said, "Ope—incoming. Priest at your 8 o'clock."

"What?"

Sarge grabbed a coffee cup, spun it right side up, and set it down on the counter in front of the stool next to mine. Moments later, someone sat down in it. I looked up and was surprised to see Jack.

"Oh. Hi," I said.

He half-smiled, half-grimaced, then groaned as he tried to get comfortable on the stool.

"How you doing, preacher?" Sarge asked.

"A little better every day," Jack said. "I was able to brush my teeth today without wincing."

"Praise the Lord," Sarge said. I couldn't tell if he was being facetious or not, but Jack took it in stride.

"You look on edge," Jack said to me.

"Is it that obvious?" I asked.

"Yes," Jack and Sarge said together.

"Huh," I said. "Well, today seemed to be the day for

unusual clients. In the morning, I got a visit from our lawyer—the clinic's lawyer, I mean—who told me that our case was not good."

"Oh, dear," Jack said.

"I told her what you found out about Maggie Edgerton," I said. "About her being a conwoman, and our suspicion that she killed her dog in order to advance the suit."

Sarge whistled. "This is what happens when we don't talk. I fall behind. I hate that."

"And what did she say?" Jack asked.

"She said she'd look into it."

"Well, that's promising," Jack said.

"Maybe," I allowed. "Then at lunch I sent a Ryde driver to Shelley's ex's house."

"And?" Sarge asked.

"Turns out he's sold the house and someone else lives there now."

"Oooo, that's hard up," Sarge said. "You know it's bad when they sell the house."

I nodded. That made it even more likely that Stephen Thomas had killed Shelley for the insurance money. At least he had motive. "And then there was this afternoon," I said.

"What happened this afternoon?" Jack asked.

"I had another visitor," I said. I looked up and met Sarge's eyes. "Massaman."

"Oh, no," Sarge said. He looked like I'd just slapped him.

"Yeah. He came in with his cat—a creepy hairless thing."

"That's Massaman, all right," Sarge said. "And?"

"And he told me that Shelley had borrowed $20,000 from him for the digital x-ray machine."

"Oh, boy," Sarge said. Shaking his head. "How much is outstanding?"

"$14,000," I said.

"Pay it and be done with it," Sarge said. "Even if you have to dip into savings. Just...just do it."

I wasn't ready to hand my retirement savings over to a thug just yet. "He only wants $500 a month. I'll talk to our accountant, figure out how to make this as above-board as possible."

"You're playing with fire," Sarge said, pointing his spatula at me again.

"Careful with that thing," I said.

"Say, what happened with the bomb thing?" Sarge asked. It was an abrupt change of subject, and I didn't quite know how to interpret it. But before I could speak, Jack jumped in. "Casey got a street location from the IP address—a place in Utah city. We went over there last night."

"And?"

Jack shook his head. "And nothing. The woman I talked to had no interest in animal rights. We didn't see any posters or bumper stickers." He shrugged. "She seemed like she was telling the truth to me."

"Their wifi had no password," I said. "So we think someone might have parked near the house and piggybacked on their system."

Jack suddenly sat up a little straighter. I could tell he was thinking. "You know," he turned toward me, excitement pricking at his voice, "when we ruled out the couple who owned that house, we instantly turned outward in our search. Maybe we should have turned inward."

"This is no time for contemplative practice, preacher, laudable as that is," Sarge warned.

"No, that's not what I mean. We instantly thought about outsiders. But we hadn't ruled out all of the insiders," he said.

"Who are you talking about?" I asked.

"Did you notice what was in the yard?" His face quickened into a bright eagerness that I found utterly endearing.

"No, what?" I asked.

"Bicycles," he said. "Kids' bikes."

I blinked. Then I sat up straighter. "Kids?" I asked.

twenty-eight

The next morning, I was hovering over my coffee in the break room. There was hardly any room on the table, but I moved a stack of pharmaceutical promotional flyers, almost causing another stack to fall off the far end. Snoopy said it was time to go see my next client, but my legs didn't want to hear it. Ellie sidled up to me and put her hand on my back.

"You look like hell, boss," she said.

"Don't call me boss. Shelley's 'boss,'" I complained.

"And now you're boss," she said. She sat down. "So...who actually owns the practice?"

"Shelley did," I said.

"Does that mean it belongs to her ex-husband?"

"That's a horrifying thought." I didn't want to have this conversation. I had avoided this conversation. I had avoided even thinking about the subject. But Ellie was right. It needed to be faced. "Maybe it belongs to her parents?" I suggested.

"Surely Shelley has a will," Ellie said.

"She has a living trust. Her father told me about it."

"But you haven't seen it?"

"No."

"Maybe you should call that lawyer. She'd know."

I nodded. "Right. You're right. I will. Things are just..."

"Moving too fast?" Ellie supplied.

I nodded again. She handed me a folder. "There's only one thing you need to do right now," she said.

I groaned and forced my legs to function. I stood, and before I knew it, Ellie's arms were around me, drawing me into a bear hug. I returned it half-heartedly. I appreciated the gesture, she just caught me off guard.

After the hug was blessedly over, I headed to Exam Room Three. I hadn't even glanced at the folder, so I went in cold. "Good morning," I said, not bothering to apologize. Doctors never do—we're always a little behind and people expect it.

A young woman rose and offered her hand. I shook it. "It's so good to meet you. I'm Kelly. You're going to be Cher's doctor!"

I blinked and looked at the dog next to her. I had seen her, of course, but now I *saw* her. "Cher?" I asked, brightening. "Well, what are the odds?" Actually, being the only practice in town, the odds were pretty good. But of course I had no idea where Cher had been placed. Now I did.

Cher sat up at attention, clearly pleased to see me. She seemed healthy and happy.

"Just here for a checkup, then, for your new dog?" I asked. "Nothing wrong?"

"No. I just want to make sure she has her shots, that she's in good shape."

"Well, I wish all dog owners were as conscientious," I said. "Let's get her on the examination table."

"Oh—I'll do it." Kelly squatted and expertly scooped all four of Cher's legs into a bundle that she raised easily, keeping her back straight and using only her legs. This girl had it together.

She placed Cher on the table and petted her soothingly. I fitted the stethoscope earpieces and listened to her lungs and heart. Strong as an ox.

I felt at her abdomen, my fingers flicking past her distended nipples as I pressed here and there. "So how did you come by Cher?" I asked. I knew the answer to that—or at least I thought I did. I was just making small talk. But I was not prepared for the answer.

"Oh, I saw her listing on Craig's List!"

I almost dropped my stethoscope. Instead, I caught myself and carefully wound it before putting it in my pocket. I consciously modulated my emotions. I cleared my throat. "Craig's List, you say?"

"Yes. I wasn't looking for a dog. Actually, I was looking for a dining room table. But there she was! Looking so beautiful and sweet. I knew instantly. I guess you could say it was love at first sight."

"Yes," I said. "I know how that is." I didn't, but I wasn't really thinking about what I was saying. "She must have cost you a pretty penny, a fine dog like this," I fished.

"Oh, no! All I had to do was go pick her up," she said.

I swallowed. "I guess the vetting process was pretty arduous."

"Vetting process?" She cocked her head, obviously confused.

"I mean, you must have filled out a form, provided references—"

"No, they didn't even take my name. I just picked her up."

I tasted blood and realized I had just bit my lip. I was sure I looked angry, and I didn't want to alienate a perfectly innocent client. "I'm just surprised. I did surgery on Cher just a few days ago. I'm surprised that..." I trailed off. "Surprise" didn't cover it. I was shocked. Horrified. Outraged. Cher should still be recovering, at home, not being farmed out the minute she could stand.

"Oh! How wonderful! You were her doctor before! That's so perfect!" Kelly sounded giddy.

"Uh...yeah. Continuity is a plus." I gently turned Cher over and pointed to the incision point. "We took out her ovaries and uterus there, about a week ago."

"I saw the stitches, but...they said she'd just been spayed."

"Well...that's putting it mildly," I said. I sighed, and let Cher scramble back to being right-way-up. "The good news is that she's healing up well, and she's going to be fine. I'm...I'm glad you found each other. She's going to be a good dog to you."

"And I'm going to be a great partner to her," Kelly said, moonfaced.

"Have you had a poodle before?" I asked.

"No."

I launched into my new-dog-owner talk, and immediately Kelly pulled out her phone and began typing notes with her thumbs. I felt my heart stir. Kelly clearly loved this dog. Good. After so many years of just being a brood bitch, valued only for her ovaries, Cher deserved to be truly loved. I drew the blood work and bid a cordial farewell to Kelly and Cher. I told her we'd call if the tests showed anything problematic. Then I closed the door behind me and seethed. "Goddam breeders," I said. It was a good thing Jack and I were headed up to the Royal Poodle. I owed Chas Dalton a piece of my mind.

twenty-nine

At lunch, I called Fuchsia Carhart, the clinic's lawyer, and left a message. I didn't know if she knew anything about Shelley's will, but I thought I'd check with her first before tearing up Shelley's office again. If I was lucky, I'd hear back from her. If I wasn't lucky...well, then she was just a typical lawyer.

I glanced at Snoopy and saw that I still had a half hour. I hopped on the computer and did a search for Stephen Thomas' sister. I vaguely remembered that her name was Pam, which must be short for Pamela. Luckily, she had either never married or had kept her maiden name. Her picture came right up, smiling to beat the band. "Arlington Realty. We find homes, not houses." I clicked on her picture, noting just how similar she looked to Stephen Thomas. She had the same sunken eyes, the same hooked nose. She was not what you would call conventionally attractive, but she bore her own idiosyncratic brand of beauty with dignity. I dialed her number and waited. It went straight to voicemail, of course. "Uh, Pam, you probably don't remember me. I'm Casey Gibbons, a friend of Shelley's, your brother's ex. Listen, I don't know if you had heard that Shelly died, but...I'm trying to get ahold of Stephen Thomas and...well, I'm not having any luck. I hate to bother you, but if there's any way you can put me in touch with him, I'd be so grateful. There are...some sensitive issues that I need to discuss with him. Timely issues." I left my number, repeated it, and said goodbye. Then I hit the red button and sighed.

I visited the restroom and took my time. When I came out I got the stink eye from one of our techs, who brushed past me in a huff. "'Bout freakin' time," she whispered, slamming the door behind her.

"Okay, then," I said. "Sorry!" I shouted at the door.

My pocket vibrated. I took out my phone and noted a number I had recently dialed—Pam's. I hit the green button and put the phone to my ear. "Pam, thank you so much for calling."

"Casey, I'm so glad you called. It's been a long time. How are you?"

"Well, exhausted, to be honest. And...okay, I'm a little freaked out."

"I don't blame you. I'm so sorry to hear about Shelley."

"You didn't know?"

"No. What a shock. I'm just...I don't know what to think."

"I understand completely," I sympathized.

"Can I ask what happened? I mean, how did she...die?"

"The police ruled it an accident, but I think they're wrong. I think someone killed her."

"Oh my God," Pam said. "Do you know who?"

"Well, there are a lot of possibilities," I said. "So I'm...I guess I'm running them down."

"That's tragic."

I didn't know if she meant that Shelley's death was tragic, or the fact that the police didn't believe me was tragic, or the fact that I was investigating was tragic. I guess I could take my pick.

"You wanted to contact Stephen Thomas," she said.

"Yes," I said.

"Wait," she said, her voice catching. "Do you...do you think he had something to do with her....you do, don't you?"

"I don't know, Pam. I'm just...I'm running down every lead I've got."

"Oh, holy cow. Stevie, Stevie, good lord..." She trailed off into a mumble. "He's desperate, Casey. I don't want to think that he did it, but...you know, he's never been in dire straits like this. I mean, even for him, this is...I can't imagine...except that I can. Oh, God." Her voice started to crack. "Oh, God, and you know what the worst part is, Casey?"

"What?" I asked, suspecting that I did.

"The worst part is that, deep down in my gut, I know that he could have. He totally could have. He...oh, Jesus." Her voice tightened into a squeak.

I took a page from Jack's playbook and just kept my mouth shut, letting Pam have her feelings. After a few seconds, to my great surprise, it wasn't awkward at all. I was just breathing deep, being with this old acquaintance as she emoted. It was fine. What do you know?

After a while, I realized my time was running out. I cleared my throat. "Uh, Pam, I have to get back to work, so... Look, I know you don't want to do anything that might hurt Stephen Thomas."

"No..."

"But Shelley deserves...well, she deserves the truth. She deserves justice."

"Yes..."

Okay, which was it? I took another deep breath. "I wonder

if you would reach out to him for me. Just...give him my number and ask him to call me. How's that?"

"Then you'd know," she said.

"What do you mean?" I asked.

"If he called you, you'd know he didn't do it. If he didn't call you..."

"Pam, this is Stephen Thomas we're talking about." Pam knew her brother better than anyone. I didn't need to soft-pedal this for her. "There are a million reasons why he might not call me back—everything from getting beat up for a gambling debt to his cell phone falling into a lake...and literally everything in between."

"True..." she said. "Okay. I'll find him. I'll...he'll call you. I promise."

I knew there was no way she could make good on such a promise, not absolutely. But I was grateful that she was willing to try. "Thank you, Pam. This means a lot to me."

I looked at my watch and waited for her response. Snoopy's left-most hand was inching past the six. 1:30. Time to work. Pam sniffed. "I liked Shelley. A lot."

"I know. She was...she was a really good person."

"Thank you for calling, Casey."

"Thank you for calling me back. Take care of yourself."

"You too." She hung up. I leaned against the break room counter and paused. There was an intensity of emotion just under the surface, but I couldn't discern what it was. "Off-pissédness," I said out loud. I didn't know if it was right or not, but it was a damn fine guess.

thirty

After work, I picked up Jack. He was moving with greater ease, and I was glad to see it. His range of motion had improved and he seemed to be in much less pain. The stab of guilt that I typically felt upon seeing him suffer diminished just a bit.

As usual, he didn't say much at first. I glanced over at him and saw a slight smile as he sat back with his eyes closed. His right elbow hung out of the window, and he seemed to be relishing the feel of the wind on his face. I'm not sure why seeing him enjoy such a simple pleasure made my own heart leap, but it did.

In the back seat, Scout sat upright, her nose sniffing at Jack's open window, moving up and down like a bobblehead doll. All of a sudden, she lifted her muzzle and emitted a howl. Jack sat up with a jerk and looked behind him. He gave me a "What the hell?" look, and in answer I raised my own chin and let loose with my own howl, blending my voice with Scout's. Jack laughed. Raising his gaze to the car's ceiling, he added his own howl to the mix. I'm not sure that what we produced was technically harmony, but it was certainly a glorious cacophony.

"What was that all about?" Jack asked after the howl had run its course.

"It's just a thing we have," I said. "It's how we connect."

"She's not in pain...or upset?"

"No!" I said. "I mean...well, she howls for a lot of reasons, but right now it probably means she's outrageously happy. Sometimes she howls for the sheer pleasure of it—but more for the pleasure of doing it together, I think. The first time it happened was when Dennis and I split up—he's my ex. I was sitting on the couch, crying my eyes out. Scout was on the floor looking up at me, whining. And then she just let loose with this blood-curdling howl. It shocked me right out of my cry!" I laughed, reliving the memory. It was so fresh. "I think that howl was about empathy, or sympathy, or something. Anyway, she kept doing it, so I just joined her. And do you know what? I felt a lot better after."

It was Jack's turn to laugh. "I don't think I've ever howled before. I totally understand how it can be cathartic."

"Well, dogs eat grass when they're sick, and they howl when they have strong feelings. They know what they're doing."

"The dog has Buddha nature," Jack said.

I made a pained face. "What on earth does that mean?"

"Well, a dog eats when it's hungry, sleeps when it's tired, scratches when it itches. We don't do any of those things. Dogs are much more in touch with their true selves than we are. The dog is in touch with its inherent Buddha nature."

"How does that fit in with your Christianity?"

"Why does it have to?" Jack asked.

"Huh. I guess it doesn't," I conceded.

"I can appreciate and enjoy another paradigm without

living inside it," Jack said. "I find the Buddhist paradigm fascinating. I read a lot of Buddhist theology."

"Huh," I said. "That would be like me reading journals on acupuncture."

"Exactly," Jack said. "If we're not careful, we both might learn something."

"You are a very weird man," I said.

"I'll take that as a compliment, unless you tell me otherwise."

"And your glass is always half-full."

"Not by nature. That's a spiritual practice," he said.

"It is?" I asked.

"Of course. We're hard-wired by evolution to focus on the negative. Focusing on the positive is hard work. Good work too."

"Well, you could have fooled me. You do it well."

"Hey, if I didn't have anything to show for twenty years of spiritual practice, I should give up and go do something else."

"Does that mean that you're holier than the average bear?" I asked.

"Not by even a little bit," he laughed. "I'm just a screw-up and a sinner."

"Why would you say that about yourself?" I asked. "That's terrible."

"Well, I guess the truth hurts sometimes," he said. "But if you don't start with the truth, nothing you do has any integrity, does it?"

I would have to think about that one. My head was beginning to spin. Fortunately, we were pulling into the driveway of the Royal Poodle, and I could set Jack's baffling metaphysical assertions aside.

"Stay," I told Scout. She whimpered the tiniest bit, but that was the extent of her protest.

Jack's face froze in a momentary grimace as he got out of the car, but he straightened up and a fresh smile quickly returned to his face.

"You okay?" I asked.

"Yeah, I'm fine," he said.

"You'd tell me if you weren't, right?"

"Would you tell me if *you* weren't?" he asked.

"No," I said.

He laughed. "Let's go," he said, and to my great surprise, he took my arm as we walked up toward the office.

To the left was a large, two-story farmhouse that looked to be about sixty or seventy years old. It was, however, in impeccable shape, facing away from us and looking out over the vineyards and dry brush of Gold Valley. It was a spectacular view. Straight ahead were a series of squat, cinder-block buildings surrounded by chain-link fencing. I couldn't tell how far back they went, but the size of the place was impressive, gauging by just those buildings that I could see.

I expected the office door to be locked—it was after hours, after all—but to my surprise it was open, and we let ourselves into a comfortable waiting room dominated by a large desk. Behind the desk was a plump middle-aged woman on the phone. She held one finger up to us and we took a seat. In front of her was a pile of blue striped envelopes—I surmised she was in the middle of a promotional mailing project. I had seen that pattern printed onto the envelopes before, but for the life of me, I couldn't place it. Before I could wrack my brain any further, however, Chas Dalton himself entered from a door just behind the woman's desk.

His face brightened to see us and he offered his hand. We shook, and, keeping his voice low, he said, "Carly is working late tonight—getting caught up after her vacation. Let's go in back where we can talk."

He led us past the desk through the same door he had entered through, and we found ourselves in a sizable storage room. There were large plastic bins marked "kibble-adult" and "kibble-puppy," and lots of gear proper to kennels. None of it surprised me.

"Mr. Dalton, this is Father Jack Mornington—he's the Episcopal priest I was telling you about."

Chas offered Jack his hand. "Ah, yes, Fr. Mornington. So good to meet you again."

"Have we met?" Jack asked.

"I believe I beat you in the egg-on-a-spoon relay race at the town picnic a couple of years ago," Chas said. "Tough luck with your teammate tripping over that stump."

"Ha!" Jack laughed. "I remember that! I hope you'll forgive me not remembering you though. I was pretty focused on the job at hand."

"Not at all. Dr. Gibbons said you're interested in adopting one of our older dogs."

"I'm not sure 'interested' is the right word...maybe 'exploring the idea' is really more where I'm at."

"Well, it's a big commitment, so we don't want to you rush into anything," Dalton said with an affable smile. "Follow me, won't you?"

He led us out the back door, across a gravel stretch overgrown with weeds and into another of the cinder-block buildings. My nose twitched, assaulted by the odor of wet dog and disinfectant. That was normal enough, but I also caught a whiff of feces. I felt my ire rising and fought to keep it under control. The air was thick with the sound of dogs whimpering and crying. I love dogs, of course, and it cut at my heart to hear such obvious despair. Kennels are necessary, but I always found them depressing and heartbreaking. It's why I almost always found a house-sitter to stay with Scout when I had to go away. A dog belongs with a loving family. A kennel is no place for a dog—not for any length of time.

Dalton stopped by one of the pens. Inside I could see two poodles—one black, the other, gray. Their hair was shorn close, and they seemed to be healthy enough. I could tell from their salt-and-pepper muzzles that they were in middle age—probably about six or seven years old. They jumped to their feet at the sight of us, wagging furiously. Dalton opened the gate and the two rushed out, jumping all over us.

"Off!" Dalton bellowed. The dogs, slightly cowed, refrained from jumping, but were still exuberantly sniffing us with glee. I wasn't surprised to see they were both females. Males can be used for stud until the day they die, but brood bitches have a sell-by date, after which they cannot bear any more litters. These bitches had reached that date.

The look on Jack's face was sheer ecstasy, and I relaxed a bit. Bringing him here, adopting a dog, I felt sure it was the right thing. But I still had a bone to pick with Mr. Dalton.

Giving the dogs a final pat, I left Jack sitting cross-legged, reveling in doggy love. I walked over to Dalton, who was leaning against a wall. He seemed enjoy watching Jack as much as I did.

I leaned against the wall next to him, and lowering my voice so that Jack couldn't hear over the sound of the bitches' panting, said, "So, Mr. Dalton—"

"Call me Chas, please."

"So, Chas," I started again. "Craig's List?"

He frowned. "I'm sorry. What?"

"I saw a mutual friend of ours yesterday. Middle-aged poodle bitch, goes by the name of Cher. Mangled ear and everything. Her new owner brought her in for a checkup."

Out of the side of my eye I saw Dalton's shoulders deflate. "I see. And...how was Cher? She checked out, didn't she?"

"She's in fine shape for her age," I assured him. "That's not what concerns me. You listed her on Craig's List?"

"It's a good tool—"

"Did you do any vetting at all, or did you just toss her into the back of the first car that came along?" My voice was starting to quake with anger, and my hands were shaking. I put them between my butt and the wall to still them.

"Doctor, what are you implying?"

"I'm not implying anything. I'm asking you to explain yourself. A reputable breeder vets the new owner. Cher's new mom says she didn't even fill out a form. She says she just drove up here and you delivered the dog to her, no questions asked, no name or address taken."

Dalton said nothing. Jack laughed and pushed one of the poodles away before his face got any wetter.

I continued my attack. "Cher is lucky she found a good home. What if the ad had been answered by dog-fighters looking for warm-up bait?"

"That's a terrible thought," Dalton said.

"Damn straight, a thought you should have had."

Dalton sighed. "I didn't break any laws."

"No, more's the pity. But there's a difference between illegal and immoral. Just because you didn't breach the former doesn't mean you didn't transgress on the latter."

"I'm afraid you lost me," he said.

"No I didn't. Don't play stupid with me," I said.

"I treat my dogs well," Dalton said.

"Your dogs are healthy enough. That's not my complaint. Don't change the subject."

"You seem...irritable."

"Don't patronize me, you prick. I'm not irritable, I'm outraged."

"I—"

"Shut the hell up and listen. I'm not on my period. And I'm not misdirecting grief about Dr. Capra's death, or whatever other nonsensical psychological rationalization you're about to spew."

"I—"

"I'm pissed because you owe a debt to life. You've been blessed, you've been well taken care of in this life. You have a duty to protect the life in your care. You failed in that duty. I want you to do better."

This time he did not try to protest. He fidgeted, then cleared his throat. "I promise you...I shall do better."

"Jack will fill out a form. You will do a background check."

"You don't trust him?"

"You're missing the point. Focus," I said. "Not just Jack. Everyone."

"Or...what?"

"Or you no longer get to present yourself as a reputable breeder...and I don't have to pretend you are one."

He nodded. "Message received," he said.

thirty-one

The next morning at work was blessedly slower paced. I'm not sure how it happened—and I wasn't curious enough to ask. I just wanted to enjoy it. We were still packed with appointments, but at least they weren't stacked on top of each other, and I had a bit of time to breath between clients.

I was still seething from the encounter with Dalton, but I'm not sure who I was more mad at—him or myself for not seeing him for the snake he was. Had the signs been there all along, and I just hadn't seen them? I wracked my brain for wisps of memory from our first encounter, when he had brought Cher in, but nothing stood out.

I picked up the phone and dialed Eureka Acres Dog Farm. A few minutes later, I heard Nancy's voice answer. "Hello? Eureka Acres."

"Nancy, hi. This is Dr. Gibbons. I'm calling to check in on the puppies."

"Oh, Doctor. Hi."

There was a swirl of emotions in her voice that I could not untangle. She seemed mildly glad to hear it was me, but did I sense shame as well, or was I just projecting that? I couldn't tell. "Are they improving?"

"Yes. They're much better. Harry's home now. I showed him how to do the medicine. He's been regular as clockwork about it."

I sat up straight, my eyes popping open. "Your husband is *home*? How—" I bit my tongue so as not to say anything that might offend her.

Apparently I had caught it in time, because she said, "Your friend—the priest—he paid Harry's bail."

"He did?" I said, shaking my head back and forth slowly.

"He did." Her voice tightened up, and I realized she was trying not to cry. "And we're so grateful. Would you please... would you please tell him thank you...from me?"

"Uh...okay." I couldn't think of anything else to say. "Uh, is Harry there?"

"He's out in the kennels, but I'll ask him to call you if you like."

"Sure, that would be great. I just want to get some specifics."

"Of course. I'll tell him. Bye—and thanks."

I hung up and just sat there at the workbench next to the centrifuge. "Jack, I have no idea what to make of you," I said out loud. Did he have a private fortune he could dig into? Did he borrow against that creepy house of his? Except that it wasn't his house, was it? I thought it belonged to the church. I'd have to ask him...but then, it was none of my business. I shrugged. That didn't mean I couldn't be curious about it. *He can always tell me to mind my own business*, I thought.

It was time for the next client—which should have been simple enough: a checkup and a nail trimming. The checkup went well enough, but this dog—a husky malamute with one blue eye—did not want to have his nails trimmed. In the end we had to sedate him to the point where he was so blissed out he didn't care *what* we were doing to his paws.

Afterwards, as I was heading for the restroom, my phone buzzed. I didn't recognize the number, but it was local, so I answered it anyway. "Casey Gibbons," I said.

"Dr. Gibbons, this is Myra Lind. You...you and your friend came by the other night to...well, to ask us about animal rights, I guess."

I cocked my head, intrigued. "Yes, Ms. Lind. Thanks for calling. Uh...what's up?"

"Well, I'm sorry to bother you, but...is there any way you could come over again? We have someone...well, there's someone here you should speak to."

"Huh. Okay. What about tonight?"

"Tonight would be just fine," she said. "About six?"

"Great," I said.

"And, doctor...you might want to bring...you know, some evidence."

"Evidence...like pictures or something?"

"Yes. Something like that."

"Okay," I said. "We'll see you tonight." I hung up. *That was strange*, I thought. I pulled up the text app and texted Jack.

> Utah City couple asked to see us tonight. You free?

A few minutes later my pocket buzzed. I looked at the screen and saw Jack's reply.

> I can be. Time?

I texted back and put the phone back in my pocket, and resumed my trip to the bathroom with a bounce in my step. I didn't know if that was because of Ms. Lind's mysterious call or because it meant I'd see Jack tonight, but I had a strong suspicion it was the latter.

But I couldn't help wondering what the cryptic phone call had meant. Were the terrorists back in play? Had they killed Shelley after all? Stephen Thomas was at the top of my suspect list, but on my internal scoreboard I moved the terrorists into second place.

At lunch I sped home and took Scout for a quick walk. Then, tossing her a handful of dog biscuits, I shut the door and walked back out to my car. But before I could get into it, a sheriff's car rolled to a stop in front of the house. I watched as Gus got out and waved at me.

I had already opened the door of my car, but I shut it again and walked across the grass to where Gus was standing. He picked the hat off his head and gave me a shy smile. "Casey."

"Gus," I said. I crossed my arms. "To what do I owe the pleasure?"

"Well, uh, I was just driving by and—"

I could instantly see that wasn't true. He'd come here for some reason. But I didn't call him out on it.

"—and, well, I was wondering if maybe you'd like to...uh... catch a drive-in sometime. A movie. You know...like a drive-in movie?" He looked at his shoes. One leg was bouncing up and down.

I felt a moment of vertigo. I put my hand on his squad car to steady myself. "Uh...Gus, I'm...I'm honored, but..."

"I know you've been seeing the Father, but I didn't know if maybe you were just friends, or what...so I thought I'd just... you know, man up and ask." He looked me in the eye now, but it was a look I'd seen before—the look of a dog afraid he was about to be hit.

The fact was, though, I didn't know if Jack and I were just friends myself. There was something sweet about Gus, but until that moment I'd never seriously entertained the idea of going on a date with him. I didn't know what to think.

"Uh, if you want to think it over, I'm—"

"No, it's not that," I said, even though it was. "I...well, to be perfectly honest, Gus, I'm not a juggler. I've never been good at keeping two balls in the air, let alone three."

He squinted, not making the connection.

I gave him my most compassionate look and said, "I don't know where things with Jack are going...but I think I need to find out before I start...looking elsewhere. You know?"

He looked down at his shoes again and nodded. "Yes'm. I do. Well, if you ever...if it doesn't...if you want to pick up where..."

"I'll call you," I said. "I promise. And thank you."

He gave me a pained smile and tipped his hat again. Then he climbed into his squad car and disappeared down the county road.

"Hoo-boy," I said to myself. "What just happened?"

thirty-two

Afternoon brought an unexpected breather when one of our clients didn't show for her appointment. I was worried about that too, because it was a follow-up on her cat, Tolstoy, who had been receiving subcutaneous saline infusions at home. I was anxious to follow up. Ellie had already left a voice mail, but there was nothing to do but reschedule.

I felt my phone vibrate and quickly checked the screen. I didn't recognize the number. It was probably a sales call, but there was enough going on that I didn't want to risk it. *What the hell*, I thought, *I can always hang up.* "Hello? Dr. Casey Gibbons here."

"Casey? Oh, God, it's you, it's really you."

I frowned, not recognizing the voice. It was a man's voice, a rough voice—sounding as if the speaker had been chain-smoking for a couple of years.

"Who is this?" I asked.

"It's Stephen Thomas," he said.

I snapped to attention. "Stephen Thomas? Are you...it doesn't...are you okay?"

"Uh...not sure how to answer that," he said.

I glanced at my Snoopy watch. "Tell me what's going on," I prompted.

"Well, I...uh...I lost my job. And my...I had to sell my car."

That was bad. San Jose was not a city with decent public transportation. If you didn't have a car, you couldn't really live there. You could survive, I suppose, but you couldn't *live*. "I'm so sorry to hear that, Stevie," I said, using his old endearment.

"And I...I've been using."

"Using what?" I asked. "You can tell me, I'm a doctor."

"Smack," he said.

Heroin. Damn. "How long have you been using?" I asked.

"A couple of months. Since I lost my job," he said.

"And how are you paying for it?" I asked.

There was a long silence. "I'd...I'd rather not say."

"Okay," I said. "You don't need to tell me everything."

"Thanks," he said. "So...Pam told me about Shelley."

"Yeah," I said.

"Oh, geez, Casey," his voice rose an octave, and it sounded like he was trying not to cry. "Oh, man, I just..."

I kept my mouth shut. If Stephen Thomas was going to hang himself, I didn't want to move the rope.

"I just...I still love her, you know? I can't even believe that she's not—guh..."

And then he sobbed. I felt my own throat swell up as I listened to him. After about a minute, when I thought he might be at the end of his crying jag, he began to keen. It sounded just like Scout's howling. I reminded myself not to join in, although I must confess, some grieving animal part of me wanted to.

Finally, though, the keening stopped, and the sobs gave way to retching. He was throwing up. I grimaced and held the phone so tightly to my ear that my fingers began to ache. I switched hands—and ears—and waited until Stephen

Thomas had finished letting his emotions sweep through him.

"I'm sorry," he said.

"It's okay," I said. I had one ace up my sleeve. It was time to play it. "Um...Stephen Thomas, listen. I was going through some of Shelley's things and there's an envelope here with your name on it." That was true. It was a 9 x 12 manilla envelope with "Stevie" scrawled in Shelley's almost unreadable doctor script. "I don't know what's in it," I continued. But that wasn't true. I'd opened it up and discovered a whole cache of documentary evidence detailing the history of their relationship. Apparently she'd shoved everything about their life together into that one envelope and then tucked it away in a drawer, much the same way she'd compartmentalized it in her own head, I imagine. *Time to set the hook,* I thought. "I did peek inside it, and there's some cash...probably several hundred dollars." That was another lie.

"Oh, geez, oh geez, that would be so..."

"Thing is, I don't really trust the mail. You'd need to come get it. How soon can you be here?"

"I..." There was another silence, but this one was awkward. "I just don't see how I can do that," Stephen Thomas said. "I mean, I want to, but...I don't...it would be so hard...I don't...I'm just not thinking straight enough to..."

He didn't finish his sentence. He didn't need to. If you dangle several hundred dollars in front of the nose of a heroin addict and he can't find a way to snatch at it, then... It told me all I needed to know.

I heard a squeak, and I realized that Stephen Thomas was crying again. But this time, I sensed that he wasn't grieving over Shelley. He was despairing over the waste he had made of his life, the utter helplessness that he felt. Jack would probably say that he felt abandoned by God. And who knows, perhaps he had been.

"Stevie, give me an address—a safe address—and I'll send it by FedEx. I'll have it insured."

"Yeah. Yeah, okay." He gave me the address of a church, and I wrote it down on a Post-it.

"It was good to hear your voice, Stevie."

"You too, Case. I'm...I'm sorry..."

"It's okay. Just...take care of yourself, okay?"

I hung up and steadied myself against the counter. I shook my head. I remembered when Stephen Thomas was strong, successful, whip-smart. He didn't catch Shelley's eye for nothing. But then...

I'd send the package on my next day off. There wasn't actually any money in it, but I'd put some in. I owed Massaman a hefty sum, but a few hundred dollars wouldn't change that. And I knew it would all go into Stephen Thomas' arm, but that was the price of knowing for sure. There was no way he could have held it together well enough to even get to Gold Valley, let alone orchestrate his ex-wife's murder and make a clean getaway. No way in hell.

thirty-three

"So you don't think he could have done it?" Jack asked.
I had picked him up at his house and was filling him in on my phone call with Stephen Thomas. "No," I said flatly.

"You don't think he could be playing you? He is an addict, after all."

"I know, but...my gut tells me he's just too broken to pull something like that off. Plus...you didn't hear him crying when he found out about Shelley. He was...completely undone."

"Poor guy," Jack said. He sprawled in his seat, looking for all the world like a crab that had found itself on its back.

"You okay?" I asked.

"Yeah, just...my shoulder really aches today. It's hard to find a comfortable position."

"Are you sure you feel up to this?" I asked.

"Are you kidding? I've been looking forward to this all day."

I raised one eyebrow, wondering how a meeting with strangers in Utah City rated. And then I realized that it wasn't the activity he was commenting on, but the company. I felt a flame of affection bloom in my chest.

"So where does that leave us with our suspects?" he asked.

"I think we've ruled out Stephen Thomas and Harry Clementine," I said.

"I think it's safe to say Maggie Edgerton isn't your girl," Jack chimed in. "Which leaves us where?"

"Without any of our prime suspects," I groused. I exited the freeway and turned onto the county road.

"There's still the animal rights wackos," Jack said.

"Father! You surprise me," I said.

"What?"

"I don't know. It's just so...unkindly put."

"Oh. Sorry about that. You know, underneath the collar, I'm just a regular guy."

"You'd better be," I said, before I could stop myself. I looked over at him and watched him grin. I realized we were flirting and felt blood rush to my face.

"You're blushing," he said.

I changed the subject. "And then there's Massaman."

"Right," Jack said. "I almost forgot about him. But surely he didn't do it. He wants to be paid."

"Maybe Shelley threatened to stop paying him," I said.

"Why would she do that? She borrowed the money. From everything you've told me, she strikes me as the kind of person who honored her commitments."

"She was," I agreed. No matter how I tried to place that puzzle piece, it didn't fit. "But he has violent tendencies."

"So...means. But no motive," Jack said, referring to the hat trick of "means, motive, and opportunity" that can point to just the right suspect in most cases. "Whereas the animal rights group has motive, but..."

"But we don't know enough about them to establish means or opportunity."

"Maybe we're about to find out," Jack said.

"Maybe," I agreed. I pulled to a stop outside the house. There were still bicycles in the yard, but they had been moved since the last time we'd been there.

"Kids," Jack winked at me. "Mark my words."

"We'll see," I said. I got out, grabbed a file folder, and walked beside Jack to the door. I pushed on the doorbell and waited. A few moments passed before the door swung inward, revealing the same woman we'd met a couple of nights before. She didn't meet my eyes, but rather looked downward. If I didn't know better, I'd swear she was staring at my chest.

"Come in," she said. "Please. I'm so sorry about this."

"Thank you," I said. Once inside, I waited for my eyes to adjust. The place was small, and the walls were a dingy yellow. There were attempts at homespun decorations, but they were more sad than cheery. This was a house that had seen more than its share of wear and tear.

She led us through a short hallway into the kitchen. Just beyond it was the living room. A brown shag carpet looked in desperate need of cleaning or at least a good vacuuming. The air smelled of animal fur and grease. Outside, a dog barked his objection to our presence.

Sitting on a threadbare couch was a man in his late 30s, which I took to be the woman's husband. Next to him was a teenage girl. A scowl marred her face and her arms were folded tight against her chest. She refused to look at us.

The man rose and offered his hand. I shook it. Then he shook Jack's hand.

"I'm Ben. You've met my wife, Laura."

Now I had names. "Ben. Laura," I said.

"And this is Bonnie." He indicated his daughter.

"Nice to meet you, Bonnie," Jack said. He still had his clerical collar on. I wasn't sure whether that was going to work for us or against us. I decided it didn't matter. This was Jack, and it was part of the package.

Bonnie said nothing. She still didn't look at us. *What do you know?* I thought. *Jack was right. Damn him.*

I sat down in a chair on the other side of the coffee table. Jack hovered behind my chair protectively, one hand on the headrest. I wasn't sure if I liked that or not, but decided not to be distracted by it.

"Thank you for your phone call," I began, not knowing where else to start.

"I think it was the least we could do," Ben said.

"After your visit, we started...looking around," Laura said.

"I take it you found something," I said.

Laura looked at her shoes. I could tell she was feeling shame. I intuited that the shame was not really hers, but as a mother... I looked at Bonnie.

Wordlessly, I placed the file folder I'd been holding onto the chipped, stained coffee table. I opened it. I placed a color copy of a photo in front of Bonnie. It showed the outside wall of the clinic, with the words "Killers" and "Animals are people too" in bright red spray paint. "Did you do this?" I asked.

Bonnie's eyes glanced at the printout, then back to whatever point in space she had been staring at before. She said nothing.

I put another photo in front of her. It was harder to make out because of a lack of contrast, but if you looked closely you could make out the vertical slashes someone had cut into my tires. "How about this?" I asked.

Once again I saw her eyes flick to the paper and away again, but this time I saw her shoulders deflate. She seemed to shrink into herself.

I hesitated to go further. I had one more photo, and it was intense. I struggled with whether it was too intense to show to a teenager. But the value of seeing her reaction overrode my caution. "And...did you do *this?*" I asked, and put the photo of Shelley lying on the kitchen floor before her, blood spattering her hair and the linoleum. I saw Ben rear back at the sight of it. Laura startled and then bit her lip, but did not object. But Bonnie jumped up instantly. "No! I didn't do that! We—never. We didn't do that one!"

Jack's voice was soothing. "We believe you," he said. "And it's okay. Everything is okay. No matter what you're feeling, and no matter how scared you are, everything is going to be okay."

I could see the effects of his words immediately. I also marveled at them. I was angry and hot for vengeance and blood. A teen's tender feelings were not my top concern. I was grateful that it was his.

Slowly, she sat back down, but this time, her eyes moved more freely, and the defiance was gone. She was scared, and it showed. Her fingers were trembling. "We did the other two," she confessed.

"Who is we?" her father asked.

"Me and Billy and June," she said.

"They're her friends," Ben said. "I thought they were good kids."

"They are," Bonnie protested. "We didn't do anything wrong. We were trying to save the animals."

"You were trying to save the animals from me?" I said.

"Yes," Bonnie said.

"What is it I'm doing to the animals that is so terrible?" I asked.

"You're killing them," she said.

"I save their lives every day," I protested. My voice rose with a bit of defiance of my own.

"Do you mean when she has to put them to sleep?" Jack asked.

She looked up at him hopefully. She nodded. "I heard Mom and Dad talking about euthanasia...you know, for people. And they said it was wrong. How can it be wrong for people and not for animals?"

It was a good question. I felt something shift inside myself. My stomach loosened its death grip on my spine. I felt my whole body relax. *This is a teaching moment*, the voice in my head said. *Don't blow it.* "Bonnie, there are ways that animals are like humans, and ways that they aren't. One of the ways they're different is that they're not self-reflective—"

"What does that mean?" she asked.

"You can know something," Jack offered, "and you can know that you know it—you can think about the fact that you know it. Animals can know things, but they can't reflect on the fact that they know things. You need language to do that."

"So?" Bonnie asked.

"So we all feel pain, but only humans can reflect on their pain and find a meaning for it," I said. "For animals...well, they can only suffer. They can't find meaning in their suffering."

"Are you saying that we let people suffer because they can find meaning in it?" Her brows screwed up in confusion.

"I guess I am," I said. "We don't think people should be in pain—we try to alleviate that, of course. But we don't end human lives before their time...at least, we didn't used to. It's becoming more common. But that's a dangerous, very slippery slope."

"Why?" Bonnie asked. "Why is it okay to kill dogs but not people?"

I realize my "meaning-making" argument was going nowhere. "If euthanizing people is okay, where do we draw the line?" I asked. "Why not euthanize homeless people? They're suffering, right? Wouldn't it be merciful to put them out of their misery?"

"That's horrible," Bonnie said.

"It is," I agreed. "Or people who are disabled, or really sick? Or how about addicts? Or even old people? If they become a burden to a family, why not just put them down? They probably have a lot of health problems anyway."

Bonnie's face started to screw up. I realized she was about to cry. I leaned back, cursing myself for pushing too hard. I glanced at Bonnie's parents, and saw that they were concerned. I felt the moment slipping out of my grasp. I had messed it up, just as I had suspected I would. I opened my mouth to say something—anything—that might fix it, but before I could make it worse, Jack did something utterly unexpected. He started singing.

> When peace like a river, attendeth my way,
> When sorrows like sea billows roll;
> Whatever my lot, Thou hast taught me to say
> It is well, it is well, with my soul.

And then, despite how weird the moment felt, it got weirder still when Bonnie's parents joined in on the chorus.

> It is well, with my soul,
> It is well, it is well, with my soul.

I looked over my shoulder and stared at Jack. He gave me a compassionate look. I turned back to Bonnie, feeling utterly lost. She had regained her composure. For several minutes we sat in silence. Then she asked another question. "So why not make sure animals aren't in pain? Why do you have to kill them?"

I took a deep breath. "Animals can't talk to us. They can't tell us how much pain they're in. All we have to go on is their behavior. Sometimes, we have to guess. I'm sure that we guess wrong sometimes. And that does make me sad. But I have to believe that I'm relieving more pain than I'm causing."

She didn't look convinced. "I think sometimes people have their dogs and cats killed when they become too much of a bother."

That was insightful. "Yes, that happens sometimes. I try to talk them out of it. But sometimes I can't."

"But why do you go along with it?"

I struggled whether I should say what I was thinking. I was afraid it was too brutal for her to hear. But there was a defiance in her eyes that made me think that she could handle it. I took the plunge. "Because there are freeways."

She looked confused. So did her parents. Then I saw recognition break over Ben's face, then Laura's. They looked horrified. They should be. "What does that mean?" Bonnie asked.

I looked up at Ben, then at Laura. *Do you want to explain it, or should I?* my eyes pleaded. Ben closed his eyes and nodded. I cleared my throat. "It means that if people decide they don't want their pet anymore, sometimes they...they do terrible things to get rid of them. Like dump them onto a busy freeway. Or feed them rat poison. Or....well, you get the idea."

Bonnie's eyes were large as saucers. Water welled in them. I didn't blame her for a second. "So when an owner says they want to put an animal to sleep, I have a choice. If it's well enough to go to a new home, I try to convince the owners to take it to a shelter. If it's not, I can give it a shot, and end its life peacefully, with dignity, and without pain...or I can let their owners do something...terrible. And painful. And wrong."

Bonnie swallowed. Then she nodded. I felt my shoulders

relax. I had gotten through. I felt like thanking Jesus, even though I didn't really believe in him—that was Jack's job.

I had one more question nagging at me, though. "Bonnie, do you really think that animals shouldn't be kept as pets?"

She scowled and looked thoughtful. "That was Billy's idea. He got that from a website. But it sounds good to me."

"So, you don't want your dog—what's your dog's name?"

"Astro," Bonnie said.

"So you don't want Astro to live with you anymore?"

She looked genuinely frightened. "No...I mean...I don't want Astro to go anywhere."

"If we suddenly turned all of our dogs and cats out onto the street, what do you think would happen to them?" I asked.

"I don't know," her voice turned up, an indicator that she was feeling vulnerable. I understood.

"They would starve, and the big ones would kill the little ones for food. Is that what you want?"

"No," she said.

"The truth is that dogs and cats and humans have evolved together, as kind of a family of species, for hundreds of thousands of years...maybe even millions. We need them, and they need us. We're like Siamese twins—we're joined at the hip. If you try to surgically separate us now...we would both suffer, and they would most certainly die. And we...I think we'd die inside."

She looked shell-shocked. Then, slowly, she nodded.

"Do you still think I'm a terrible person?" I asked.

She looked me in the eye then. "I...I don't know what to think," she confessed.

"Well, that's fair," I said. "These are complicated issues... even for adults. It's not easy to sort them out. I struggle with them too. I mean, when Astro is sick, where are you going to go?"

Her face said, *Not to you,* but she didn't say it. But that answer would have been okay. There were plenty of fine vets around.

"So what now?" Ben asked.

"Someone took the life of my friend, long before her time," I said. "That is my number one concern. So if you promise to stop attacking the clinic—and sabotaging my car—I say we just let this go."

Bonnie looked like she might cry again. She sniffed and nodded.

"Do you think you can convince Billy and June to stop?" I asked.

"Don't worry about them," Laura said. "Their parents are friends. We'll talk to them."

I nodded. "Okay then. Because if there is even one more threat, I'm going to let the sheriff handle it. Does that seem fair?"

Bonnie nodded. I looked up at Ben and Laura. They looked relieved and grateful. Ben shook my hand. "Thank you, Doctor."

I turned to Laura. "Thank you for calling."

She looked tearful herself. "Thank you for...for..."

"The grace," Jack interjected. "It's called grace."

thirty-four

On the way home, I realized that I was fresh out of suspects. I sighed and wondered if all my effort had been for nothing. I was no closer to finding Shelley's killer than I had been the day I had found her. "I'm sorry," I said out loud to her...wherever she was. Then I realized I was talking to the air, and felt stupid.

I also realized I was bone tired, and that if I wasn't careful, I could spiral into despair. I resolved to stay as positive as I could, if only for Scout's sake.

When I finally arrived home, Scout was so glad to see me that she leaped a full three feet off the ground, pogoing better than I ever did to Debbie Gibson in my mildly misspent youth. We had a little lovefest and I got her dinner ready. She dug into it with gusto and I poured myself a whiskey. I had picked up an expensive Scottish single malt. I told myself it was homework, but in reality it was all about comfort. I was just about to collapse on the couch when my phone rang. I was surprised to see Jack's name on the screen.

I pushed the green button. "Some people might call this

obsessive," I said, since I had dropped him off not fifteen minutes ago.

I was relieved to hear him laugh. "Just so long as you don't think so," he said.

"What's up?" I asked.

"Um...tomorrow is your day off, right?"

"Yeeeeahhhh," said, drawing it out playfully. "What did you have in mind?"

"I was wondering if maybe you and Scout would like to come over for breakfast. I make a mean frittata."

"Do you have Tabasco sauce?" I asked.

"I have Topatío," he said.

"I like that even better," I said. "What time?"

"I don't want to take away from your sleeping in. What's a good time for you?"

"I don't sleep in. Scout makes sure of that. I'm up at 6am, rain or shine. Don't you have to work?"

"I do," he confessed. "How about eight, then? That gives us time for a good, leisurely breakfast before my first meeting at ten."

"That sounds lovely. Do you want me to bring anything?" I asked.

"Just that beautiful dog of yours," he said.

"You know how manipulative that is, don't you? Playing off a girl's feelings for her dog?"

"What? It's the truth. Scout is a beautiful dog. Just like her owner."

I was glad he couldn't see me blush. "Um...Jack, is this a date? Like a real, formal date?"

"You mean as opposed to whatever it is we've been doing up to now?" he asked.

"Exactly," I said.

"Do you want it to be?" he asked.

I held my breath while my brain froze. "Uh...yeah. I think so. Yes," I managed.

"You don't sound too sure," he said.

"I'm not," I confessed. "This is...it's been a long time. I'm..."

"Scared?" he asked.

"I was going to say 'cautious,' but sure...'scared' will do."

"Me too," he admitted. "Let's be scared together."

That settled it. I wasn't likely to sleep at all that night. More whisky was in order. "I'll see you in the morning. Thank you...for the invite...for the date."

"I'm looking forward to it," he said. "See you in the morning."

I pushed the red button and hung up. A warm glow came over me, but I don't think it was the whisky. I downed the rest of the glass and as it shot its relaxing tentacles into every part of my brain, I realized I was hungry too. I walked to the kitchen and opened the refrigerator. I peeled the breast off of a rotisserie chicken and put it on a plate. I added some frozen broccoli and put the plate in the microwave. I knew the chicken would be done before the broccoli was, and I waited for the timer to go off, fork in hand to remove the steaming chicken. It wasn't the most elegant way to work this particular process, but my mind wasn't really on it.

After eating, I watched a rerun of *Law & Order* with Scout's snoring head in my lap. I'd helped myself to a second glass of whisky and I was seriously nodding off. I turned off the TV and announced it was time for bed. Scout yawned loudly, rolled over and fell off the couch, fortunately landing on all four feet. I turned off the lights and headed for the bedroom. Scout leaped up on the bed first and turned in place four times on the side I don't sleep on—that was her side.

I had just plugged my phone in for the night when it rang. "Damn," I swore, squinting at the phone. I didn't recognized the number, and I was tempted to let it go to voicemail. I should have. But for some reason, I didn't. "Hello?" I asked.

"Dr. Gibbons, hi. This is Chas Dalton."

"Oh, Mr. Dalton. Uh...hi. It's...late."

"I know, and I'm so sorry about that. The problem is that I...I have a bit of a medical emergency. One of my brood bitches —Britney—she's been in labor for four hours now, and—"

"Let me guess, no puppies?" I yawned.

"That's right. It's not the first time this has happened, and I'm sure it happens all the time, but she seems to be in a lot of pain. She won't lie down, and she keeps turning in place and whining. I've seen a lot of whelping, but I've never seen a bitch like this. The amount of distress she's in...it isn't normal."

"Well...ordinarily I'd say just keep her comfortable and call me if it gets worse, but—"

"It's bad," he said. "I can feel it."

"Okay, okay. Can you bring her down to the clinic?"

"She's in too much pain. I don't think I can move her that far. I don't want to try."

I sighed, catching myself halfway through it. "Okay. I've got my bag. I'll...I'll be there in about twenty minutes."

"Thank you, Doctor. I'm forever in your debt."

"Uh...sure. Okay, see you soon."

I hung up and blearily looked at Scout. "I don't think I can drive," I said. "Can you?" She wagged her stubby tail. I went to the bathroom and slapped cold water onto my face. Then I made a mug of instant coffee—dreadful stuff, but still... caffeine in a jar. Then I held the door for Scout and walked out to the car.

I might ordinarily have left Scout at the house, but I'd left her alone too long that day, and I felt bad about it. She'd have to stay in the car at Dalton's place, but I knew she'd appreciate the car ride.

I was probably over the legal limit, but not by much. I drove just fine, or so I thought. It took me a little over ten minutes to get to the Royal Poodle. I rolled down the window before I got out and turned to face Scout. "I'm sorry, girl, but I have to work. I want you to stay here until I get back, okay?" She'd use the open window if she needed to use the yard, but otherwise I knew she'd stay put. But Scout wasn't even looking at me. She was panting happily and looking at the ceiling.

"Whatever," I chuckled. "I'll try not to be long." I gave her a pat and got out, shutting the door firmly behind me.

I opened the hatchback and snagged my medical bag. Then I shut it again and walked briskly to the front door, trying not to weave. Before I could even knock, Dalton opened the door. "Doctor, thank you so much for coming." He was wearing brown corduroy pants that had seen better days and an over-sized t-shirt that said, "Purple Goat Kibble." Purple Goat was the kind of chichi kibble a breeder would never use in a million years, and I instantly assessed that the shirt was swag from some long-forgotten dog show.

"I don't normally make house calls," I said, more grumpily than I'd intended.

"Well, then I'm doubly grateful," he said. There was sincere concern on his face. "I have her in here," he said, leading me through the house, though the kitchen, to a large mud room. That was good. Whelping bitches shouldn't be in the cold, and I could tell that this mud room had seen a lot of whelpings. It was kitted out with everything one might need—blankets, paper towels, an electric kettle, a first aid kit. The whole setup spoke well of Dalton. I still hadn't forgiven him for the whole Craig's List affair, but just seeing this whelping room raised him a notch in my estimation.

In the corner, underneath a row of coat hooks, a white PVC whelping box had been set up, a perfectly square structure about three-and-a-half feet on each side, its walls extending up about twelve inches. It was lined with waterproof material and padded with soft, comfortable blankets. Lying atop the blankets was a gray standard poodle bitch in obvious distress.

I set my bag down near her and rolled up my sleeves. "So this is Britney?" I asked, not expecting an answer. "Looks like she has finally lain down."

"Every now and then, but then she gets up again," Dalton said.

Britney was panting and her eyes were wild. She was obviously pregnant, which isn't always the case with dogs. She struggled to rise, but I put my hand out and scratched at her withers. "Shush, girl, it's okay. Just relax." I took out my stethoscope and pressed it to her ribcage. Her heart rate was fast but strong. I pulled the stops out of my ears and eased Britney back so I could have access to more of her tummy. I gently placed my fingers on her stomach and began to probe. Just as I suspected, one of the pups was transverse—turned at a right angle to the birth canal, and was blocking the way for all the others. Britney's contractions were regular and strong, and the poor girl was working it, but to no avail.

"I need hot water and soap, please," I said.

Dalton pointed at a utility sink I hadn't noticed—I'd been too focused on the dog. I rose and washed up past the elbows. Then I pulled on a set of blue nitrile gloves. I searched for and found a tube of KY jelly in my bag and began to apply it to my right hand, rubbing up past the wrists. Holding my right hand up, I shouted to Dalton, "Clean towel, please." He handed me one, and using only my left hand, I wiped the glove clean. I figured I'd work the misplaced pup from the outside with my left hand, and from the inside with my right. I turned to Dalton. "Okay, I need you to hold her head and try to keep her calm. If you can't, I'll need to sedate her. But the fewer drugs the better."

Dalton sat cross-legged and cradled Britney's head in his lap. He cooed at her and stroked her ears. I nodded my approval. Dalton was definitely good with dogs, and he seemed to care about them—which made the Cher thing even more baffling. Using only a couple of fingers, I reached inside Britney's uterus and felt around. The dog started at the unexpected intrusion, but Dalton had it under control. I went deeper, and felt the edge of the pup's side, blocking the canal like a cork. I rested my fingers there and closed my eyes. "The pup is dead," I said as soon as I was sure. "Probably the pressure from the others."

Dalton scowled but said nothing, other than doubling down on his calming noises.

The dead pup was unfortunate, but there was an upside—I didn't need to be nearly so careful with it. I could press much harder in order to get it to move 'round the right way. I couldn't hurt it, after all. Carefully placing my left hand, I felt for the outline of the pup, and with a coordinated effort using both hands, I shifted the pup's corpse. Britney yelped, and instantly leaped to her feet, nearly knocking Dalton on his back with the force of her movement. I quickly withdrew my right hand before she twisted my wrist.

"And she's up," I said. "She's getting in position. Get ready to catch," I said, leaping up myself and heading for the utility sink. Over my shoulder I watched the bitch strain, her legs trembling with her natal efforts. I quickly washed and dried my hands and returned to the dog. I bumped Dalton aside and took up my position just below her crowning vagina. "Get her head," I barked as the first of the puppies slid out and into my waiting hands.

It was dead, just as I expected. I quickly laid it aside and hoped for better results with the second pup. It slid out of Britney covered in black slime, wriggling like a caught trout. I pinched open and removed the fetal membrane so that the puppy could breathe. I then gently laid it on a nest of blankets and waited for the next. It wasn't long in coming. Britney's breathing was labored, and she whined now and then, no doubt from the discomfort and probably confusion. Something was happening to her—something ancient, something holy, but undeniably something strange.

"Is this her first litter?" I asked Dalton.

"Second," he said.

Okay, so not so strange, I thought. That was actually good. The bitch would be less freaked out if she had gone through it before. A calm bitch is a good bitch while whelping.

Over the next two hours, four more pups made their way out into the world. Each time a new pup emerged, I expected it to be the last. I expected Britney to get up and start doing what momma dogs did—cleaning each of the puppies, directed by an instinct older than time. But she didn't.

"Do you know how many pups there are?" I asked.

"No," he said.

"You didn't get an x-ray?" I asked.

"No."

"Damn," I said. "Okay, let's just keep her comfortable and calm and hope for the best." But as the hours dragged on, I grew more and more worried. Britney was still obviously in pain, and the puppies were going uncared for. It wasn't good. I checked for signs of internal bleeding, but there was so much blood and mucus from the birth it was hard to tell.

"I'm sorry, doctor," Dalton said, a little after 3am. "I didn't realize it would be *this* difficult."

"I'm just glad you called me," I said. I stood up and felt pinprick pains running up and down my legs. I stretched and stripped off the nitrile gloves. "I need a restroom break," I said.

Dalton nodded. "I'll start some more coffee. Uh...the restroom is down the hall, there, to your right."

"Thanks." As I walked down the dark hallway, my brain was flooded with thoughts about Britney. It was possible that there was another dead pup in her womb. While the first had been pushed out by the live puppies, this one would be trickier —if my guess was right, that is. There were drugs I could try to move things along, but I didn't have any of them on me.

I was lost in my head, and wasn't really paying attention to where I was going. I'd found the hallway all right, but sleep-deprived and moving on autopilot, I opened the first door I came to. I flipped on the light, and then just stood there, momentarily confused. It wasn't a bathroom, as I'd expected, but a bedroom. There was a bed—either full or queen sized, by the look of it. There was also a small desk and a bookshelf full of books, adorned with knickknacks. *Maybe the bathroom he was referring to is en suite*, I reasoned, and looked for a door. There was a closet at the far side of the room. Just to make sure I wasn't missing something I stepped into the room and turned around. No door. No bathroom. Just—

My attention was immediately arrested by a framed photo on the bookshelf. I blinked, not making sense of it at first. Unconsciously, I moved toward it and picked it up. It was obviously a photo of Chas Dalton, that was clear—he was younger, but it was definitely him. He had his arm around a woman who looked strangely familiar. My eyebrows bunched as I wracked my brain searching for the face. I have a strange quirk about me—I have a hard time recognizing people if they are out of context. That was the problem here. I knew this woman, but in a different context. *She's older now too*, I thought. And that's when it hit.

"Nancy," I breathed. Nancy Clementine. My mind raced, and I flashed back on the first time I had met Dalton. I heard his words echo in my head, *There was a girl I loved...once. Nancy. She had an infection, and...well, she couldn't have children after that.* Chas Dalton knew Nancy Clementine. Had been in love with her—so much so that he still keeps a picture of the two of them together. Gold Valley was a small town, so it didn't surprise me that two dog breeders knew each other, but... I wasn't sure what it meant, but I knew it had to mean something.

I heard a rustle and looked up. Dalton stood in the doorway, staring at me with wide, shocked eyes. The color drained from his face. He glanced quickly between the photo and my face. He must have seen something in my eyes, because I certainly saw something in his. I knew something, and he knew that I knew. His eyes narrowed into a look of steely resolve that I didn't like one little bit. Clumsily, I put the picture back on the bookshelf. "That must be Nancy," I said nervously, awkwardly. "I remember you telling me about her... when we first met."

I backed away as Dalton entered the room, moving toward me with slow and grave resolve. Before I knew what was happening, he shoved me—hard. I felt a momentary pain as my head hit the wall behind me, and I sank into oblivion.

thirty-five

The first thing I was aware of was pain—sharp and dull at the same time. My hand went up to feel the back of my head and found a painful knot. I tried to open my eyes, but a harsh light prevented me. I held my hand in front of my face and tried again. Everything was a little bit blurry, but I gradually discerned that I was lying on a cement floor. There was hay around me. The place reeked of antiseptic and dog. The light above me was coming from a single naked bulb, hanging from its cord.

"You're awake. Good. She needs help." It was Dalton's voice. I had to squint to see him. He was outside a metal gate drawn across the entry to the cell I was in. His features were lost in shadow, but I could tell it was him.

"What the actual hell?" I squeaked through a dry throat. "Why did you hit me?" I rose shakily and moved toward the cell's gate. It was padlocked. I shook the gate, trying to shake it free, but also using it to hold myself up. It was secure. "And why the hell am I...locked in here?" I could feel the adrenalin rising in my system as the panic took over.

"I can't just let you go free," Dalton said, his voice a little too calm and even. He was sitting on a stool just outside of the gate. "Now that you know."

"Know what?" I asked. "Now that I know what?" I suspected it had something to do with seeing that picture of Nancy, but I still didn't know what it meant.

"Britney," he pointed at his dog. "She needs your help."

I looked around me on the floor and saw Britney lying on her side. Her tongue hung out one side of her mouth like an unrolled hallway carpet. Her breathing was fast and labored. Her eyes flicked toward me, but she did not otherwise acknowledge my presence.

My head felt thick, and my body moved clumsily, but instinct kicked in and I held open her eyelids and checked her pupils. I looked at her gums. They weren't blue, but they were paler than I would have liked. I put a hand on her belly, but didn't feel anything.

"There's another dead pup in there," Dalton said. "And it's not coming out."

My medical bag was not in the cell. I did not have my stethoscope. I put my ear to Britney's stomach and listened, but I couldn't hear much of anything. "She needs a cesarian," I said. "I need to get her to the clinic."

"No," Dalton said, raising his voice. "No. You'll do it here."

"If I do it here," I said, turning toward the voice, toward the shadow that I knew was Dalton, "she'll die. I need an operating room."

"If she dies, you die," he said.

I cocked my head. "Excuse me?"

Dalton said nothing at first. Then, calmly and slowly, he said, "If she dies, so will you."

"Are you threatening me?" It was a stupid question. He had

already attacked me, and now I was locked inside a cell. I felt for my phone. It wasn't in my pocket.

"It's not a threat," he said. "It's just a fact. Save her, but save her *here*."

"I can't," I said.

"You mean you won't," he said.

"No, I mean I can't. I don't have the equipment."

"I'll give you your bag," he said.

"I don't have everything I need with me."

"You have anesthesia. You have a scalpel. What else do you need?" he asked.

"How about lights? How about assistants? How about specialized equipment? How about a whole pharmacy at my disposal? How about IV fluids? How about a sterile environment?"

"You don't need any of those things," he said. "Now get to work, or I'll kill you now."

"You'll kill me?" I asked.

"I will," he said.

"I don't believe you."

I caught a sparkle in the gloom—his eyes. They were black and unblinking. "It won't be the first time," he said. "And the first time is the hardest."

"What does that mean?" I asked. But no sooner were the words out of my mouth than I felt the bottom drop out of my stomach. I knew exactly what that meant. I'm not sure how I knew, but I did. A couple of pieces of the puzzle fit together. "You killed Shelley?"

He didn't answer. I took that for a "yes."

"Why? Why did you kill her?"

Again, Dalton said nothing.

"Why did you kill her, dammit?!" I yelled.

His voice growled with menace. "Just. Save. Her."

I looked behind me at the struggling bitch. Dalton was right. I didn't have what I wanted to do proper surgery, but I probably had the bare minimum to do the job. I didn't have a general anesthesia, but I had enough lidocaine for a local. "Bring me my bag," I said. "And some hot water and clean towels."

He nodded and left, his face disappearing into the darkness. I knelt by Britney and placed a calming hand on her side. My mind raced. *Chas Dalton killed Shelley,* I thought, over and over, trying to tease some sense out of it. I thought of Nancy, the discovery of the photo that had set him off—had made him violent toward me. There had to be a connection. Nancy was married to Harry Clementine. Nancy and Dalton had been an item...once. I know I didn't keep pictures of my old flames around, which meant. "The flame is not out," I whispered. Dalton still loved Nancy...loved her enough to kill.

Just then I heard a howl. And I knew that howl. "Oh, God," I said aloud. I wanted to shout, "Run, Scout, run!" but there was no way she'd hear me. There was only one thing to do, so I did it. I raised my chin and answered her mournful cry. She'd hear that. More than that, she might understand it a little bit. She'd know that I was missing her too. I tried to infuse more meaning into it—danger, concern, fear—but I knew it was just wishful thinking. Scout was just a dog. She was a great dog, but she wasn't magical, she wasn't a genius or anything, she wasn't super-canine. She was just a dog, and I couldn't expect more of her than what a dog could give.

I heard her howl again, an answering howl, high with alarm. I opened my mouth to respond, but before I could utter a sound, I heard the explosive report of a shotgun blast followed by a high-pitched yelp.

"Oh no..." I said. "No. Scout. No..." My body was suddenly awash with adrenaline, dread, and terror. My knees buckled. I listened desperately for another sound from her, but there was none. I curled into a ball, my head resting on the cold cement of the cell, and then I howled again. But this wasn't in imitation of a canine howl. This was an authentic howl of rage, of grief, of desperation. My chest shuddered as tears slid down my nose. My hands balled into fists.

And then Dalton was there again. He passed my bag through the bars of the cell. "Water is on the way," he said.

"You killed my dog," I managed, through gritted teeth, my voice not cooperating.

"I told you. I won't hesitate," he said. "Now *fix her*."

thirty-six

I held the scalpel over Britney's abdomen, but my hands were shaking too much to make a clean cut. I wiped tears out of my eyes with my sleeve, being careful not to touch the nitrile gloves to any part of my face. I gritted my teeth and bit back on the rage and despair and grief that threatened to undo me. *Get a grip,* the voice in my head told me, cool as a clam. *The only way you stay alive another minute is by continuing to be useful.* I shut my eyes and tried to clear my head of thoughts. But as soon as I did, the only thing I saw was the dead body of Scout, slick with blood, splayed out across my mind's eye.

I felt paralyzed. It was only with Scout that I felt competent. If I didn't have her... I suddenly felt like I'd lost my own soul. *No Scout, no Shelley,* I thought. *No Jack.* I felt bereft. I suddenly very much doubted I could be of any help to Britney at all.

In my desperation I did something Jack would have approved of, something that I hadn't done in almost twenty years—I prayed. It wasn't much of a prayer. It was basically two words: *Help her.* And as those two words unspooled in my thoughts, I almost howled again.

But then somehow, miraculously, the grief subsided and I was able to focus on my breath. In. Out. *Nothing else exists,* I thought. *Only the breath going in, only the breath going out.* I felt the muscles in my stomach unknot the tiniest bit. I kept at it, holding the blade about four inches from the dog's belly, eyes closed. Breathing.

"What are you doing?" Dalton's voice broke through the calm.

My eyes snapped open. My hand was still. I lowered the knife and made the incision. Britney began bucking. "This would be a lot easier if you were in here to hold her head and comfort her," I said, trying to soothe her with my free hand.

"You're doing just fine," he said. I heard approval in his voice, now that I had made the cut. I don't know why a part of me was relieved to hear it, but there it was.

"Shh, girl, you're doing fine." I had given Britney more than the required dose of lidocaine. If I had to do this by myself, I didn't want her to feel so much as a pinprick. I put my right hand into the incision, feeling my way past the viscera and uterine tissue.

As I worked, though, my brain was working too. Dalton had killed Shelley. Why? He was in love with Nancy Clementine—or had been at one time. He was too reactive by far for that to be the end of it, though, I reasoned. Those two facts were connected somehow—in a way that was obvious to Dalton, but not to me.

I reached toward the back of the bitch's womb for where the errant pup should be, but it wasn't there. I began to feel around, keeping my left hand on Britney's shoulder, rubbing it soothingly. What I was doing couldn't have been comfortable for her, no matter how much lidocaine was on board. But she withstood it, bless her. And then my hand found it—a deformed mass that might have developed into a puppy, but hadn't, stuck to the uterine wall very near the birth canal. *No wonder the other pups had so much trouble coming out,* I thought. *They had to go around this one.*

I needed both hands for this, so I stripped off the left hand glove with my teeth, and used my right hand, still slick with blood, to pull on a fresh one. Then I prised the uterine wall back to give me space to get the scalpel in, and cut the mass free.

It was out of place, I thought. And then I froze. I'm not good at recognizing things that are out of place. I suddenly flashed on the image of the blue-striped envelopes in Dalton's office, and I remembered where I had seen another just like it. In Shelley's files. In the file on Eureka Hills.

My mind raced as I threaded the catgut and began to stitch up Britney's tummy. And one by one, all of the pieces fell into place. I tied off the suture and replaced the small scissors to my bag. I began to bathe the wound in antiseptic solution.

I knew there was no way out of this. He was going to kill me—he had to, because there was no way I was not going to go directly to the police, and he must know that. I couldn't overpower him. He was holding all the cards. So, I reasoned, if I was going to die anyway, I wanted to best him the only way I could. So where I probably should've kept my mouth shut, I didn't. Typical me.

"So you tried to frame Harry Clementine," I said.

"What?" Dalton asked, as if coming to. He rocked forward so fast I thought he was going to spill out of his chair.

"You tried to frame Clementine. I think you fed Shelley information about his puppy mill so that she'd expose him in the press and make him lose face. Then maybe Nancy would see him for the bum that he is, maybe she'd remember why she loved you...once."

I stripped off the gloves, soaked one of the towels in water, and began to clean my hands.

"That's a lie—" he began, but he wasn't terribly convincing.

"I don't think so. I saw one of those envelopes you use in your office—the ones with the blue stripes. Those are unusual. I've never seen anything like them before. But there was one of them in the folder Shelley was keeping about Eureka Hills. I'm guessing you slipped it to her anonymously."

He opened his mouth to protest, but before he could deny it, I pressed ahead.

"But it didn't work, did it? You didn't count on Shelley getting pushback from her editor. A story about puppy mills just wasn't going to sell enough papers, and it was going to piss off valuable advertisers besides. There was another way to make sure that information got out, but you had to raise the stakes. The paper might ignore a disreputable puppy mill, but they couldn't ignore a death...especially a murder. You couldn't kill Harry Clementine directly, because it would lead straight back to you. But if you could pin a murder on him—that would do the job fine and dandy. So you killed her."

I watched Dalton's eyes as I spoke, and his stone-faced resolve confirmed every point as I made it.

"But that didn't play out the way you expected either, did it? Turns out that you kind of suck as a murderer—you made it look *too* much like an accident, and the police didn't even investigate. You left the crime scene too clean. You messed up. Lucky for you Harry Clementine is a trigger-happy weasel anyway, and he was in jail just the same."

"Was?" His eyes grew wide.

"Yes. Out on bail."

Dalton looked away and swore. I could see his eyes moving back and forth, thinking hard.

"But it still did the trick. Nancy is beginning to ask 'what if' questions."

Dalton looked like I'd just struck him across the face with a cold fish. "She is?"

I nodded. "Heard it from her own lips."

Hope welled in his eyes. "I...I...I...I've got to see her..."

"Good luck with that," I said, standing up. We stared at one another for a long time. "How long has it been since you've seen her, anyway?"

He looked away. "A long time. I write her, though."

I frowned. "How often?"

"Once a week. Every Sunday. I disguise the letters as bills."

"Does she ever respond?" I asked.

He shook his head. In spite of everything, I felt myself soften toward him. He was pathetic, and I pitied him.

There was an awkward silence. Finally, I said, "You can't let me go."

"No," he agreed.

"But you also can't kill me," I said.

"Why not?" he asked, sneering. "You've put enough dogs down in your time. Turnabout is fair play, surely."

"Uh...from a karmic perspective...I suppose..." I didn't think for a moment that Dalton had a problem putting dogs down. As a breeder, he had as much blood on his hands as I did. "But what I meant was..." I pointed at Britney with my nose. "I didn't sew her up right. I used a half curl instead of a full curl in my sutures. It'll hold...until it doesn't." This was all nonsense, of course. There is no surgical knot called a "half curl"—or a "full curl" for that matter—and I had sewn her up just fine. But he didn't need to know that.

"You bitch," he snarled.

"You say that like it's a bad thing," I said.

"You fix her right now. Right now!" he yelled, pointing through the gate at his dog.

"No," I said. "Because the moment I do, I die."

A vein bulged in his forehead. He looked like he might have a stroke. Then I watched a change come over his face. He became calm, his eyes narrow and dark. "I've had enough of you," he snarled. "And I don't care if she dies."

I didn't think that was true, but there was no ignoring the flash of silver as he pulled a revolver from his pocket and pointed it through the gate—directly at me. *So this is it,* I thought. *This is how it ends for me.* My shoulders drooped and I shut my eyes, backing up until I felt the cold cinder-block wall of the cell behind me. I braced myself for the sound of the shot, and wondered if it would hurt. The only comfort I felt in that moment was when I realized that wherever Scout was right now, I was going to be with her.

thirty-seven

My eyes squeezed tight, it occurred to me that I might never see light again. Or Jack. Or Scout. And then—as if my thought had summoned her—I heard it. A howl—a high alto siren swooping up, then down. It was a voice I knew. A voice I loved. It was Scout, and she was alive! And she was close. *But how?* I wondered. But it didn't matter. I opened my eyes and felt hope bloom within me. Dalton didn't seem to notice. His aim did not waver. I raised my chin and answered, howling my response with everything I could muster.

Apparently, my behavior was enough of a *non sequitur* to throw Dalton off. "What the hell are you doing?" he asked. His eyebrows bunched in confusion and the muzzle of his pistol lowered ever so slightly.

"What does it look like I'm doing?" I asked, in my snarkiest are-you-an-idiot tone. "I'm howling."

Scout howled again. I chanced a look at Dalton's face. He didn't recognize her—this was a kennel, so of course there were dogs howling all damn day. But I knew my dog's voice. I'd know it anywhere. I howled again in response.

"You're mad," Dalton breathed.

"You got that right," I said. "I'm mad as hell."

Just then there was a banging sound and a series of shouts. Dalton's eyes snapped open wide and his head whipped to his right. I couldn't see what he was seeing, but I could tell it wasn't a welcome sight. He raised his gun again, just as I heard pounding footfalls on the cement. I heard a blast of gunfire, but there was no flare from Dalton's muzzle. Instead, Dalton crumpled in front of me, gun dropping from his hand.

"Here!" I yelled. "I'm here!" I didn't know who it was, but it didn't matter. The odds were very high that whoever it was, they did not want me as dead as Dalton did.

And then Gus' goofy face peeked around the corner, his hat slightly askew. "Casey?" he asked.

"Gus!" I said. "Thank God!"

"Thank God indeed!" another voice said. I knew that voice too. A split second later, Jack burst past Gus and grabbed the grate of the gate that held me in. "Oh God, Case. I'm so glad you're okay."

"'Course she's okay," said a third voice. Sarge sauntered into view a moment later, a shotgun slung over his shoulder. "She's tough as nails, aren't you, Case?"

My knees gave way and I stumbled. A sob of relief escaped my throat. I steadied myself with one hand against the wall behind me.

"Are you hurt?" Jack asked.

"No," I said. "Just..." My head snapped up. "Scout?"

"She took some buckshot," Sarge said. "But your pal Ellie fixed her right up."

"She's okay?" I asked.

Jack nodded. "She'll be fine. She's outside right now. We tried to leave her at the clinic, but she wouldn't have it."

I cried then. I'm ashamed of it now, but I supposed I knew

that it was the fastest and most efficient way for my body to shed the trauma, the fear, the danger, the relief. When I was done, when I came to my senses, I discovered my head on Jack's shoulderas he hugged me and rocked me and shushed me. I squeezed him back. Shakily, I got to my feet. He held my arm, steadying me, waiting to catch me should I collapse again.

But I stood firm. I was still a bit shaky. I felt drained from the crying. I was exhausted. But I was alive, and I would walk out of there on my own two feet. I clasped Jack's hands in mine and looked into his eyes. "This poodle needs to get to the clinic...and..." My voice quavered and I fought to bring it under control. "And I want to see my dog."

epilogue

When I heard the knock on the door, I had three reactions. I stopped breathing, my pulse began pounding, and I grabbed the baseball bat from its place under the coffee table. Scout began barking wildly, and I leapt from the couch.

Slowly I approached the door, the bat resting on my shoulder, ready to swing. Scout was sniffing under the door, and her stubby tail began to wag with joy. Then I heard Jack laugh—he must have heard Scout. I lowered the bat and opened the door.

Jack smiled, but his eyebrows stood at full attention at the sight of the bat. "Was that for...uh...was that for me?" he asked.

"Sorry...I'm a little jumpy," I said. "Come in."

"You should have called me when you were ready to come home from the hospital," he said, stepping across the threshold. I shut the door behind him.

"I..." I faltered. I leaned the bat against the doorframe. "Gus was there to take a statement. He brought me home."

"Oh." A complicated set of emotions paraded across his face. "That's good...I guess."

I smiled, and despite myself, enjoyed his moment of jealousy. "Coffee?"

"Sure, sounds good." Jack knelt to give Scout a good rub and a nuzzle.

I set the coffee on the small table in the breakfast nook and he slid into one of the seats. "Thank you," he said. He searched my eyes as I took my own seat. "Are you okay?"

Scout sniffed at Jack's leg, but a moment later turned a quick circle and lay down, half-under the table.

"Yeah," I answered. "More psychological damage than physical, if I'm honest." I couldn't believe the words coming out of my mouth, but I trusted Jack.

"That sounds about right," he said. "Are you going to see someone?"

"You mean, like, a psychologist?"

"Yeah."

"Do you think I should?" I asked, narrowing one eye.

"It's not like that," he said. "*Anyone* would need help processing something like this. You're not Wonder Woman, you know."

"No...she's prettier than I am," I quipped.

Jack laughed, but returned to his serious face quickly. "You know what I mean. You're not...special."

"I'm not?" I wasn't sure how to take that.

"No. You're as fragile as the rest of us mere mortals. It's foolish to pretend otherwise. If you're wounded, you go to the doctor." He reached out and put his hand on one of mine. "You're wounded, whether you want to admit it or not." I grasped his hand and held it tightly. I didn't answer, but I didn't think I needed to. "Case, you've experienced trauma. You almost died. We're all going to have to deal with that. You can bet I'll be talking to my therapist about it, and my spiritual director, and I've already been talking it over with God." He sighed. "I just want to make sure you have the support you need to get through this."

I didn't want to admit it out loud, but he was probably right, damn him. I hated to show weakness, and going to a therapist definitely smacked of weakness to me. But Jack saw a therapist, and did I think of him as weak? I didn't. I felt a moment of vertigo as my moorings to a long-established way of thinking were undermined. Maybe I should see a therapist. Who would have to know, and what could it hurt? I had a hard time understanding my own emotions, even in the best of times. Maybe a little professional help didn't mean I was crazy, but just...could it really be that I was just normal? I hated it when Jack made sense.

"Are you at least going to take some time off?" he asked, interrupting my reverie.

"Not...not right away. I have to be at the clinic this afternoon—I need to check on Britney."

"What happened to the pups?"

"I called the local poodle rescue. They're being cared for. The other dogs, too."

"Well, that's a relief," Jack said.

"Yeah," I agreed. "Plus, the Clementines are bringing their puppies in for a progress check this afternoon. Nancy is making sure Harry ups his dog care game."

"Well, that's good, isn't it?"

"It is," I agreed. "This whole affair might have been just the shakeup their relationship needed, or so it seems to me—not to mention their business."

"God works in mysterious ways," Jack said. Then he looked down. "I...uh...have a confession to make. I might have had something to do with that."

"Oh?"

"Yeah. After I paid the bail for Harry, we had a drink

together. He apologized. He asked if there was some way he could make it up to me."

"What did you say?" I asked.

"I said, 'Why don't you let Casey help you upgrade your operation?'"

"You sly devil," I said, slapping his hand. I grinned at him.

The grin faded as several minutes of silence passed. Tentatively, Jack asked, "Do you feel like telling me what happened? I mean, I know the broad strokes, but I don't know what it was like for you...or what you were feeling. And if you don't feel like it, or it's too painful...that's okay too."

"No, it's okay," I said. And over the next half hour, I told him what had happened, leaving out no detail that I could remember. While I talked, his face was both grave and compassionate, and he never let go of my hand. As I talked, I realized that I was probably learning more than he was. I felt pride as I talked about figuring out, at long last, who Shelley's killer was. And although I had been terrified, I was proud of how I had held up under pressure, how I had kept my wits about me, how I had been able to focus. It also occurred to me that, despite all my self-doubts, I was a damn fine veterinarian. As I held his hand, I wondered if perhaps I wasn't quite as hopeless in the romance department as I thought I was. Maybe...just maybe I wasn't as much of a failure as I thought I was.

When I finished, I refreshed our coffee cups and reached for his hand again. "Your turn," I said. "How did you find me?"

"Well, you can thank Scout there, for that," Jack pointed with his chin at the Boxer. Scout's ears pricked up at the sound of her name, and she lifted her head off of her paws for a few seconds before settling back down again.

"How so?" I asked.

"If you recall, you were supposed to come over yesterday morning for breakfast."

"Eight o'clock," I said. "And I was only supposed to bring my dog."

"But you didn't. You didn't show, and...I know we don't know each other that well, but...it just didn't seem like you. So I hopped in the car and drove over here to see if you were okay."

"That was sweet of you," I said, moving my thumb across the back of his hand.

"And that's when I saw Scout," he said. "Running around loose outside. Sitting by the front door. Unable to get in. And... bleeding. That's when I knew that something was really, really wrong."

"What did you do?" I asked.

"Well, first I knocked, and I thought maybe you were passed out inside. So I jumped the fence and—I'm sorry, but the back door *was* open—and you weren't there, so I went back out and called Scout to come get into the car, and took her to the clinic as fast as I could go. It was just opening up, and Ellie was there—nice girl, by the way—"

"She is," I said. "She's my right arm."

"I told her where I found Scout. She's no vet, but she patched her up as well as she could—"

"She did a great job," I said, making a mental note to let her know that.

"And then she pulled out her phone and told me exactly where you were—some app she had, I guess. I asked her to call Gus, and I phoned Sarge on the way to the door." He leaned over and patted my dog. "And Scout was right behind me. She wasn't taking 'stay' for an answer."

"That's my girl," I said, smiling at her. The stub of her tail buzzed back and forth like a butterfly's wings.

"And we all just kind of arrived at the same time, and...and you know the rest, really."

I looked at our intertwined hands and nodded. "Thank you," I said.

"I'm just so glad you're okay."

"You'll be proud of me—I prayed," I confessed.

"I'll bet you did," he smiled. "But I'd be proud of you anyway. You're one of the bravest people I know." He squeezed my hand extra tight. I squeezed back.

"I'm sorry you didn't get a poodle out of all of this," I said. "I can put in a good word with the rescue people."

"No, I..." A strange smile came over Jack's beautiful lips. "... I've been thinking. We both know of a dog—a good dog, a brave and noble dog—that needs a home."

"Who?" I asked.

"Tripod," Jack said. "I know Ellie has been fostering him. Do you think...?"

My throat swelled up and I blinked back tears. How many guys were there in the world willing to adopt a middle-aged, three-legged mutt? This guy. *My guy*, I thought, before I could stop myself. "I think...I think that's wonderful, Jack. That will be a great relief for Ellie, and...well, I think you and Tripod will be perfect for each other."

"I think so too," Jack said. "God is a master at making beauty out of broken things."

It might have been a cryptic thing to say, but I instantly understood. Everything about the past couple of weeks had been broken...if not devastated—Jack included. "Speaking of broken things...how is Dalton?"

"He'll live. Still in the ICU, although Gus assures me he's handcuffed to the bed."

"Surely not," Jack scowled.

I shrugged. "Maybe he just told me that so I wouldn't

worry." I fell silent for a moment. Then I said, "I have to confess, I didn't see it coming. Dalton. I was sure it was Massaman. Weren't you?"

"To be honest, I really had no idea."

"I've never trusted poodle breeders...not really." I scowled.

"Now you're just playing with me," he said.

"I am," I said, and met his eyes.

"There's still the lawsuit," he said. "What's up with that?"

"The hearing is set for the month after next," I said. "It should be a thrill-a-minute. Wanna come?"

To my amazement, he brought my hand to his lips and kissed it. My hand was not where I wanted those lips, but I wasn't complaining. I felt a thrill ripple through me.

"I wouldn't miss it for the world," he said.